Entangled

Barbara Ellen Brink

Visit this author at www.barbaraellenbrink.com

Cover photo by Barbara Ellen Brink

Cover design by Katharine A Brink

Author photo by Barbara E Brink

Entangled

ISBN-10:1493658859
ISBN-13:978-1493658855

DEDICATION

Big hugs to my husband for supporting this insanity of mine
to write fiction, and for being pleasantly surprised
when he read and liked it.

I also want to thank Ruth Ann, Patty, and Nancy for being
awesome critique partners in the early stages of Entangled.

Becky and Elaine—what can I say? Thanks for reading my work
and encouraging me along the way. I love you guys!

.

CONTENTS *Fredrickson Winery Novels*:

Crushed

Savor

~~~

Second Chances Series:

Running Home

Alias Raven Black

~~~

Split Sense

~~~

The Amish Bloodsuckers Trilogy:

Chosen

Shunned

Reckoning

Entangled

For my Mom

Prologue

For years I've had nightmares. They started when I was fifteen--after the night Paul attacked me and tried to rape me. I dream of wine, and blood, and a desperate struggle. After tossing and turning, I end up staring into the darkness of my room, wondering why the past continues to have a chokehold on my life.

Sleeplessness is a common feeling, always craving one more hour of rest, but never getting it. Finally I sleep, but it's far into the night. In the predawn of morning my body is pulled from slumber with a jolt of remembrance. Something unspeakable sits in the shadows waiting to be recognized.

But weariness soon settles in and hides the night's truth with a blanket of fog. It feels as though only moments pass and I awake at the sound of my alarm. The sun streams through the blinds, and I curse the hands of time.

Chapter One

Mother often chose to call when I was the busiest, informing me that her ESP just clicked on and gave her no choice. I'm sure what she really meant to say was she felt lonely and assumed I must be too.

"Uncle Jack died?" I switched the receiver to my left ear as I tried to sign the papers Jody placed before me on the desk.

"Yes, a massive heart attack."

Jack was my father's half-brother but I hadn't seen him since I was a little girl and couldn't even remember what he looked like. I assumed my father and he had a falling out of some sort.

"He liked to travel but when he bought that winery and vineyard out in California he was always too busy to visit." She sighed. "We didn't see him after your father died. I sent a Christmas card or two, but he never responded."

I'd heard it all before, but Mother needed to say it so I continued to listen while deleting Spam from my email inbox. She told me she was going to California for the funeral.

"Why do you feel obligated to fly out there? Doesn't he have a family to take care of things?" I asked. Fridays were always busy and I had another appointment in ten minutes.

"That's the problem. He never married and we *are* the only family. Your father would never forgive me if I abandoned Jack in his time of need."

Mother's sense of drama was always rich. "They're both dead. Neither will know if you choose not to go."

"You can't be serious! Your father would turn over in his grave."

I rolled my eyes and reached in the desk drawer for the small mirror I kept there. "How's that possible? I thought he was in heaven."

"Of course, honey. It was just a figure of speech."

"Which? Heaven or turning in his grave? Because if it's the latter,he probably needs to turn over. He's been in the same position for thirteen years."

"Wilhelmina Fredrickson! That is disrespectful."

"Sorry, Mother." I lowered the volume on my headset and tried to touch up my lipstick. "I've really got to go. I have an appointment."

"I understand, but I haven't told you the real news yet," she said.

"Can I call you back when I get home?" I asked. "I've really got to go." I clicked off before she could respond. I'd probably pay for my rudeness later, but right now it was worth it. I put my head down on the desk and closed my eyes, a feeble attempt to ward off the headache I felt building.

*****

"Jody, go home to your kids. I'm going to finish up this brief before I leave. No reason for you to hang around." I pulled open the top drawer of my second-hand desk and rummaged around for a paperclip. An ancient coffee stain spread out from the middle of the drawer's bottom like a one-celled organism magnified to scary proportions. My father built the desk before I was born. He said he felt the need to do something useful with his hands during my mother's pregnancy. She said it would have been a heck of a lot more useful to build a bassinet. But in hindsight, at twenty-eight and unmarried, the desk served me better.

Jody stood with her arms crossed over her chest, staring out the narrow window behind me. "Looks like a storm's setting in," she said. "Abigail hates storms. I imagine I'll be sharing my bed tonight." My secretary, a former client that needed a job after her husband gambled everything away, was a sweet lady, but a little too touchy-feely for me. I preferred to take charge of my emotions, lock them away during the day, and only take them out at night if they were completely incapable of staying hidden any longer. Emotions were messy, better left turned off during business hours.

I smiled. "She's thirteen, isn't she? Don't they ever grow out of that?" I asked, even though I still fought the urge to leave a nightlight on.

"Ann didn't ask me to tuck her in after she turned ten. But Abigail has always been my little girl." She walked to the door. "Don't forget you promised to call your mother back," she said.

I waved her away. "Goodnight. Have a good weekend."

Alone in my office, I dropped my pen on the desktop and leaned back with my hands above my head, stretching the kinks out of my back. I needed to go to the gym and spend some time on the machines. But I had an appointment with Kent to meet at the Bullpen for dinner.

"Appointment," I said aloud. "Why do I call...?"

Probably because Kent always called during business hours and set our dates up with Jody as though we were meeting to discuss a civil suit rather than to spend intimate time together.

The Bullpen was a raucous sports bar, where food and fun meant loud and greasy. I preferred the dimly lit, quiet ambiance of an Italian restaurant after a day at the office, but Kent couldn't be more than twenty feet from a television screen.

I finished, slipped the papers into a folder, and stood up. Maybe I would call Kent and cancel our evening. I was tired and still had to return Mother's call. If I didn't, she would be sure to call me. I flipped the lights off and had my key out to lock the door when the telephone rang. Hopeful that Kent was on the other end of the line and I could back out of our date gracefully, I set my briefcase beside the door and picked up the phone on Jody's desk.

"Fredrickson Family Law."

"This is Handel Parker. Jack Fredrickson's attorney."

I picked up a pen and scrawled the unfamiliar name across the top sheet of Jody's notepad. "What can I do for you, Mr. Parker?"

"Not a thing. It's what your uncle did for you. He named you sole beneficiary of his estate."

"Is this some kind of joke?" I asked. My brother Adam and his college buddies had pulled senseless pranks on me before but this didn't have the same immature flavor.

"I can assure you this is no joke."

Why would a man I'd met only once leave everything he owned to me? It made no sense. Nearly everyone had friends or a lover -- someone. "Mr. Parker, why --?

Could we arrange a time to discuss the details after the funeral?" he asked.

"Yes, of course, but could you tell me something about this winery? After all --"

"I'd be happy to answer all your questions when you get here, but right now I'm running late for an appointment." He left me his office phone number and asked that I call his secretary to let her know when I would be arriving so that someone could meet me at the airport.

Moments later I hung up, and stared down at the meager notes I'd scribbled. The thought of owning and operating a winery brought up a dozen questions. What kind of wine did they bottle? Was the business solvent or were there debts to pay? How many employees were involved? Was there a manager in place or had my uncle run things alone? But the question uppermost in my mind was -- what am I supposed to do with it?

It might seem romantic to own a California winery, but as a Minnesota divorce attorney my life was quite the opposite. I couldn't imagine depending on such an iffy thing as weather conditions to make a living. Gardening had never appealed to me for that very reason. I liked knowing what to expect, and getting what I expected or a close proximity. When you file a divorce you get what you ask for.

*****

At home the winery situation continued to occupy my mind as I changed into jeans and a sweater. When I returned Mother's call it was to inform her that I was going with her to California. She didn't seem surprised, but she was ecstatic. She kept me on the line for twenty minutes before it suddenly occurred to me that I had never called Kent to cancel our date. It was too late now. He would already be at the Bullpen, watching the ever-present television screens while he waited for me to show up.

"Mother, I have to go. I forgot about Kent."

"How could you possibly forget that man? He's adorable. Even if he does talk sports all the time."

"Yes, well, learning I'm the owner of a winery might have something to do with it."

I grabbed my jacket and keys and flew out the door. A light rain fell, slowing traffic already thick with the Friday night crowd. I pulled into the Bullpen parking lot twenty minutes later, glanced in the rearview mirror to reassure myself I didn't look as tired and drawn as I felt, and hurried inside.

The Bullpen was revved up. Most of the tables were full, and the bar was swamped. Sport spectators knocked back beers and argued at the top of their voices about the latest game. I spotted Kent sitting at our usual table, his purple Vikings cap on backward and his arm around a woman I didn't recognize.

He did expect me to meet him tonight, right?

His preoccupation with the woman nearly sitting on his lap gave me the seconds I needed to sum up what was going on. As I hesitated, she ran her hand along his cheek and pulled him in for a kiss. I stared a moment, then spun on my heel, and hurried for the door, nearly colliding with a waiter carrying a tray of drinks. My departure was so fast I'm sure not even my perfume had time to linger.

Chapter Two

Mother and I flew out to California on Monday morning. She sat puffed up with importance as though I were receiving a title along with my inheritance. She touched up her makeup before disembarking from the plane, no doubt afraid that some reporter would seek us out and take our picture for the National Enquirer.

"I always knew there was something special about Jack," she said as she powdered her cheeks. "He and your father were opposites. Jack was an adventurer, while James was down-to-earth responsible."

"Does that mean Dad wasn't special?" I asked as I glanced out the window at the runway. The plane turned slowly and headed toward the buildings in the distance.

"Billie, why do you always turn everything around that I say?"

I patted her arm and grinned. "Because it's fun."

She lined her lips with a darker shade of mauve. "I just meant that he was different. Exciting in a romantic way. He traveled to places most folks would be afraid to set foot in. He tried new things, wasn't afraid of taking a chance." Her voice dwindled and she sat back against the seat, releasing a quiet sigh. "James once asked me if I was in love with Jack," she confessed.

Now it was my turn to be aghast. "Mother!"

She shrugged her shoulders and laughed lightly. "I guess maybe I was once." She met my horrified gaze and patted my cheek. "A long time ago. But only for a minute. I fell too much in love with your father for it to last."

As she stuffed her cosmetics back into her carry on bag, I watched her, and realized how little I really knew about my own parents. She could be loving, sometimes to the point of suffocating, but other than as my mother I didn't really know much about her. Did she kiss on the first date when she was a girl, smoke cigarettes in the woods, or run on the track team at school? Was she popular? Would she rather run in the rain or build a snowman? And did she and my father have the kind of love that would last, or was his death a blessing in disguise?

A man in a chauffeur cap met us at the gate. He held a sign with **Fredrickson** in big black letters. "I'm Wilhelmina Fredrickson," I said.

After collecting our luggage, he led us to a limousine and opened the door. "Here we are, ladies."

I let my mother climb in first and then followed. A man waited inside, his dark suit blending into the shadows. He smiled, his teeth white against tanned skin. "Hello. I'm Handel Parker," he said.

I don't know if it was the surprise of the man being the exact opposite of what I'd expected, (old, stout, balding, and short), or the instant attraction I felt when he took my hand, but I nearly fell into his lap as the limo edged into traffic.

"Sorry," I breathed as I caught my balance and sat

firmly next to my mother, opposite Handel Parker.

"It's quite all right," he murmured, turning to answer the phone that blinked beside him. "Excuse me."

His quiet conversation went on for five minutes or more while we watched San Francisco roll past our window. We were headed toward the Napa Valley, wine country.

"Sorry about that." He replaced the phone and sat back, his attention complete on his guests now. I thought I detected a thread of mistrust laced with curiosity in his gaze. "When's the last time you visited this part of the country?" he asked.

I hadn't been out of Minneapolis except to attend law school in Chicago, never taking the time for a real vacation. "I've never been to California."

A slight look of surprise crossed his face before he resumed the bland lawyer persona. "Really?"

"Sure you have, honey," my mother interjected. She patted my knee as though I were still a small child. "We came here to visit Jack when you were six or seven. No -- actually, you were closer to eight. I was full-blown pregnant with Adam on that trip. I'm surprised they allowed me on the plane."

Handel Parker didn't ask any questions, but apparently he showed a glimmer of interest that only my mother picked up on. She continued with her story, reminiscing about the past with so much vibrancy I began to suspect she really did have feelings for my father's older brother.

"My children are nine years apart," she explained. "Just when you get used to the idea that your child is in school and growing up, along come diapers and late-night feedings. Jack never met my son Adam, but he bonded with Billie instantaneously on that trip. Obviously, more than anyone knew," she said with a slight shake of her head. Her salon perfect hair never moved. "Jack and Billie were both early risers and each morning they went out to the winery where he let her explore, and explained the wine making process to her."

I felt uncomfortable under the spotlight so I chewed at my bottom lip, and stared out the window, distancing myself from the conversation with inattention. I had no memory of that time or Uncle Jack, and yet I had been eight years old. How was that possible?

The countryside rushed past without me really seeing it, my thoughts turned inward, struggling to dredge up something from that time to call my own. Mother's memories were foreign to me, a life apart from who I now was.

Handel Parker unbuttoned his suit coat and clasped his hands loosely in his lap. My gaze strayed from the window to his face. He had a firm chin, full lips, and deep set eyes. His blonde hair grew thick and curled up along the collar of his dress shirt, a good month past due for a trim. Definitely not as conservative as most lawyers I knew.

"So how long were you here for that specific visit?" he asked my mother. His voice was modulated, trained to sooth clients and convince juries of his version of the truth, no doubt.

I glanced her way, curious myself since I had no memory of the events.

She smoothed one eyebrow as she had a habit of doing when thinking. "Just under three weeks. As I recollect, James planned for a month, but he suddenly got a call from the office and we had to leave that very day. There was an emergency of some kind." She reached out and patted my arm. "Funny thing though. Billie didn't even throw a fit like I thought she would.

After all the fun she'd been having, working with her Uncle Jack, and learning new things, she was thoroughly ready to go home."

"I suppose Jack was disappointed," Handel said, ever the perfect host, keeping the conversation from lagging. He held my gaze as my mother opened her purse to search for a mint. "He must have felt lonely after having a family around."

Mother looked up, her brow wrinkled in thought. "I don't really know. Jack was off somewhere when James got the call and we had to leave before he returned."

"How strange." If I hadn't been looking directly at him I wouldn't have caught the flash of cynicism that crossed Handel's face, immediately replaced with a polite smile as he shook his head. "But it sounds like Jack. Always the perfect host. He might have forty people scheduled for a wine tasting and he'd just disappear. If it weren't for the terrific staff, the place would be bankrupt by now."

I watched his eyes light up when he spoke of Jack and the winery, and wondered what their relationship entailed other than attorney/client. Were they friends, or just acquaintances? "How long did you know Jack?" I asked.

He pushed the hair back from his forehead. "As long as I can remember. He and my father were friends since high school. My folks worked for the previous owner of the winery and then my father continued to work for Jack when he purchased it. I must have been about ten when I started doing odd jobs around the place. As a teenager I helped harvest the grapes. After I graduated from law school Jack insisted that I be his personal attorney, although I specialize in criminal law."

"You worked only for Jack?"

He raised one brow, a look that would be considered condescending without the smile that accompanied it. "Of course not. Jack wasn't that well off. He couldn't afford to hire me full-time. I agreed to take care of any legal matters for him when and if they came up. After all, he helped pay my way through college."

"Well, wasn't that nice," Mother said. "I knew Jack was a philanthropist at heart."

Handel Parker nodded slowly, his expression indecipherable. "Yes, he was."

*****

Rows of vines in neat symmetrical lines stretched as far as the eye could see, rolling with the hills and dells, parting smoothly to encircle a cluster of olive trees left standing guard like gnarled, elderly, gentlemen keeping watch over the tender grapes. A neighbor's vineyards butted up to Jack's, the lines running in the opposite direction, and according to Handel, Fredrickson's biggest competitor.

"New winery's are spreading all over the country," Handel informed us as we slowed to turn into the long gravel driveway.

"I read something about that," I said. "Didn't the number of registered winery's double in the past couple of years? Last year over 600 permits were issued. Wine is becoming the fastest growing agriculture in America. I have a friend from college who lives in Washington State. She said wineries are popping up all over there too."

Handel's look of surprise at my knowledge warmed my heart. For some reason he didn't seem to like me very much and I enjoyed the thought of besting him at something. We were both attorneys, and maybe that accounted for the competitive streak in me. But the man was obviously jealous I'd inherited Uncle Jack's holdings. Had he expected them for himself?

"Yes," he said, buttoning his jacket in anticipation of our arrival. "They've spread along the entire West coast, as well as Virginia, the Carolinas, and any other state conducive to growing grapes. In fact, I believe Minnesota has a few vineyards as well."

I opened my mouth to expound once more from my well of winemaking knowledge, but my mother laid a hand lightly on my arm and squeezed, a warning to *save it*. She knew from experience between my brother and myself that I wouldn't quit until I had the last word, something I'd failed to grow out of. I expelled a frustrated breath and watched as the buildings came into view.

According to Handel, the house had been rebuilt in the fifties after the original was destroyed by fire. The owners at that time decided to go with brick to save themselves another heartache. Spreading out like a child's Lego creation with one addition after another, it appeared a living, growing, entity. The brick was the palest pink, shimmering in the sun like a watercolor painting. The outlying buildings, storage sheds, barn, and winery were painted white with black trim, in sharp contrast to the deep cerulean California sky, and rather modern when compared to the neighboring wineries with their monastic style buildings.

The limo pulled up to the house and stopped behind a red Porsche. The chauffeur opened the back door for us before emptying the trunk of our luggage. I climbed out first and stood looking around, my gaze resting briefly on each building as though memories would suddenly start flooding back and I would remember that summer with the clarity Mother seemed to have. But nothing looked remotely familiar.

Handel took Mother's arm and walked with her up

to the house, not even waiting to see if I would follow. I glanced back at the limo, but the driver had already climbed in and was pulling away. There were two pickups parked across the yard in the shade of a huge, oak tree and I caught a glimpse of someone watching from the shadowed doorway of the winery. I shivered in spite of the warm rays of the afternoon sun, and turned toward the house.

Handel held the door for me and I stepped into the coolness of the darkened entryway. Bells of recognition still had not started ringing inside my head and I wondered if they ever would. Obviously, those weeks of my childhood had not been as remarkable as Mother made them out to be.

Handel led us down a hallway to a large room, cavernous in its simplicity. A single chair sat close to the brick fireplace, a piece of stray furniture lost and alone. An old, brown, leather couch and end table were pushed close against a far wall, as though someone had cleared the floor for a dance. However, the walls were not empty; paintings filled with bright splashes of color adorned them like jewelry on a naked woman.

Mother stopped in the middle of the room and gazed around, her eyes wide with something akin to shock. "What in the world happened to Jack's beautiful furniture?" she asked. "I remember he had wonderful pieces that he picked up all over the world."

Handel paused in his guided tour, his eyes narrowing as he looked around, as though just noticing the bareness of the room. "Oh -- well, Jack gave it away," he said with a slight shrug. He met my look of incredulity and I swear there was resentment in his gaze. My initial attraction to the man was quickly fading. "I was surprised when he willed everything to you. I thought he'd have the place sold and give the money to those in need or designate shares to all of the employees. He had a heart as big as anyone I've ever known."

Something about that statement made my stomach turn, but I didn't know if it was Handel's attitude toward me or my own sense of justice. I knew that inheritance didn't necessarily have anything to do with deserving. Lazy, worthless, children inherited their hard-working parents' fortunes everyday just because they had matching DNA. I certainly didn't feel that I deserved my uncle's money, but he had made the decision to leave it to me of his own free will.

I tore my gaze from Handel's accusing one and fixed my eyes on the huge painting above the fireplace mantel. Streaks and wild dabs of paint adorned the canvas like a food fight gone creatively abstract. I imagined anger rather than fun emanated from the framed art. For some reason it frightened me, and I no longer wanted to be in the same room.

"I would like to take a tour of the winery if you have time to show us around before we settle in a hotel for the night," I said. My voice seemed over loud in the hollow space and I felt another headache coming on.

"I'm sure that can be arranged, but aren't you planning on staying in the house while you're here? I had rooms prepared for you." He spread his hands as though in supplication. "It is your property now."

I was not seduced by his placating words. I knew he resented me for being Jack's niece. I cleared my throat and looked at mother. "Well, of course we'll stay if it's all prepared. I just didn't want to presume."

Mother laughed lightly, her eyes crinkling at the corners the way I liked to see. A person that laughed without laugh lines was not truly happy or amused. She seemed to sense my mood and wanted to lighten it.

"You aren't worried about Jack's ghost, are you honey? Because if he's hanging out around here, I'm sure he's a friendly ghost. After all, he gave the place to you."

I released a breath and hoped the tension I felt would expel from me as well. "Please show us to our rooms then," I said, looking at Handel silently waiting.

"Right this way, ladies."

*****

My earlier notion of touring the winery was forgotten as quickly as Handel Parker left the house, speeding away to town in his red Porsche. He needed to attend to some things, he said, but then he would be back to take us to dinner. The thought of spending more time with the man made my heart thud in my chest, anxiety filling me like a teenage girl on her first date, except it wasn't anxious excitement over the prospect, but an incomprehensible foreboding that I couldn't quite put my finger on. I knew he questioned the validity of my receiving my uncle's holdings, as though I'd conspired to put a voodoo curse on Jack before he died, which was preposterous since I was raised Lutheran.

The bed in the room prepared for me was one of those monstrous, four-postered things that take up nearly the entire room. Three steps were built into the side so that anyone other than Paul Bunyan could get in without a catapult. I spread out and closed my eyes, relaxing into the soft comforter, imagining myself the Raggedy Ann doll that I once owned. The cloth doll was literally torn to shreds when my father ran over it with our riding lawnmower one summer, leaving me heartbroken and him guilt-ridden. He replaced it with another doll, similar in looks and clothing, but I knew it wasn't mine and refused to play with it. Mother placed it on my bookshelf. Limp and bent over at the waist, it continued to grin down at me, an evil doppelganger.

The house seemed hushed as though even the walls knew there had been a death in the family. I could hear faint sounds from outside my window, birds chirping happily, a motor of some kind humming, but in this room only my quiet breathing broke the silence. I turned over, curled up into a fetal position and slept.

Chapter Three

Dreams of shadows hovering over me stole the restfulness from my sleep, and I woke still tired and irritable. I got up and moved about the room, admiring the view from my window, and taking a closer look at the artwork on the walls. In here too was an assortment of paintings, abstract and bold in composition, frightening in intensity. I didn't like them and blamed the room's heightened atmosphere for my less than adequate nap. I promised myself that I would take them down and store them in the back of the closet before I slept in here again.

I stole into my mother's room and saw that she was still sleeping, a little mascara smudged beneath her eyes, but her hair quite perfect in its protective shell of spray. Mother was one of those people who always woke fresh as a spring flower, happy and talkative. When I woke, no matter how long I slept or how still I lay, I always looked like Attila the Hun after a night of pillaging and mayhem.

The sound of a child singing wafted through the open window, and I tiptoed past the bed where Mother slept to lift a slat of the closed blinds and peer out. Our rooms were situated at the back of the house where the view of the vineyards was obscured by dozens of full-grown oak, redwood, and eucalyptus trees. A small boy of about six was sitting in a tire swing, suspended from the branch of a tall oak. He pushed his bare feet against the ground for momentum as he sang at the top of his voice.

"Mamas, don't let your babies grow up to be cowboys..."

I watched him for a moment, a smile on my lips, as he swung higher and higher, his voice floating up into the branches of the trees. Suddenly I felt a shiver run down my spine as the scene changed and I imagined myself as a little girl sitting in that tire, swinging back and forth, back and forth, like the pendulum on a clock, unable to stop or get off.

I closed my eyes and swallowed hard. What was wrong with me? I wasn't remembering this place, that swing, the week I spent here as a child. I blew out a breath of exasperation, realizing my imagination was working overtime. My father had hung a tire from a large maple tree in our yard in Minneapolis when I was seven. That's what I remembered. I'd fallen out of the thing one time and broke my arm. I turned away from the window and silently exited into the hall, closing the door behind me.

Exploring the house alone was like rummaging through a stranger's underwear drawer. I felt strangely voyeuristic. I knew it would all belong to me eventually, once the paperwork went through, but I didn't necessarily relish the idea. Inheriting "holdings" was one thing, but becoming the proud owner of someone else's toilet brush, kitchenware, and music collection was quite another. I made a mental note to schedule a yard sale as soon as possible.

The kitchen door opened into the backyard, and I went out in search of the boy. Was he one of the field worker's sons or a neighbor child wandering aimlessly, looking for entertainment in the long afternoon? I followed a path of stepping-stones through the trees to the back section of the house where I'd seen him swinging. The tire hung empty now, but still moved gently with the breeze as though a ghostly hand were in control. I stood there a moment, straining for the sound of his voice in the distance, but there was nothing but the creak of the branches above me and the rattle of leaves in the wind.

I walked toward the front of the house, following the flagstone path back past the kitchen windows and on around to the garage. Rose bushes climbed a trellis along the outside wall, reaching for the sun, their blooms a deep, startling red against the pale brick. I picked one and held it beneath my nose, breathing in the heavy, sweet fragrance that I loved, enjoying the touch of the delicate petals against my skin.

"I see you're making yourself at home."

Handel's caustic voice brought me out of my mellow mood and straight into defensive mode. "You startled me."

"Sorry," he said, stepping closer. He'd changed clothes at some point. Now wearing khaki slacks, a pale blue polo shirt, and a dark blue sport-jacket, his hair combed straight back from his forehead; he looked like a model for a sailing magazine. "Did you find everything to your satisfaction?" he asked.

I met his gaze, my eyes narrowed against the setting sun, and nodded politely the way I'd been raised to. My mother would be so proud. "Yes, thank you."

"Well, if you and your mother are interested I

could give you a tour of the winery before dinner."

"My mother is sleeping. Traveling always wears her out. But I'd be interested, if it's not a bother," I said, giving him my brightest smile. Perhaps the old adage was true, you caught more flies with honey. Not that I wanted to catch him. I just wanted to be treated with respect, and ironically, also admired for my long legs.

"No bother. Most of the employees have gone for the evening. You won't be in the way now," he said, as though my presence earlier would have set back wine production indefinitely. "Shall we go?"

I breathed in the heady fragrance of the rose bushes once more before following Handel Parker toward the winery.

A pickup was just pulling away as we approached and the man inside waved as he stepped on the gas. Handel waved back. "That's Charlie Simpson. He manages the place."

"I imagine he feels an extra weight of responsibility since my uncle's death."

Handel slowed his pace for me to catch up. I could tell from his expression that I had surprised him once again. Did he think of me as a spoiled brat, oblivious to the world around me? I'd worked to pay for my own things from the time I was fourteen, a year before my father's death, and even more so after that. I never had it easy, as Handel seemed to assume.

"I suppose he does," he said, opening the door for me. "Although, Jack hadn't been hands-on at the winery for years. He pretty much let the crew do their thing, and allowed Charlie to make most of the important decisions without him. He started traveling again off and on, and as you can see from the artwork in the house, he spent a great deal of time painting."

"Those are his?" I asked, suddenly wondering just

Barbara Ellen Brink

what kind of demons my uncle had been exorcising.

The winery was dimly lit, quiet after work hours. We passed offices, computers turned off, desks empty now, and paused in the open doors of the wine tasting room. Unlike many of the larger, fancier wineries that had separate buildings for their customers to come for wine tasting tours, Fredrickson's included it all under one roof. Long mahogany tables ran the length of the room, displays of wine bottles arranged on crisp, white tablecloths. Crystal goblets, placed upside down in rows of four, awaited the tourists that came by each afternoon to sample the best that Fredrickson Vineyards had to offer.

"Does Fredrickson's have tour buses or just individuals dropping by?" I asked, never having been to a wine tasting event myself.

"Both actually. During the summer months we usually get more planned tours. We were lucky to be included on the Napa Valley registry of wineries."

I found it interesting that Handel used the word *we*, but didn't comment. Instead, I stepped into the room and approached the tables, picked up a bottle of Chardonnay and held it to the light. Wine bottles have always intrigued me, whether from my forgotten time in this place, or my innate love of all things glass. The brown, green, and rose-colored bottles, darkened to protect the wine from harmful light, were long necked and graceful, their labels always printed in a sophisticated font and often trimmed in gold, adding to their allure. I liked the notion that until you poured the wine you didn't really know what was inside.

"Would you like to try a glass of this? It's one of Fredrickson's most popular." Handel said, taking the bottle from my hand and uncorking it as though I'd already consented.

I shook my head. "I'm not much of a drinker. I just like to look at the bottles." I raised one eyebrow as he filled two glasses anyway. "In fact, I have a collection of wine at home. But I rarely indulge."

He narrowed his eyes as he lifted a glass and held it toward me. "I see. Well, since this is all going to be yours, perhaps you should at least taste your own product."

"All right, but just a taste. The last time I drank too much it was not pretty." I took the glass and raised it to my face, pausing to swirl the amber liquid and breath in the bouquet as I knew was expected of me, although I was tempted to chug it in one gulp just to get his reaction. "Very nice," I said, after taking a sip.

"What do you taste?" he asked, raising his own glass to his lips.

I found myself mesmerized by his throat muscles contracting as he swallowed. The collar of his shirt was open at the top and his tanned skin didn't stop at the base of his throat. Obviously, he didn't wear a suit all the time. Maybe he did own a sailboat, as I'd imagined earlier.

"Grapes?" I volunteered.

He smiled and his eyes lit up, crinkling at the corners. And then he laughed. "Someone finally speaks the truth in the tasting room," he said, his voice filled with irony. "Usually amateur wine tasters detect all kinds of things that aren't there because they've read a book about wine. Having worked here in this tasting room for two summers during my college years, I can appreciate your honesty."

I shrugged and gulped the rest of the wine in my glass before handing it back. "Glad I could be of service."

"And when was the last time?" he asked, his voice curiously seductive.

"What?"

"The last time you drank too much. You said it wasn't pretty."

I shook my head and turned to study the black and white framed photos adorning the walls; they were original photographs of the winery and vineyards from its inception. "You don't want to hear that."

He stood close behind me; I could feel his warm breath on my neck as he peered over my shoulder. "I wouldn't have asked if I didn't want to hear."

"Just high school shenanigans, as my father used to say."

"And how did it turn out ugly? Were you sick as a dog?" His voice remained soft as though he'd asked if I loved sunsets. He put his hands on my shoulders and turned me to face him. His gaze held mine with unexpected warmth, foreign yet familiar at the same time.

I licked my lips nervously, tasting the clinging sweetness of the Chardonnay. "No. A boy attacked me and I hit him with the bottle. Broke his nose, fractured his skull, and didn't have another date for two years."

He dropped his hands and stepped back. "Violence seems to run in your family," he murmured. He corked the bottle and turned back to me again, suddenly all business. "Well, are you ready to see how wine is made?"

Perplexed by his comment and sudden change of subject, I glanced at my watch. "My mother is probably awake by now. Perhaps we should go to dinner and you can give me a more thorough tour after the funeral tomorrow."

The sky had darkened considerably by the time we returned to the house. Mother was sitting on the solitary leather couch reading a book when we walked in. She'd changed into a blue silk blouse and black slacks, her hair and makeup returned to perfection, and she looked beautiful. I was struck as always by my mother's presence; she exuded femininity, an alluring sexuality without being overt. At fifty years of age she still caught and held men's eyes when they passed. I was always flabbergasted when people commented on our similarity, unable to see it for myself. A matching shade of dark-brown hair did not make us equal. I would never be as beautiful as my mother.

"Well, it's about time you two returned," she said, setting the book aside and giving me the once-over, a look that spoke volumes. I could look forward to a talk after Handel Parker went home. It brought back memories of my teen years, spent trying to evade those conversations and heart-to-hearts with my mother. I had no intention of spilling my guts to her now. Besides, there was nothing to say other than, the sooner I put this place up for sale and got on with my life the better.

"Mr. Parker was showing me the tasting room. It was very nice, oak wainscot, historical photographs, and excellent wine," I said, summing up the experience quickly and simply. "You'll have to go over and see it before we leave on Wednesday."

Mother raised her brows. "You weren't drinking, were you, Billie? You know how alcohol affects you."

"She only had half a glass, Mrs. Fredrickson. At my insistence. I thought she should be knowledgeable of the product she now owns." Handel smiled easily at my mother, something that appeared much harder for him to do when it came to me. Resentment raised an ugly head and I tried to stomp it down, knowing that Mother was accustomed to attracting male attention, where as I seemed to scare them away.

"Oh. Well I guess half a glass won't adversely

affect the evening." She stood and looked at me. "Are you wearing that to dinner?" she asked, in a voice that wasn't really a question but an opinion.

I sighed and looked down at my skirt and top. "I guess not." I turned to Handel. "Excuse me, I'll only be a minute."

"Take your time," he said dismissively, his attention completely on my mother now. He smiled and asked if she would like a glass of wine before dinner.

I rolled my eyes and started toward my room. "You two could always go without me, you know. I'm really not very hungry."

"We wouldn't dream of it," Handel stated smoothly before my mother even had time to object.

*****

According to Handel, nightlife was plentiful in the surrounding towns, with hundreds of clubs, bars, theatre, and restaurants to choose from. Jazz bands were hot in the area, momentarily reminding me of Kent, who loved Jazz almost as much as he loved sports. He hadn't tried to contact me since our aborted date on Friday night and although I had no intention of making up with him, I held his passiveness against him too. I swept him from my mind, and focused on a lone sax player performing on a street corner we passed, drawing a crowd of music lovers. The bluesy tune found its way into the car, temporarily filling the space with a bone-aching melancholy until the distance became too great and the notes were lost in our exhaust.

Handel drove Uncle Jack's four-door BMW; I sat in back while Mother flirted outrageously with the man up front. It was truly appalling. Even so, twice I caught Handel watching me in the rearview mirror, his eyes probing as though he could see inside to the place no one was allowed, that room of my heart only I knew existed but refused to visit.

"I made reservations at a popular French restaurant," Handel said. "Its up highway 29 in Yountville. Not too far."

"I can't eat French food," I said. "It makes me sick."

"Billie!" Mother once again reprimanded me. I was beginning to think I'd never graduated from kindergarten.

"What do you want me to do?" I asked, throwing up my hands. "Hold my tongue now and practice Bulimia later? French cuisine is too rich and it makes me sick."

Handel tried not to smile but I caught his eyes in the mirror silently laughing. "Well, how about a sushi bar?" he suggested, knowing full well what my reaction would be to that.

"How about a hamburger? I'm from the Midwest. We like our meat cooked and everything else deep fried." Let him think of me as a redneck, I didn't care.

"Now you're just being silly," Mother said, shaking her head as though I never failed to amaze her with the crazy things I said. "We didn't fly all the way to California, get dressed up, and press this handsome man into escorting us to dinner, to eat a hamburger. I for one want to go somewhere memorable." She fluttered her mascara-laced eyelashes and placed her hand on his arm. "You take us wherever you think best and we will be eternally grateful. It's not every day we have the chance to enjoy an evening in the Napa Valley."

"Well, now that your daughter owns Fredrickson Vineyard, you'll have ample opportunities to visit," Handel said, implying, I suppose, that I would keep the winery.

My mother flashed me a look of concern, probably afraid I would make some comment to disparage that theory, but I remained silent, sat back against the glove leather seat and stared into the night outside our car, a black well of ink filling the sky like billions of words used up during the day.

The vineyards outside Yountville sparkled with hundreds of lights as the car's headlights swept past. "What in the world...?"

Handel glanced toward the fields. "Reflective foil is used to scare grape-eating birds away. It works rather well, actually."

I narrowed my gaze, taking in the metallic twinkling with interest. I could imagine how in the light of day, the birds would be startled continually by the reflection of the sun as the foil moved with the breeze. "Then why doesn't Fredrickson's have foil up?" I asked.

He shrugged. "That's Charlie's call. And it's a little early yet."

Yountville was the Beverly Hills of the Napa Valley, less populous than the city of Napa but more gentrified. Huge estates scattered further apart, shouted money and social standing. In the downtown area, wild flowers thick and lush with color, were planted along the streets, following the sidewalks set with half-moon pavers. Bathed only in streetlight, the effect was quaint and charming.

"I've had reservations for over three months for The French Raven," Handel complained, "but I'm sure some lucky couple from Nebraska or somewhere will be thrilled to take our place."

His sarcasm grated on my nerves. "Why would you make reservations three months ago? Did Jack tell you we were coming – before he died?" I asked. As soon as the comment was out of my mouth, I regretted it, but as usual, too late.

He took a right turn at the next corner. "No," he

said. "The French Raven is renowned for their cuisine. What with people driving down from San Francisco on a regular basis, and tourists flocking here year-round, it usually takes much longer to get reservations at the Raven, especially weekends. I'd planned to invite my sister and her son to go with me, but things change."

"Oh, Handel, I'm sorry," my mother crooned, her manner apologetic. "I wish you would have told us you already had plans. We never would have expected you to entertain us like this."

Personally, I didn't think he'd done that great a job of entertaining us so far, but a tweak of guilt crept into my conscience unbidden. "Yes," I said, "I'm sorry too. If you want to go to the French place, I'm sure I can find something to eat that won't make me sick."

"That's very generous of you," he said, meeting my gaze in the rearview mirror, "but I brought you to Antonio's instead." He pulled into a parking space of a brightly lit restaurant and shut off the engine. "Here we are. I hope Italian food doesn't make you sick."

I suppose I deserved his mocking tone but I didn't like it, or the accompanying laughter from my mother. Not waiting for him to open the door for me, sure he would do so just to rub salt into my wounded ego, I climbed out and looked around. Clusters of people stood about with drinks in their hands, waiting for a table inside. A bar was set up on a wraparound deck area, the bartender mixing drinks as fast as he could.

"Are you sure we'll be able to get in tonight? It looks awfully busy." I glanced at my watch. Dinnertime was six o'clock at home and here we'd already gone back two hours. I was starving! Fast food would be more than fine with me at this point.

He turned toward me with a self-satisfied smile, one side of his mouth turned up more than the other, extremely sexy but irritating nonetheless. "Don't worry. I know the chef." He let my mother tuck her hand in his arm and hesitated as though I would take his other side.

I ignored the unspoken offer and walked beside my mother, trying to appear graceful in my new three-inch heels. The dress I wore was a black sheath, sleeveless, the hem hovering a few inches above my knees. I'd bought it in a moment of weakness some time back, thinking I would wear it to a party with Kent. The party never materialized and I brought it along to California not knowing what occasions to pack for. This seemed just right, but now I was wishing for jeans and tennis shoes. I was already tired and ready for bed, but starving too. This dress was not a dress to stuff oneself in - literally. I didn't have an ounce of space to spare.

"Handel!" A man called as we stepped in. "Long time no see. Where have you been? Setting more criminals free?"

Handel grinned broadly. "Something like that," he said. He raised his brows and leaned in to speak in a quiet voice. "You wouldn't happen to have a table for an old friend, would you?" he asked.

The other man pretended to peer around Handel's shoulder. "What old friend would that be?" he asked. Then he slapped Handel on the back and laughed. "Of course! Let me have one readied for you." He glanced appreciatively at my mother standing there with her hand tucked possessively in the curve of Handel's arm, and then at me. His eyes widened with curiosity but he didn't comment, just signaled a waiter to clear a table for us.

Five minutes later we were seated in the corner of the dining room, the smell of oregano, basil, and garlic permeating the air around us as a waitress appeared in a starched white shirt and black slacks and set bread and olive oil on the checkered tablecloth. While she took our drink orders I started in on the bread, wondering if my dress would stretch to accommodate what I planned to pack into it.

"Are you sure you only want iced-tea?" Handel asked. "This is wine country, you know. We have the largest selection of wines here than anywhere else in the country."

I shook my head. "I'm aware of that, but one wine is as good as another if you're a violent drunk," I said, pointedly meeting his gaze across the table.

He expelled a frustrated breath. "I didn't mean anything by that," he said.

Mother watched us both, clearly losing the thread of thought. "What are you two talking about?"

Handel ran a hand through his hair and sighed. "It's nothing. A misunderstanding."

I shook my head but held his gaze as I explained. "I told Handel the story of my teenage drinking experience. You know, the one where Paul went to the hospital for stitches after attacking me, and then told all the boys at school that I came on to him?" I cleared my throat, still emotional about it after all these years. Date rape was a common term now, but then it was something altogether different. "Funny thing though -- they believed him, and so no one would ask me out through the rest of high school."

"You don't have to talk about this," Mother said, her voice soft with feelings floating to the surface. She'd been the one to hold me afterward when I woke from nightmares, thrashing in my bed against a shadowy villain, unable to see his face but quite sure that he would look exactly like Paul in the morning light. My father, who normally coddled me, shielded me from bad influences when he could, and naturally tried to keep me his little girl, drew away and became distant. He never came to my defense when the police questioned me about Paul's injuries, but shrugged it off as teenage shenanigans. I never understood what precipitated the change in his attitude toward me. I suppose he blamed me, as most people did.

"No," Handel echoed. "Lets change the subject."

I detected pity in his voice and I couldn't stay quiet. "Wait a minute! I want to know what you meant by your comment. Violence runs in the family." I stared him down, my hands clasped tightly in my lap. "Was Uncle Jack violent? Is that why he painted all those wacko pictures?"

He slowly shook his head. "No. Jack was very patient and kind to everyone I ever saw him with."

"Then what did you mean?" I opened my eyes wide in mock surprise. "You weren't implying that my mother has a violent streak, were you?"

"Billie!"

"Don't worry, Mother. I'll be your expert witness." I pointed my finger in Handel's direction. "My mother has never raised her hand to me in anger. She is the epitome of restraint. Although, she has been known to raise her voice slightly when she says my name."

"Billie!"

"You see?" I reached for another slice of bread. "This is really good. Thanks for bringing us, Handel."

Handel rubbed his palm along his jaw line and cleared his throat; obviously uncomfortable with the direction the conversation was going. "I wasn't referring to your mother either," he finally said. "I told you I worked at the winery doing odd jobs when I was a small boy. Well, I remember the weeks you were there... vividly. I was asked to go behind the winery and carry some old grape crates up to the equipment shed. When I rounded the side of the building I saw your father standing over Jack, kicking him in the ribs. Jack's face was bleeding and he lay curled up on the ground in pain. Your father turned and saw me. His eyes were cold and filled with rage. That's what I remember. He walked away and I ran home, afraid to tell anyone for fear he'd come after me. That's the same day you left and went back to Minnesota."

Mother made a noise that sounded like a whimper, but when I reached my hand out toward her she remained still, her beautiful face turned to stone. Petrified mother. I placed my arms on the table and leaned toward Handel, lowering my voice now that all hell had broke loose. "What are you talking about? You're crazy," I said, although I felt the truth in his words even though it was hard to believe them. Somehow I knew that my father had done the very thing Handel accused him of, and yet I couldn't dredge up even an ounce of regret.

"We never saw Jack after that trip," my mother finally said, her face suddenly pale with the shock of Handel's admission.

I guessed what she must think. Dad knew of her feelings for Jack and beat him in a jealous rage. "Mother, it had nothing to do with you. Brothers get into fights all the time, for a myriad of reasons, most of which is plain old sibling rivalry tacked on to a healthy dose of male ego." I reached out and took her hand, trying to convey reassurance. "Besides, there is no sense in becoming distressed over something that happened over twenty years ago. If Dad really did what Handel remembers, then he must have had a good reason. He was not a violent man." The one time I wished for my father's aggression, he'd remained silent and passive, letting me, his only daughter, bear the shame for something beyond my control.

"Excuse me," my mother said, rising from her chair. "I'll be right back."

I released her hand and let her walk away, knowing full well she didn't want me to follow. We were really more alike than people realized, keeping our true feelings hidden from the world as much as possible. She often tried to discuss my personal life openly, but immediately shut down when I pressed her about her own.

Handel expelled a sigh and leaned forward across the table, his fingers nervously folding the edge of his napkin. "I'm sorry. I didn't mean to upset your mother."

"But you have no problem upsetting me, right?"

The waitress returned with our drinks, and he waited until she moved on before responding. "That's not true. I'm sorry you had to hear that about your father. It must be painful."

"Don't worry about it. As they say, the truth will set us free." I didn't really believe it and I don't think Handel did either. I took a long drink of iced-tea and wished I'd ordered something stronger.

Chapter Four

The memorial service was rather simple. Jack had been cremated, per his written request, and wanted his ashes scattered by crop duster over the Fredrickson Vineyards. I for one was not going to be involved in that procedure. The urn that Jack's remains now occupied sat on a pedestal at the front of the chapel along with an enlarged photograph of Jack facing the mourners as though he didn't want to miss a thing.

Mother and I sat on the right side of the chapel, in the front row, the somewhat-grieving extended family. Well, Mother did have a tissue handy in case she got teary-eyed. Fredrickson vineyard employees sat on the left, along with a few local vintners Jack had been acquainted with over the years. Handel arrived with a pretty blonde woman who reminded me of a very young Marilyn Monroe, and the little boy I'd spied from the bedroom window the day before. His sister and nephew. They took the seats directly behind us.

Handel reached out and touched my shoulder. "Good morning. I see you found the chapel all right."

Mother and I turned to look back and I nodded.

"You gave good directions." I glanced at the woman next to him and smiled. She smiled back and nudged Handel.

"Oh, sorry. Billie, Mrs. Fredrickson -- this is my sister, Margaret. And this big guy," Handel patted the boy's knee, "is David. But he likes to be called, Davy, as in Davy Crockett."

"Mrs. Fredrickson sounds so formal," Mother said. "Why don't you call me Sabrina?"

"Its nice to meet you, Sabrina, and you too Billie. I'm just sorry that it's under such sad circumstances," Margaret said.

"Yes, thank you," Mother murmured as though Jack had actually been someone she'd often thought of during the past twenty years, and I wondered if it were true.

The nondenominational minister stepped to the front of the chapel and cleared her throat for attention. "Welcome, friends and family members of the late Jack Oliver Fredrickson."

The service was short, rather like the guest list, and no one hung around longer than it took to pay their respects and eye me, the heir to the Fredrickson Vineyards, with suspicion. Only Charlie Simpson dared approach, a solemn smile on his lips as he held out a hand.

"I'm very sorry for your loss, Ms. Fredrickson," he said. "I hope you know that I'm available whenever you want to discuss the operation of the winery."

He was shorter than he'd appeared through the window of his pickup truck the day before. His head and torso looked as though they belonged to a much larger man, but his arms and legs were stubby, reminding me of one of those miniature horses. I shook his hand.

"Thank you, Mr. Simpson. I appreciate that." I had no intention of keeping and running the winery, but this was no time to divulge that information. Other employees of Fredrickson Vineyard were standing nearby, obviously waiting for confirmation that their jobs were intact. A twinge of guilt pricked my conscience as I met their eyes across the room.

I agreed to meet with Handel in his office after I took Mother back to the house. The area was already becoming familiar and I marveled at the clear blue skies and continued sunshine after the bout of rain and clouds we'd endured in Minneapolis lately. There was something about California that drew people in, whether a combination of sunshine, year-round mild temperatures, fresh fruit, movie stars, and wineries, or just a special magic God imbued it with when he said, "and let there be California."

"Are you sure you don't want to come along?" I asked, glancing at my mother.

She shook her head. "I don't think so, honey. You can tell me all about it later. I'm going to lay down and see if this headache will go away."

She'd been unnaturally quiet since dinner last night, and I worried that she was taking my father's actions, twenty years ago, personally.

I waited as she climbed out of the car. She turned and smiled in at me before shutting the door and starting up the walk. I watched until she let herself in the house before heading back toward town.

Handel's office was located in a conventional style building, lots of glass sparkling in the sun. I took the stairs to the second floor and introduced myself to his secretary, a thin middle-aged woman in a conservative brown linen suit. Unlike Jody, my part-time secretary/receptionist/gopher/advice-giver, this woman exuded confidence and professionalism. She looked busy without appearing harried or stressed, something Jody was working on. The woman buzzed Handel on the intercom. "Mr. Parker, Ms. Fredrickson is here to see you."

"Thank you," I said.

The door to his private office opened and Handel waved me in. "You got here rather quickly. I just walked in myself after dropping Margaret and Davy off at home."

"I'm ready to get the paperwork finished up. I have clients to get back to. I can't hang around here forever, no matter how beautiful it is." I flashed him a smile, feeling more relaxed since the funeral was out of the way.

He nodded and offered me a seat in one of the chairs across from his desk. They were made of redwood with soft Moroccan leather covering the seats and backs, smaller versions of his chair except for the swivel base. His desk was massive, shining from a recent oiling, the top cleared except for a folder placed directly in front of him.

"Jack made a video that he wanted you to view before we go over the will," he began, opening the folder and pulling out a thick manila envelope. He slit the top with a letter opener and shook out a DVD disc, then swiveled his chair around and inserted it into a combination DVD/television on a shelf against the wall. With the remote in hand, he came around the desk to sit in the chair beside me.

"Before you begin," I said quickly, "I want to thank you for all your help. You have obviously gone above and beyond a lawyer's duties to accommodate everyone involved. Although you feel that you owe my uncle, you certainly aren't in any way obligated to my mother or me, and yet you went out of your way to take care of us while we were here. I appreciate it."

He raised his brows a fraction, surprise evident in his expression. "Wow. After the way I screwed up last night, I didn't expect a thank you."

I smiled and shrugged. "Let bygones be bygones. As I recall, I've said a few things lately that I've regretted."

"All right. Are you ready?" He lifted the remote and pressed play. "Jack dated the disc a week before he died," he explained as the picture blinked on.

The recording was obviously made in the living room of Jack's house. He'd positioned the chair close to the fireplace for ambiance or something, and sat in it with his hands lightly gripping the arms, as though uncomfortable with the whole process.

Jack Fredrickson was tall and thin, his black hair peppered with grey but still abundant. His face held a slight resemblance to my father through the nose and mouth, but his eyes were hooded, his brows dark and thick, and his skin weathered from living most of his life outdoors. For a man who would die within the week he looked extremely healthy. He sat stiffly, his gaze rapt on the lens of the camera as he spoke.

"Hello, Billie." He smiled and I felt as though he were looking right at me, a ghost from my past sending a chill down my spine. His voice was gentle as I imagined a wild-horse tamer's would be, and yet there was something about it, an inflection perhaps, that wasn't quieting, but frightening to me.

"It's been many years since we met, and yet each day I look out on the vineyards and relive those moments we had together. They were precious to me as I hope they were to you." He paused a moment and licked his lips as though pondering.

"I know the winery was a magical place for you then and I believe it can be again. Give it a chance. Soak up the colors and smells like a true connoisseur, live in the moment, and yet dream of the past when we were together and time stood still for three short weeks." He picked up a bottle of wine from the floor near his chair and held it up. The label was unlike any I'd seen before, the picture of a clock, obviously drawn by a young child, and the words, **Time In A Bottle**, emboldened in black.

"Remember the special wine we made together? I kept it for you." He stood up and stepped toward the camera until his torso filled the entire frame, and the camera blinked off.

Handel glanced at me, a puzzled frown between his brows, and clicked off the television with the remote. "Okay, that was strange."

I felt a tremor in my chest that began to spread outward to my limbs. "You never saw it before?" I asked, my voice cracking on the last word. What in the world was wrong with me? I felt as though I were having an anxiety attack. Something I'd never experienced personally, but had witnessed more than once with emotional clients.

He slowly shook his head, his eyes on me; probing for answers to questions I couldn't ask myself. "The envelope was sealed. Jack didn't share its contents with me. Just asked that I give it to you in the event of his death."

I stood up abruptly. "I have to go," I said. My heart was beating so hard I could hear it in my ears. "I have to go," I repeated breathlessly as I pulled open the office door and hurried out.

"Billie!" Handel called after me, and then the door closed and I was heading for the stairs.

I stopped and leaned against the wall, breathing deeply through my nose, unable to stop the acceleration of my heart. The only thought running through my head was that I needed to get to my mother. She would know what to do.

"Billie!" Handel caught up to me and caught me by the forearms just as I felt my knees begin to buckle. "What's wrong? Are you sick?"

His voice was muted as though someone had turned the volume down on his mouth. I tried to read his lips, but then the picture went out too, and everything faded to black.

*****

When I came to, I was lying on the couch in Handel's office, my shoes off and a wet cloth pressed to my forehead. I looked up and found Handel and his secretary both staring down at me, their eyes filled with concern.

I pushed the cloth away and tried to sit up. Dizziness slowed the process and I put my hand to my head, feeling the beginnings of a major migraine coming on. "I'm fine," I lied. I tried to smile up at Handel, but from the expression on his face it must have looked more like a grimace. "I'm all right, really. I just haven't eaten anything since last night. That's all."

His secretary smiled brightly. "You see, Mr. Parker, I told you she'd be fine. Funerals are very stressful. Grief affects everyone differently." She patted my shoulder as the phone on her desk began to ring. "Hope you feel better soon, dear. I'll leave you in Mr. Parker's capable hands."

"Thank you, Patty," Handel called after her as she hurried to answer the call.

I put my feet on the floor, slipped my heels back on, and attempted to stand. Handel grabbed my arm for support. "Thank you, but I'm fine," I said firmly.

He stepped back, his arms loosely at his sides. "I hate to contradict a client, but you don't look fine.

You're white as a sheet."

"I just need to eat something." I had no idea if that was the case but it seemed to be the logical explanation. Although, I rarely ate breakfast and had never fainted because of it. I walked back to the desk and picked up my purse from the chair where I'd left it earlier, opened it and rummaged for the package of airline almonds I'd stowed in there. "Ah ha! Food." I opened them and shook out a handful.

"If that's really the case, then I'll take you to lunch," Handel offered. "At least hunger makes more sense than grief."

"Very funny." I resumed my seat across from his desk and popped some nuts in my mouth.

He followed, sitting down and staring across the desk at me as though I were a high-risk flight and he was debating whether to put up my bond money. "Would you like a cola to go with that?" he asked.

"This will suffice for now. Lets get this over with. I have my return flight booked for two o'clock tomorrow afternoon."

"Oh yes. Inherit a winery one day and fly home the next. How do you expect to run the place two thousand miles away?" he asked, leaning back in his chair. "Charlie is a good manager but he needs direction. Someone to guide him to put up foil to fend off the birds, get the grapes in at the appropriate time, make sure the place is making money rather than losing it, etcetera." He folded his hands on the desk before him. "I thought maybe you could be that guiding hand. There are a lot of people counting on you. From what Jack said, you used to love the winery. Maybe you would again if you gave it a chance."

"I already have a lot of people counting on me--at home." I crossed my legs and folded my arms, realizing belatedly that my body language was speaking volumes. "Now can we get on with it?"

The will was simple. I was now the proud owner of a winery, vineyard, house, and everything that went with it, including a sizable nest egg in stocks and bonds. Jack left large bonuses to his trusted employees and a ten thousand dollar donation to the church where his funeral was held. That was all. Except for a sealed letter, to be opened by me only if I decided to keep and run the vineyard. Which at this point, I saw no such thing happening. But Handel insisted I take it with me anyway, just in case I changed my mind before my flight left for Minnesota.

*****

I pulled the BMW into the garage and climbed out. The letter was in my purse. I imagined smoke coming from beneath the flap as it tried to burn a hole through the lining to me. I was having second thoughts about the wisdom of allowing Handel to talk me into keeping it. Like a doomsday prophecy, the sealed envelope cried out to be read. Was it a list of instructions on how to run the winery, or a detailed who's who list of employees and their various idiosyncrasies? I imagined a revised will revoking everything Uncle Jack stated in his earlier will and telling me it was all a cruel joke. I wasn't sure if that last would be a blessing or a curse.

My mother was in the kitchen making a pot of fresh coffee and toasting a bagel. I smiled and took two cups out of the cupboard. "I'll have what you're having."

She popped another bagel in the toaster. "How did it go? Are you still an attorney or have you traded in your law practice for the wine business?" she asked, sitting down in a chair at the kitchen table. The small dining set was too old and beat up to be merely retro. The chrome-plated legs of the oval table had begun to peel and the cobalt blue vinyl-covered chairs were scratched and faded. I wondered if Uncle Jack bought it in the Fifties or found it in a junk shop after giving the rest of his furniture away.

I sat down across from my mother as we waited for the coffee, propping my head up on my hand. "I'll always be an attorney, Mother. Never fear. If I have anything to say about it, divorce will continue to be the number one choice for warring couples in America."

My caustic humor brought a frown to her normally smooth forehead. "You shouldn't joke about such things, Billie," she said, shaking her head slowly. "I've often wondered why you chose such a negative area of the law to work in. Divorce is so depressing, so painful, and so final."

I raised my brows. "And so lucrative," I added. "You know how they say, death and taxes, well they should add divorce to that. Make it a threesome."

"Do you really believe that, honey? That marriage ultimately ends in divorce?"

I shrugged. "The ones I've known," I said. The coffee maker stopped sputtering and I pushed my chair back and stood up. "I'm sure there are a handful of super-humans that can put up with each others quirks until death parts them, but they are few and far between."

"Marriage is not for the faint of heart, certainly, but it's much more than putting up with someone, it's about loving someone in spite of their flaws, or maybe because of them. We may not always like them, but we continue to love them, because without love we're all lost."

I poured the coffee and carried the cups back to the table, my hands shaking slightly as I set them down. Coffee sloshed over the side and I turned to find a dishrag. "Yes, I know. Love makes the world go round."

She lifted the cups and let me wipe the spill under them. "You say it, but you don't sound like you mean it. Did you break up with Kent?" she asked, as though the two went hand in hand.

The popping up of the bagels saved me from meeting her gaze. I turned to fetch them. When I brought them to the table, she peered at me across the rim of her cup, the question still posed in her expression. She sat perfectly straight in her chair as though she was the queen of England, and of course posture is very important to royalty and mothers, it gives them the edge in authority.

"What does that have to do with anything?" I finally asked, piercingly aware that she could see behind my walls like no one else.

Mother released an exasperated sigh. "You know perfectly well what it has to do with our conversation. You won't commit to a real relationship and you always find some excuse to break up with a man when things get a might too serious. We all have flaws whether we marry or not, Billie. Are you going to divorce me as your mother because I tend to be too nosy sometimes?" She reached out and patted my hand lying on the tabletop.

I laughed, trying to keep things light. "If I were, I would have done it a long time ago, mother."

"Perhaps. Is that what you did to your father - divorce him, after the thing with Paul?" Her voice, usually so strong and decisive, was soft and unsure.

I couldn't respond for ten long seconds, an eternity for a lawyer. When I spoke I looked at the bagel on my plate, unable to meet her gaze. "I never filed against my father, he filed against me. I only went along with the clauses that he set forth."

I drew a deep breath and finally looked up. She

nodded, her eyes pooling with tears. "Something happened to him that night; a door to his soul closed. I'm not sure what was going through his head, but he was never the same."

"Yes, well I know what was going through his head. He thought I deserved what I got and that Paul was only doing what any red-blooded young man would do in his situation with a girl throwing herself at him." I ground out the words, feeling the blade twist in the unhealed places of my heart. The bitterness I still felt was so sharp I could taste it on my tongue.

Mother shook her head now, tears slipping quietly down her cheeks unheeded. "You don't know what you're talking about. He never blamed you. He loved you more than you dare love a child -- knowing that God can take them at any time." She pushed the bagel and coffee to the side and leaned across the table with both hands outstretched, weaving my fingers with her own. "It was as if he gave up. He realized that no matter what he did, ultimately he couldn't keep you from harm. He was not in control of other people and their actions, the spinning of the earth on its axis, or whether or not the sun would rise the next day. He was just a man, and for some reason that made him feel inadequate to continue being your father in the way he'd always done. In fact, he was no longer the same husband either." She sniffed and gave me a watery smile. "But I never stopped loving him, or demanded a divorce. He did the best he could until the day he died."

I pulled my hands away and scraped my chair back. "Well, you can forgive and forget if you'd like, but it's not that easy for me." I stood up and crossed my arms in the defensive mode I used when I started feeling closed in. "He should have come to my defense! I was the one wronged, not him!"

Mother swiped the wetness from beneath her eyes with the pads of her fingers, slow, careful, movements that felt drawn out. I could see that the subject had opened old wounds for her too, and she desired closure, but I wasn't ready for that yet. Only red-hot fire could cauterize a wound and I still needed to burn a few degrees hotter.

"You can't stay mad at him forever, honey. You've got to let it go. Try to remember the good times you shared," she said, her voice pensive. She slipped out of her chair and came around the table. "But no matter what, I'll always love you." She leaned in and kissed my cheek and I felt a section of the wall crumble beneath her touch. I opened my arms and pulled her into them, my chin resting snugly against her shoulder.

"I love you too, Mom."

She laughed, a sound rent from tears and surprise. "You haven't called me that for years," she said.

"Sorry," I said, pulling away.

"Don't be. I like it." She took my face in her hands. "Are you sure you're ready to go home tomorrow? Maybe you should stay here a few more days and think things over. Living in sunny California might be kind of nice, you know," she said, her smile wistful. "I could stay too, if you want me to."

I made a face and shrugged. "I don't know. Life in Minnesota's not so bad. Besides, I don't know how to be anything but a divorce attorney. It's what I am."

She shook her head. "You're a beautiful, kind, compassionate, loving woman. And my daughter. Divorce law is what you do, not who you are. You can do anything you want to do, even become a wine vintner. Don't sell yourself short. You have depths of talent you haven't even begun to plumb."

I grinned. "And I suppose they were all inherited

from you."

"Of course. My genes are top-notch."

"Yes, they are," I agreed.

She went to the sink and poured her cold coffee down the drain and refilled it with fresh from the carafe. "You never did say what happened with Kent," she stated over her shoulder.

"Didn't I?" I picked up my purse and dropped the car keys on the counter. "I've got some thinking to do. I'll see you later. Feel free to take my new BMW for a spin if you'd like."

I hurried to my room before she could press me further. I still didn't want to get into it. Mother never really liked Kent, but I knew she wanted me to find someone to settle down with and eventually get married so I could procreate and give her half a dozen grandchildren. She would make a wonderful grandmother, spoiling them and filling them with treats, then turning them back over to me to deal with the repercussions, but doing it all with love.

My cell phone broke into a rendition of Beethoven's Fifth as I climbed up on the edge of the bed, the ring tone informing me that it was a call from the office. I took it out of my purse and flipped it open. "Hello, Jody."

"Hey. Just wanted to touch base with you before I went home for the day," she said. I could hear young voices arguing in the background and wondered if her kids had been there all day.

"Okay. How's it going?" I lay back on the bed and stared at the ceiling, imagining the office being used as daycare for three teenagers. Hopefully they didn't break any windows or get gum on my wood floors.

"Everything is fine," she said, although her voice sounded strained and tired, probably from yelling.

"Well, Mrs. Booth did call three times today. She said her husband has been making threats."

My grip tightened on the phone. Violence was one of the things I dealt with as a divorce lawyer, since many of the women that came to me were in abusive relationships and needed to get out. I didn't advertise for these women, but through word of mouth a continual trickle of mentally and physically wounded walked through my office doors looking for a savior. I was perhaps the only person willing to fill those shoes. They very seldom could pay, but the relief and gratefulness in their eyes were compensation enough.

"What sort of threats?"

She must have placed her palm over the receiver because I could hear her muffled voice as she spoke to her kids. Then she was back on the line. "Sorry about that. The girls are here." She cleared her throat. "He threatened her bodily harm. Told her he would see her dead before he would let her go."

"I see. Well, you know what to do. Make sure she files a report with the police. I want every threat well documented." I pushed up on one elbow and faced the painting above the headboard. A motley assortment of objects pressed out from the canvas as though trying to escape. I thought I saw a cat, an ax, a giant ant, and a pitchfork amid the blotchy colors, but it could just be my over-active imagination. Everyone probably saw something different in this sort of art.

"I already did." Jody coughed lightly, and I knew she was running her hand through her short brown hair as she always did when she talked on the phone. She paused. "The building manager came by this morning right after I got in," she said, her voice quieter.

I frowned. "Ted Churchill? What did he want? I'm not behind in my rent and I haven't been smoking on the premises like old Betty does down the hall."

"No, but you haven't signed the new lease. The rent was raised and additional charges added to pay for remodeling of the public restrooms." Jody sounded apologetic, as though it were her fault. She had complained louder than most about the dilapidated facilities.

"Great! Like the rent wasn't high enough already. They finally remodel something that should have been done ten years ago, before I ever moved into the building, and now they want me to help pay for it," I grouched. I'd actually gotten rather attached to the slate rock exterior and dark, dimly lit interior of my office building. Like a bear returning to its cave in winter, I traversed those familiar halls each day, my home away from home. "So Churchill expects me to sign on for another year, huh?"

"Actually," she said, "he wants you to sign on for five. It's the new policy."

I closed my eyes and drew a deep breath. Five years? I no longer felt sure what I would be doing in five weeks, much less five years.

"Oh–I almost forgot," she said quickly as though just realizing she'd called long distance and was trying to make up for lost time. "Kent called this afternoon. He wanted to set up a date for Wednesday night to meet for dinner. I told him you were still out of town and he asked where you went. I figured you told him on Friday night, but he seemed surprised, said he never met you Friday." There was a pointed question in her voice.

I was glad for the thousands of miles separating me from the office because in person Jody would have the entire story out of me in under a minute. She knew when I was being evasive and became a pit-bull in her questioning. She should have been a lawyer. I sat up and stared at my open purse beside me on the bed. The edge of the letter stuck over the lip, begging to be read.

"No, I was tired and went home instead."

She was silent for a second as though letting that information sink in. "Do you want me to go ahead and set up the date or wait until you get home tomorrow night and you can talk to him yourself?" she asked.

I chewed the inside of my jaw, my thoughts a jumble of options. If I used my return ticket I would be home tomorrow afternoon in time to deal with Kent, the Booths, my new lease, and any other problems that cropped up in my absence. I suddenly wished they'd all disappear.

I pulled the letter out and stared at it long and hard, my finger itching to peel back the flap and have full disclosure. Instead, I sat and held it in my lap, debating whether it would be easier to solve the growing problems of home, or familiarize myself with the winery and its potential problems. Never having run from a difficult case, I found it strange to suddenly feel insecure, desiring peace more than controversy.

I pushed my fingernail under the flap and ripped the letter open. Two sheets of heavy paper were folded together in thirds, stiff and crisply white with importance. I slipped them out of the envelope and smoothed them open on the bedspread. The pages held no words, only a key taped directly under the second fold, a key that brought forth more questions than it answered.

"I'm not flying home tomorrow after all." My sudden decision shocked even me. I held my breath a moment, waiting for Jody's response.

"Then when are you coming back?" she asked, worry filling her voice.

"I'm not sure. There are things I need to take care

of first. Probably just a few days. If you want to close up shop and take some time off, that would be fine. I know there isn't much for you to do when I'm gone, other than answer the phone."

Her girls were arguing in the background again, their voices rose in consternation. Jody shushed them loudly, not bothering to cover the receiver. "I could do that," she said, although I detected hesitation. She was probably worried about the lack of income.

"Jody," I said, "I'm going to have my mother bring you a check when she returns tomorrow. I appreciate your hard work, but don't think you need to keep the office open while I'm gone. Have the calls forwarded to an answering service and let me know if there are any emergencies that need to be taken care of right away. Don't worry; I intend to pay you for your time off. Have a good rest and I'll talk to you later, okay?"

"Billie, is everything all right?" she asked, before I could disconnect.

"Of course. Goodbye now." I flipped my phone closed.

Uncle Jack wanted me to have this key if I made the decision to take over running the winery. Why? I shook my head, simple reason eluding me. There were no instructions with the key, no treasure map to guide me to a chest of gold, no word at all of what it unlocked, just a brass key to secrets I might never find.

Chapter Five

"Are you sure you don't want me to stay?" Mother asked once again as she waited in line for her turn to go through the metal detector. She held a small overnight bag. She'd checked her suitcase already along with a case of Fredrickson wine. Just a few gifts for her friends at the Bridge Club, she said. People with no carry on luggage bypassed the line and went directly through the metal detectors on either side, hurrying to their flights.

"You have to go home, Mom. You don't want to miss your dinner date tonight. They only get fewer and farther between as a woman ages," I teased. Her banker had asked her out before we left; a middle-aged widower, average in every way except for the uncanny ability to make her laugh. To Mother, laughter made up for everything else that might be lacking.

She pulled me in for one last hug as we neared the beginning of the line. "All right, smarty. I'll go, but if you need me don't hesitate to call. I can be back out here just like that," she said, snapping her fingers.

"See you later, Mom." I smiled as she placed her bag carefully on the conveyor belt, slipped off her heels and put them up there too, then walked in her stocking feet through the detector to retrieve them on the other side. She slipped her shoes back on, hoisted her bag and waved one last time before hurrying off to board her plane.

I watched until she was out of sight down the long hallway. I missed the freedom of pre 9-11 when family members could go to the gate and say their goodbyes, watch men with huge ear protectors out on the tarmac scurry around performing their jobs like synchronized swimmers, the sound of engines roaring to life, escalating until the plane began its slow roll toward a place in the line near the runway, and then waving them off, although you could never tell which window to wave at, everyone was so small at that distance.

Handel had brought us to the airport, but decided to wait in the car, circling endlessly so he didn't have to park. I was glad the weather was nice as I stood for fifteen minutes waiting for his next round. I wore a short denim skirt and t-shirt, summer attire in Minnesota, but fine for the month of May here. The sun beat warmly down on my bare arms and I felt lethargy seeping into my bones before I finally spotted the car pulling up to the curb. I hurried over and climbed into the front seat. He exited from the airport before speaking.

"I knew you'd stay." Handel's bold statement was an absolute lie of course, but his surprise at my decision had been masked well.

"Sure you did."

He glanced my way and a car cut in front of him.

"Watch the road!" I yelled, not yet used to the traffic congestion or rude California drivers. "I'd prefer to live long enough to enjoy my newfound wealth."

He grinned and zipped into the flow of cars. "You'll

live. I promise."

"You shouldn't make promises you can't keep," I said, remembering how my father gave up after realizing he wasn't really in control of anything.

Handel glanced my way again, his eyes narrowed into slits against the sun. "Could you check in the glove box for a pair of sunglasses? I forgot mine this morning."

I pushed the button and let the little door fall open. A flashlight, the car's instruction manual, and a package of tissues filled the small space. "Sorry. Don't see any." I pushed it closed again.

"Terrific," he grumbled, adjusting the visors at the best possible angle.

I opened my purse and handed him my shades. "Here, try these. You drive like a girl anyway."

"Red?"

"They match your shirt."

He smiled and put them on. "Thanks for noticing. So - was the girl remark derogatory or complimentary?"

"I said girl, not woman. You figure it out."

"Ouch. You've wounded me to the quick." He pressed his hand to his chest where his heart was supposed to reside, and then accelerated, passing cars one after another until I thought we'd suddenly run onto the Indy 500 track. I gripped the door handle hard enough to turn my knuckles white.

"How's this?" he asked, his lips curving into a self-satisfied grin.

"Now you're driving like a woman with a death wish."

He laughed and slowed down, moving into the center lane. "Did you read the letter? Is that what changed your mind?" he asked, his curiosity undisguised now.

I reached for my purse and pulled the envelope out of the side pocket, holding it up for him see. "Is this what you want to know about? Are you driving like a maniac so I'll spill my guts?" I asked. "No pun intended."

"Nope, the driving is a bonus. I'm just curious. You're an attorney. Doesn't it bother you when a client leaves you completely in the dark, hiding information you might possibly have used for their defense? Not that Jack needed defending. You know what I mean." He chewed at his bottom lip as he drove, one hand guiding the steering wheel, the other resting in his lap.

I watched him drive, his attention equally divided between the task at hand and the information he was trying to pull out of me, not even diverted by the length of my bare legs stretched out beside him. I tugged at the edge of my skirt, my own thoughts making me self-conscious. Did I want him to notice me?

He reached up and scratched at his jaw in that slow way I'd noticed before when he was deep in thought. Of course, I didn't know if his deep thoughts were about the exorbitant amount of road-kill on the highway this morning or something deeper. "Don't want to tell me, huh?" he finally asked when I made no response.

I pulled the pages out and spread them open. I'd taken the key off earlier and slid it into my coin purse, but for some unknown reason kept the empty letter also. "You might be a bit disappointed when you see what he wrote," I said, turning the pages toward him.

Handel looked down and his jaw tightened, a frown forming tiny little lines of age that weren't there before. He made a scoffing sound and glanced back at the road. "What's this?" he asked, as though I were telling him a joke. "Where's the letter?"

I cleared my throat. "This is the letter. Two pieces

of blank paper."

He suddenly looked like a small boy who dropped his ice-cream cone upside down in the dirt. "No way. Jack wasn't a practical joker. What are you trying to pull?" He locked his eyes back on the road, but his grip on the steering wheel had tightened considerably, both hands now in place at eleven and two o'clock.

I released an exasperated breath and stuffed the blank pages back in the envelope, my movements deliberately angry. Every time I felt the least bit of attraction for this guy I instantly regretted it. "I'm not trying to pull anything. But unless Uncle Jack wrote in invisible ink and thought I owned a decoder ring, he didn't leave any message in this envelope other than a key." I hadn't meant to bring up the subject of the key, but now it sat between us like a giant mime waiting to be acknowledged.

I stared straight ahead, watching the bright white lines of the highway unfurl before us, mile markers come and go, vineyards, lush with leaves and blooms stretch off past my peripheral vision. I felt his gaze on me more than once but he didn't speak, not until we turned into the long drive of Fredrickson Vineyard and pulled up to the house, tires crunching on gravel as dust stirred behind us and slowly settled back down, leaving a layer of white on the once shiny black car.

"I'm sorry. It's really none of my business..." he began.

"No, it's not." I opened the door and climbed out, then turned back to glare in at him. "My uncle left all of this to me, and you hate me for it. What – did you think because he paid your way through college he thought of you as a son? Haven't you heard? Blood is thicker than water." I slammed the door and started up the walk, fumbling in my purse for the house key.

I heard the other car door slam as I turned the key in the lock. I didn't look back but I knew he was following me. I kicked the door shut and headed for the kitchen, desperate for a cup of coffee and some aspirin.

My cell phone rang as I dropped my purse on the dining table. I pulled it out and flipped it open on my way to fill up the carafe with water. "Hello?"

"Billie? It's me." Kent's familiar voice stopped me in my tracks. I stood with the pitcher in hand, staring out the window above the sink, as Handel knocked insistently at the front door. I couldn't say anything. "Are you there? Billie?"

Handel wasn't stymied for long with an unanswered door. He strode into the kitchen looking like a hellion come to wreak havoc. Criminal lawyer and criminal were very close to the same thing in my book. "Billie, I want to talk to you," he said, the apologetic tone replaced now with frustrated anger. He didn't seem to know what to be more upset about, the letter, my accusations, or my shutting the door in his face.

At the look in his eye I suddenly forgot Kent was on the line and lowered the phone to my side. "What are you doing in my house?" I demanded. I pointed the phone at him as though it were a weapon. "Take your accusations, your intrusive behavior, and your nasty California temperament and get out!"

"Billie? Billie! What's going on? Who are you talking to?" Kent asked, his voice tinny and small, coming through the airwaves from Minnesota.

A smile stretched over my face, a mask of perfect timing and revenge. It all depended on which one I wanted to hurt more. Kent drew the short straw. Handel paused in the doorway as I raised the phone to my ear. "Kent? Sorry I didn't get back to you. Just been having too much fun around here."

He was silent for a moment. "I see. Well, why didn't you tell me you were going to California? I could have rearranged some things and flown out with you. Maybe caught a game in San Francisco while we were there."

I didn't ask the question in my mind; what sort of things would you rearrange, Kent, the women you meet at the Bull Pen; but just laughed lightly. "That's quite all right. I have plenty of male companionship right here. In fact, I'm with a man right now. So I've really got to go. Bye." I flipped the phone closed and met Handel's gaze, his lips curved in amusement. He tried to hide it but failed miserably.

"Is Kent your significant other?" he asked, taking a seat at the table without being invited. It seemed to be his way.

"No." I turned back to the sink and took my time filling the carafe. My hands shook slightly and I took a deep steadying breath. "He's not significant or mine. Just another man I have no time for."

He tapped his fingers lightly on the table and cleared his throat. "Look -- I'm sorry about the conversation in the car, busting into your house, everything. Can we start over?" he asked.

I finished my coffee preparations before turning to face him, crossed my arms and leaned against the counter. "Start over? Start over the morning or start over from the moment I laid eyes on you?"

"Whatever works best."

I shook my head, trying to keep a straight face, but a smile broke through. "You're a piece of work, aren't you? I think I'd have to go back to the moment I first laid eyes on you. Nothing less will do."

"Okay, but its going to be hard to squeeze myself back into that tire swing."

"What are you talking about?"

He stood up, and turned slowly in a full circle until he faced me again, as though modeling his khakis and red polo shirt on a runway in Paris. "Don't you recognize me? We met the first time you visited Fredrickson Vineyard, twenty years ago. You called me Handy." He held his arm out at chest level. "I was about this tall, skinny as a grape vine, and in love the moment I laid eyes on you."

I bit my lip, ignoring that last bit because I didn't know how to process it. He'd told Mother and I that he worked here back then, but for some reason I hadn't put two and two together until now. I stared at him hard enough to see through the man he'd become to the boy I knew so long ago. I caught a glimpse of shaggy blonde hair, a pair of cutoff overalls and bare feet, and gasped. I nodded. "I do remember you. I called you Handy because you were always fetching things."

"That's right." Handel moved toward me, stopping within arms length, and smiled. "I'm also handy in other areas. All you have to do is ask."

I straightened up from the counter. "Such as?"

His mouth curved up on the left side. "Finding locks for keys to open."

"That's what I thought." I moved around him to the coffee pot and poured myself a cup, automatically filling one for him too. "Here," I said, thrusting it toward him, and took mine to the table.

"Gee, thanks." He followed and sat across from me, cradling his cup between his palms.

I dug through my purse until I found the little tin of aspirin at the bottom. Took three and swallowed them with a sip of coffee. I didn't know if aspirin worked well with caffeine, but I figured if one thing didn't do the trick maybe the other would. He didn't comment, just watched me patiently, one finger following the rim of his cup around and around.

"Are you saying you know what my key unlocks or are you just grasping at straws, hoping to be included in the treasure hunt?" I finally asked.

He sipped his coffee, watching me closely over the rim of his cup. His hands were tan and lean, like the rest of him, showing two sides of his personality. The thin white scar across the top of his thumb pointed to the dare devil boy he once was, but the professional manicure spoke of how far he'd come since those days. A criminal lawyer has to think a bit like a criminal to get his clients off the hook. Handy knew where the dead bodies were buried and Handel would have them dug up.

He shrugged and tilted so far back on the rickety chair legs I half expected him to go down. "I always liked a mystery. Besides, now that you've decided to stay, I thought maybe we could renew our friendship."

I laughed, finally able to see past the veneer of uptight lawyer to the holy terror I vaguely remembered. "You know, my memory of those weeks is truly obscure. In fact, you're only a shadow on the screen of my life. I would hardly call what we had, friendship. Acquaintance, perhaps."

"Really? I'm amazed I didn't make a bigger impression. After all, I saved your life," he said, crossing his arms and weaving on the back legs of the chair.

I heard the groan of weakened metal and picked up my cup to keep it from spilling. "I wouldn't do that if I were you," I warned.

He frowned. "Do whaa...?" The chair collapsed beneath him, sending him crashing to the floor. His foot jerked up and kicked the edge of the table as he hit, sloshing coffee out of his cup and all over the legs of his perfectly creased, tan slacks.

I started laughing, stood up and backed away, my day pretty much made by the look on his face. I didn't like to think someone else's misery could make me happy, but there are exceptions.

He glared daggers at me. "You knew that was going to happen, didn't you?"

"No." I set my cup in the sink and turned back to face him, still grinning. "I can't see the future -- I can only hope."

"Nice. Very nice." He rubbed the back of his head as he struggled to his feet. "I have a good case to bring a suit against you," he said, lifting the broken chair and eyeing it thoughtfully.

"Really? Bring it on."

He looked up and gave a short laugh, part amusement, and part amazement. "You'd like that, wouldn't you? A nice courtroom drama to fuel your resentment."

I counted to five, not able to make it all the way to ten before I answered him. "Resentment against whom? You?" I raised my brows, curious to know what twisted perception he held of me. I watched as he calmly set the broken chair on its side, slid it out of the way, and starting mopping up the spilled coffee with a towel left sitting on the counter. On his hands and knees he looked rather appealing, like a servant boy, docile and willing to obey. "While you're down there perhaps you should pray for enlightenment." I walked out of the kitchen, leaving him to his work.

I settled into the chair by the fireplace, ignoring his presence in my house, and glanced around the room from my new perspective as a homeowner. Brighten up the walls with a fresh coat of paint, maybe a more vibrant color, and add a set of sofas and chairs, comfortable enough to fall asleep on, and it would be livable. The paintings would definitely have to go. I couldn't stand seeing my uncle's tortured soul twisting and writhing on canvas in the daylight, much less at night in an empty house.

I stood up and started pulling the smaller works of art from the walls, setting them in a stack against the couch. I couldn't reach the large gold-framed canvas over the fireplace without a ladder and some help. It looked as though it weighed quite a lot.

"What are you doing?" Handel asked from the doorway.

I turned to face him, brushing the dust from my hands. "A little housecleaning. You want to help?"

He looked up at the painting I'd been contemplating and stated the obvious. "You want that one down too."

"Yes," I said. "It's horrible. Perhaps I could sell them all to a rich, California snob who thinks art is anything that resembles half-digested food."

He laughed lightly and placed his hands on his hips. "Don't look at me. I'm not that rich. I'll get a ladder though. I think there's one in the garage."

"Thanks," I said, as he turned to go.

The sun filtered through the sheers covering the front window and spotlighted the scratched and dulled finish of the oak flooring. Another job to be done. Obviously, Uncle Jack had not spent time in home upkeep. I sighed just thinking about the work it would entail. Whether I sold the place or kept it, I would have to make it livable again.

New drapes needed to be ordered, the woodwork stripped and re-stained, and carpeting replaced in the bedrooms. The kitchen was a construction nightmare all its own. I didn't even want to think about that right now.

"Here we go." Handel arrived, lugging a ten-foot ladder, which he set up under the picture. He climbed three rungs, took hold of the frame on each side, and paused to gaze down at me. "Are you sure about this? Up close and personal its much more artistic," he informed me, crossing his eyes and making a face.

I laughed and stood closer to take a hold of the frame as he lowered it. "It looks heavy."

"Yeah, probably worth its weight in gold." He stepped carefully down, supporting his end of the painting and then some, surprise showing on his face. "Actually, its pretty light for solid gold. Guess it's not worth as much as I thought."

I ran a hand over the intricate design carved into the wood of the frame. "I bet this frame is worth more than Uncle Jack's entire collection of paintings. It's a work of art all by itself. I wonder why he would use such an expensive frame on this. Did he think he was Picasso?"

Handel shrugged and set it carefully against the stack of pictures already accumulated. "Don't know. The other frames don't look so special."

I narrowed my gaze on the stack of art. "No, they don't."

"So where do you want them?"

"Well, I'd say put them in the basement, but nobody has basements near the coast, do they? I think it's a state law in Minnesota to put a basement under every house. Not so much for fear of tornadoes, as most people think, but because we accumulate so much junk. Well above the national average. We need lots of storage space. Believe me, its murder living in a condo."

"We have attics," he offered with a shrug. "But I think you should store them in one of the extra bedroom closets until you find someone rich enough to recognize true art. That way you don't have to lug them up and back down again."

"Good idea. I already removed the pictures from the walls in my room. We can add these to the collection in the closet. That doesn't leave much space for my clothes though."

"Since you've decided to stay a while, you should move into the master bedroom. Much more closet space."

We carried Jack's masterpieces down the hall and stacked them in the closet with the three I'd already hidden away. Handel offered to help carry my clothes to the other room, but I declined.

"I'll do it later. Why don't you give me that tour of the winery you promised. We never got past the tasting room the other day."

"Are you sure you want me to take you through? Charlie Simpson would be a better guide. He'd know the answers to all your questions, or be able to find out. I'm just counsel." Handel folded the ladder and prepared to return it to the garage.

I felt disappointed at his words but nodded in agreement. "You're probably right. Besides, I wouldn't want to keep you from the office any longer than I already have."

"That's not what I meant," he said, stopping in the doorway, one hand steadying the ladder, the other pushing the hair back from his forehead. I liked the way his hair tumbled forward, fighting free from the restraints of his grooming, messy and boyish and familiar.

"Its all right. You've done enough today. Driving to the airport, cleaning up spilled coffee, fetching and carrying," I said, ticking them off on my fingers. "Go. I'll be fine."

He sighed, his face a mixture of relief and frustration. "Okay. But if you need me, call." He lifted the ladder once more and turned.

"You never did tell me how you saved my life," I called after him.

He stopped and looked back, his eyes narrowed in thought. "You don't remember?"

"Don't feel bad. I have very little memory of those weeks. Just flashes really. Images of a time I couldn't place until now. You, the tire swing, a couple of other things. But a near-death experience was not among them."

He grinned, reminding me once more of the boy from my past. "That's too bad," he said and started off again.

"You're not going to tell me?" I asked, following and opening the front door for him.

He kept walking, cutting across the yard toward the garage. "It's a long story, requiring dinner and conversation. I can be back out here by seven if that works for you," he said over one shoulder.

I watched him, my mouth hanging slightly open, wondering how this man could appear so confident when he so recently fell on his backside. Not sure how to respond, I closed the door and leaned against it. Was he asking me out on a date, or did he expect me to cook for him? And why was I wondering about it at all? He probably made the whole thing up about saving my life. I wasn't afraid of water, small spaces, or crossing bridges. I might have a slight phobia about the dark, but who liked being in the dark? Nobody, that's for sure! They didn't make dark beds to lie in and soak up creepy feelings and nightmares, charging you by the minute. They made tanning beds because people craved the sun, light, warmth, and security.

A couple minutes later I watched through the front window as Handel pulled away in his red Porsche, heading to town and his law office. I missed my own practice, mostly for the time spent solving other people's problems, my thoughts turned outward rather than inward, my days filled with work and research. At night I had no time for dreams or self-discovery, but fell into bed exhausted enough to sleep uninterrupted until morning when I would do it all again. But here things were different. Here I was actually trying to find out what I wanted, what I had or something new, a law practice or a winery, an exhausting but fulfilling job, or... a life.

Chapter Six

"I always prefer the red wines. The rich color makes me think it tastes better. I'm not much of a drinker," I explained as Charlie Simpson took me through the winery.

Charlie nodded, his eyes alight, eager to share his love for the wine making process. "You're absolutely right."

"What did I say?"

He chuckled as though we shared a joke. "You said the color makes you think it tastes better. The color is sort of an optical illusion. The eye tells the brain your tongue is going to taste a more concentrated wine, but in fact the color is not necessarily connotative of depth of flavor."

"Really? So, what makes wine red? Darker grapes?"

He put out a hand and placed it on the side of the wine press machine. "Not always. The same grapes can be used for white, but when the grape berries are crushed in the press, we immediately separate the skins and seeds from the free run juice. That eliminates most of the color. For red wine, the grape berries are introduced whole into tanks."

We walked on as he pointed out other machinery and explained their part of the process. By the time he'd gone through clarification, filtration, and aging, showing me step by step the birth of a new wine, explained temperature and humidity control, and introduced me to many of the employees, I was exhausted.

I stared up at the oak barrels lining the decanting room and shook my head slowly. "Wine making is truly an art, isn't it?"

Charlie smiled, his top teeth protruding slightly over his bottom lip. "I never thought of myself as an artist, but I guess so. Harvesting the grapes at the exact right time, the separation process, everything you do decides the outcome of the wine, whether it's a good year or a terrific one." He seemed pleased by my acknowledgement and his bulky chest puffed up even more.

"Well, I'm certainly no expert, but it appears you've done a good job running the place, Charlie. I understand my uncle wasn't much of a hands-on vintner."

He cleared his throat and looked away when he answered. "Jack was busy with other things. He left the running of Fredrickson Vineyard and Winery to me most of the time. Every so often he would come take a look around, check things out, and make sure there weren't any catastrophes to speak of, then he'd be off again. Either traveling out of the country, or on his sailboat."

"Was that what kept him busy? Traveling and sailing?" I asked. Didn't he like Uncle Jack?

He met my gaze, his brows nearly connecting in a thoughtful frown over pale blue eyes, faded with sun and time, edged with dozens of tiny lines caused by squinting into the light. "That and something else. He has a workroom here, an underground cellar that was built years before he bought the winery. He spent a lot of time down there. He said he was perfecting a wine that would revolutionize the world." He shrugged, his palms raised toward the ceiling. "Whatever that means. He would carry grapes and supplies down for making small batches, but I never saw a finished product." His tone spoke volumes about what he really thought. He believed Jack was a nut. It was as simple as that. But that deeply ingrained sentiment, Never speak ill of the dead, kept him from saying so.

"I see. Where is this cellar?" I asked. "Have you gone down and checked it out since he died?"

"Can't. Not unless I have the door taken off. Thought I should wait for the new owner's approval," he said with a grin. "Jack installed a lock and didn't bother to leave me with a key." He led me through another doorway and pointed ahead. "But I can show you where it is."

I followed eagerly, suddenly energized by the thought of discovery. Could this be the door I had the key for? We passed through two other rooms filled with wine barrels and finally stopped before a door marked *Private*. He jiggled the knob as though just this once it would be open and we could explore.

"This is it. The secret cellar," he said with a smirk.

"You mean no one has been down there except Uncle Jack?" I asked.

He shook his head. "Not that I know of. Not since I've been working here."

I had no intention of exploring the room with Charlie watching over my shoulder and so I made no mention of the key I kept in my purse. I would come back later when everyone had gone home for the night. On the video disc Jack presented the special wine we made together when I was eight years old, and I was curious to know if it was the same secret concoction he'd continued to work on over the years, alone in this cellar, without any other soul knowing what went on down there.

I thanked Charlie for the tour and promised I'd be back to learn more. I wanted to know exactly what I'd gotten myself into and whether wine making was something I might be good at. There was certainly a lot to learn and it wouldn't come about through osmosis. It would take time and patience working under Charlie's mentoring, along with a significant amount of perseverance and natural talent.

Dusk was settling into night when I waved Charlie off in his pickup and headed back to the house. I hadn't left a light burning, and shadows blanketed the interior, still unfamiliar enough to cause me to stub my toe against something in the hallway. I reached the living room before finding a light switch, illuminating the sparsely furnished room now complete with empty walls.

The light blinked on the answering machine at the kitchen counter and I listened to a rambling account of Mother's flight and subsequent ride home from the airport with my brother Adam before she collected her thoughts, her voice becoming warm as fresh muffins as she ended her monologue.

"Honey, I just want you to know that you can call me anytime, day or night, if you need to talk. I love you. I'll catch up with you later." The machine was quiet after that with no more messages to impart.

I sat down at the table and looked around. The house remained quiet, unwilling to intrude upon my thoughts with creaks and groans as it had the night before when I tried to sleep. The yellow flowered wallpaper pressed in around me, ebbed and flowed as I breathed in and out, and I knew I'd gone too long without adequate sleep. My eyes started acting up when I was tired.

Thoughts of the locked cellar door and what I might find down there clashed in my mind with the more pressing concern of Handel's dinner invitation, or intrusion, however you looked at it, sending me hurrying off to shower and change before he showed up. Exploring my uncle's secret room would have to wait.

*****

Handel brought a bucket of fried chicken, biscuits, and potato salad, holding them out at the door like a peace offering. "How's this? Deep-fried heart stoppers. What do you think? Is it mid-western enough for you?" he asked with a grin.

I waved him in. "It'll do."

He followed me to the kitchen and set the food on the table while I searched the cupboard for plates. Uncle Jack's old china still remained, chipped and marred with hairline cracks, edged in faded Morning Glories, odd numbered stacks of five plates, three cereal bowls, six cups and saucers. Obviously, I was unprepared to give a formal dinner party.

"So, how was your tour of the winery?" Handel asked, as he reached for a third piece of chicken. "Did Charlie answer all your questions to your satisfaction?"

"Only the ones I could think of."

"What does that mean?"

"It's a lot to take in. He showed me around and tried to explain all the machinery involved, the creation of wine, etcetera, but I'm sure what's really needed is in-depth research and hands on involvement to fully understand everything. Or even know what questions to ask." I sat back and stifled a yawn.

"You're right. I've lived around the winery most of my life, but I don't know if I'd be able to explain all that goes into wine making. My father always lost me when he started droning on about clarification and the like."

I picked up my plate and carried it to the sink. Outside the trees were lit up, individual leaves reflecting the moon's yellow glow, sparkling gaily as they moved with the breeze. A perfect night in wine country.

"I thought the purpose of your return tonight was to tell me how you heroically saved my life so long ago," I said, filling the sink with soapy hot water. "Or have you forgotten the details as well?"

"That isn't possible. A boy doesn't become a hero every day, you know."

I turned around, a small smile of encouragement curving my lips. "I expect not. So...? What's the story?"

He wiped his fingers on a paper napkin. "You were playing hide and seek one morning. You climbed into an empty barrel and pulled the lid on. I happened to be skulking around, looking for something to do, and saw you. Your uncle walked right by the barrels and on into the winery. A couple minutes later my father showed up. He noticed the lid was loose and stopped to tap it down with the hammer he always kept on his belt. Lids have to be tight around here or mice tend to move in and occupy the joint." He grinned. "Free room and board. Anyway, I knew you were stuck and probably finding it hard to breathe. I waited until my dad went around back of the buildings before running over to help you. By the time I got that lid back off you were white as a sheet. You threw your arms around me and held on like a cocklebur."

I narrowed my eyes. "That's how you saved my life?" I asked. "By opening a lid? I could have yelled for help and any number of people would have let me out."

His blue gaze darkened like the sky before nightfall. He shook his head. "You would have stayed in that barrel for hours and never cried out. Being sealed in there frightened you, but something outside frightened you even more. All I know is, you were pretty happy when you opened your eyes and saw me."

"My eyes were shut?" The notion seemed odd. It took my mother years to wean me from the nightlight in my room. I'd wake in the dark, my eyes wide with the strain of trying to see beyond the veil of shadows. Wasn't it natural to try to see even when there was no light?

He bit at his bottom lip as though thinking back. "Yeah," he said with a nod. "Until I spoke your name."

I turned back to the sink and washed my plate and glass. The full moon caught my attention through the window and pulled my thoughts like the ocean tide.

"Would you like to go for a walk?" Handel asked, reaching around me to set his plate in the sink. I felt as though he'd read my mind when he said, "The moon's full enough to light our way. Besides, I need to work some of this off." He patted his stomach, but his body looked firm and well toned in the jeans and yellow t-shirt he wore. I knew from experience that an office job was not compatible with staying in shape. It took running at least four times a week to maintain the size I'd been since high school. He obviously worked out at a gym on a regular basis.

"Sure," I said. He didn't step back when I turned, but stayed where he was, filling my personal space like an extra passenger on a single person raft. My lower back pressed into the edge of the counter as he leaned in, his face mere inches from mine, like a butterfly's antennae feeling me out for approachable sweetness. I cleared my throat and the moment was gone.

He drew slowly back, his eyes dark and hooded. "Okay, let's go," he said, moving away, suddenly intent on escape, leaving the impression of warmth on my skin and a debilitating fear in my heart.

Taking a chance was something I'd never truly done. Kent was not a man I took seriously. I knew in my heart that his actions at the sport bar, although hurtful to my pride, were something I'd almost expected. He thought football was the cornerstone of America and families were just an afterthought in God's plan. But Handel was something else entirely. I had no idea where he fit into the scheme of things. Or whether he would fit.

In my small world-view, women mooned after men, then realized they were married to a werewolf and wanted out. I helped them break the tie that binds, but more often than not they went right out and did it again. Divorce law could definitely be lucrative if you took the right clients, but not fulfilling. Why had I ever thought so? It made me tired, depressed, and leery of all men, approaching them as wild stallions that would bolt and run at the first hint of trouble.

The back door was our quickest escape. I followed Handel out onto the flagstone path, feeling the cool breeze caress my heated cheeks, and waited for his lead. He seemed to know where he was going, a plan of some kind already formulated in his mind. He took my hand and headed through the trees to the vineyards beyond, his fingers entwined securely with mine and yet loosely enough to pull away if I had the urge to be free.

"Have you ever walked through a field at night?" he asked, his voice soft as the night air around us, blending with the cricket's music and the tune that the breeze played on the leaves of the trees.

I shook my head, afraid to break the spell of perfect peace.

"I used to sneak out at night when I was a boy, pretend to be lost in a jungle. The vines were well over my head, thick with leaves, and mostly impenetrable. Of course, if I looked hard enough I could find a hole to scoot through to the next row, imagining that I was cutting through with my machete."

We started down the dirt track between the rows, our steps muffled, the vines on either side reaching toward the night sky, their leaves a green staircase to heaven. Looking ahead, the end of the row was hidden in a canopy of distant darkness, perhaps secreted away below a hilly drop-off, waiting to be discovered at our approach. Like hide-and-seek. A game that children play. Only no one was hiding.

I glanced at his shadowed profile against the light of the full moon and pictured coming here at night with a tow-headed ten-year-old boy, running through the vineyard in our bare feet, cotton pajamas flapping against our young bodies like sheets on a line. The scene was so clear in my mind that I wondered if it were a memory.

"Did I sneak out one night, while we were here, and meet you in the vineyard?" I asked, my senses filled with damp soil, grape leaves, moonlight, and a hint of the spicy aftershave Handel wore.

His fingers tightened slightly around mine as he stopped to face me. "Then you do remember," he said, his eyes reflecting the heaven's lights. "I knew if I brought you out here it would all come back."

I licked my lips; afraid his expectations were slightly higher than my own. "I don't remember anything; it's more of a picture in my mind. Feelings, snapshots, even smells, but nothing definitive."

He rested his hands on my shoulders; his fingers warm against my skin. "That's what memory is. Sounds very definitive to me." His lips curved up. "Unless of course, Minnesotans have a different definition for memory."

"You don't understand. I can't tell whether the images are memories or just imagination." I pulled away from his hands and started walking again, setting my course for a dark clump of Olive trees about a half mile away.

"So, you're prone to a lively imagination then?" His teasing tone, softened by the night air around us, felt too intimate. He kept pace with me, kicking at dry clods of earth as though the tow-headed boy had possessed his feet.

"Not usually." I pulled a leaf from the vines we passed and absently tore it to shreds, letting the pieces flutter lightly to the ground. "Imagination isn't something I've needed a lot of since I became a lawyer. My clients provide more than enough of their own."

He laughed quietly. "I know what you mean."

We walked on without speaking, letting the symphony of the night play on our ears; a cricket's chirp blended with the whisper of the wind in the vines and away in the distance a lone dog howled at the moon. Handel reached out and took my hand again, making it appear a natural thing to do, guiding me around a low spot in the trail as though I wouldn't have noticed it.

"Don't you find it strange that your memories of this place and the weeks you spent here are forgotten?" he finally asked. "I know you were young, but so was I. Those weeks are very clear in my mind."

"Everyone's not the same. Our brains don't all

work the same. Maybe you remember that time because it meant something special to you. I forgot it because it wasn't special to me." I pushed the hair back from my face and sighed. Why did he care whether I could remember three weeks of my life at the age of eight?

"Now you're just being mean. Your mother said you were very excited about the winery. You spent a lot of time with your uncle, learning and exploring. And we became friends. I know we were just kids, but a bond like that doesn't disappear." He shook his head when I looked at him. "It might fade with time, but it doesn't disappear."

I stopped, his gaze piercing my psyche like a needle in my thumb. "We were children, Handel. Just children."

"I know." He reached up and pushed a strand of hair behind my ear that the wind had pulled loose. "Children that found solace in one another."

I narrowed my gaze, a questioning frown furrowing my forehead. "What do you mean?"

He shrugged, his eyes filled with sadness and an underlying anger. "I came here at night to get away from my father. He was an abusive alcoholic. I was his favorite target." He paused. "I don't know what your personal secret was. You didn't say."

My eyes widened with comprehension. "You think my father was abusive too," I gasped. I shook my head, surety in the strength of a lifetime of memories not forgotten. "My father was a very passive man. Believe me, I would know. Just because he had a fight with his brother once doesn't mean he would ever hit a child. He didn't even believe in spanking."

Handel didn't appear convinced. He stood there, a towering block of disbelief in the middle of the vineyard. The dog howled again, sounding closer this time, and I looked back toward the house. The kitchen light gleamed from the window, a beacon to moths and a woman fluttering against life's realities, hoping for a safe haven filled with warmth and peace.

"We should go back," I said softly.

"If that's what you want." Handel pushed his hands in the pockets of his jeans and tilted his head back to look straight up. "Have you ever seen such a perfect night sky?" he asked.

I followed his gaze. The velvet expanse was riddled with stars, a thousand pinpoints of light making the moon's fullness appear like a big brother showing off. The star-strewn, midnight blue sky stretched over the edge of the horizon, God's blanket tucking us in for the night. I felt like a small child again, helpless to fight against... something.

He was watching me. I cleared my throat and glanced at the dark face of my watch. "Well, I'm tired. If you want to stay out here for a while, be my guest, but where I come from it's past my bedtime."

He nodded. "I'll finish my walk if you don't mind, then I'll be on my way."

I didn't know if I liked the idea of his being outside in my vineyard while I slept, but I couldn't bring myself to tell him so. I hesitated, unsure of how to end the evening between us. Should I leave him here without another word, or tell him what a good time I had and thank him for dinner?

While I debated, he leaned in and kissed my forehead. "Goodnight, Billie. Sweet dreams." He didn't wait for a response, but turned and started walking away.

I headed in the opposite direction, picking up my pace as I neared the house. I suddenly wanted to be inside where the shadows could be dissipated with the flip of a switch, and strange sounds could be wiped out entirely by the noise of a television set. I turned at the door and looked behind me, but the only movement was the listing of the trees as the wind picked up and blew everything eastward.

It wasn't until I crawled into bed and turned out the lamp that I remembered my plan to go to the winery and try my key in Uncle Jack's private cellar. Exhaustion won out over curiosity and I closed my eyes, deciding that procrastination could be a good thing.

*****

Sometime during the night it started to rain, a gentle patter on the roof and windowpanes. The steady rhythm lulled me further and I couldn't bring myself to get up and shut the bedroom window. I dozed off again, dreaming of tiny drummers locked inside a wine bottle, trying to get out by tapping at the glass.

When I woke, the room was pitch black, no light filtered through the blinds from outside. Had the moon been obscured by the storm? I lay in bed; unnaturally warm as though I had a fever, the blanket pulled down to my waist to catch the breeze from the open window. I tried to see into the space around me, my eyes wide and strained with the effort. Suddenly I was smothered, a hand covered my mouth and nose, the weight of a body pushed down on mine. I tried to scream but could only manage a desperate moan against the pressure on my face. I twisted and writhed to be free, as the faceless monster pressed closer, his other hand moving purposefully over my bare skin.

I struggled to push off this nebulous creature, my thoughts frantic and hysterical with incoherence. My mind splintered into shards, thoughts flying every direction as I realized I had no hope of dislodging my attacker or changing the course of time. Vines of fear began spreading their tentacles across my bed and winding over my body, pinning me down further still. Leaves unfurled and covered my face with their soft, smooth, skins.

I wrenched myself free and sat up in bed. My heart beat loudly in my ears, my throat felt raw with strain, and my body was covered in a cold sweat. I looked from one side of the room to the other, searching every seeable nook and cranny for the nameless dread that lived on in my head. The room was just as it had been the night before when I shut off the light and went to sleep. Only the bed looked as though a struggle had taken place, the sheets twisted at my feet, the pillow thrown to the floor.

I scooted back to lean heavily against the oak headboard, my hands clenched tightly around my drawn up knees, my body tense and brittle with the aftermath of a dream I'd hoped never to repeat. I glanced toward the window. The blinds were closed, swaying gently in the breeze coming through the screen, the fresh scent of a newly washed world beckoning.

A new day was here although it wasn't quite light outside, but I would never get back to sleep now. I breathed deeply and moved toward the edge of the bed. My muscles were tense and knotted, my head pounding as I stood and made my way toward the bathroom. I needed to run, loosen up, and dispel the ghosts from my mind. They belonged in the past, not here, not now.

Why did this place bring back the nightmares? I had almost forgotten how horrible they were, how panic-stricken I became in my sleep, waging a life and death struggle in the dark. Only my mother had been able to calm me after an episode, her soothing hands and tender voice bringing me back to reality. Now I was in a strange house, away from everything familiar, and the dream returned to me full-force. After ten years of freedom from its bondage I suddenly felt the chains of terror again. Why? Why now?

I hadn't really given Paul a second thought for a very long time. I'd felt anger more than fear at his drunken, groping, assault. Anger that he dared touch me that way after I said no, anger that he lied about the circumstances later, and anger that my father seemed to believe him. But my dream didn't spark anger, only mind-numbing terror.

After pulling on a pair of sweatpants, a t-shirt, and my running shoes, I headed outdoors. The sun was spreading shades of pink along the horizon, inching slowly higher as I started out at a brisk walk. The gravel crunched beneath my rubber soles as I hurried toward the highway. The pavement was still damp from the recent rain, slick in spots. I moved to the hard-packed dirt shoulder and broke into a jog.

I hated feeling helpless. I'd worked hard to overcome my childish fears, and I had no intention of letting them back into my life. Helpless was a word to be stomped into the ground, burned up by the light of day, and relegated to infants in the womb. Billie Fredrickson would never be helpless again.

The cool morning air cleared my head, my thoughts running in a straight line as my legs led. Too early for commuters to be out yet, I had the stretch of road to myself. I ran faster, letting the dream evaporate beneath the sun's morning rays. Thirty minutes later I headed back the way I'd come, my pace slowing as I neared the turn off to the winery.

The pinks of sunrise spread upward, white light emerging from the color, waking the day with its all-encompassing warmth. Birds chirped their remarks back and forth, gossiping mothers foraging for food, fathers keeping an eye on the nest of young. Songbirds sang the melody God gave them at birth, repeating over and over the string of notes, the tune forever stuck in their heads.

Charlie's pickup truck was already parked out front of the winery when I stopped to stretch my calves before heading inside the house. I wanted to try my key in the cellar door, but knew that Charlie would insist on accompanying me down those stairs. I understood his curiosity after years of wondering what Jack did down there, but it would have to wait to be satisfied. I needed to explore that room alone. Jack gave me the key to his private cellar, a place only he visited.

A strange feeling coiled in my gut and worked its way up, trepidation threatening to turn to fear. Or maybe I was just hungry. I shook off the niggling worry at the back of my mind and went inside to forage for breakfast.

*****

"I'm fine, Mother. I just called to see how your date turned out." I leaned against the kitchen counter, nibbling at my last whole-wheat bagel. I needed to restock the refrigerator if I intended to stay much longer. My food choices were running low.

"My date turned out wonderfully." Mother yawned into the receiver, and I realized I'd woken her. She never slept in past eight and according to my watch, which I had yet to set to Pacific Time, it was well past nine o'clock in Minneapolis. I'd spent the morning moving my things to the master bedroom and straightening up around the house, mostly wasting time until it was safe to call.

"I guess it did. You sound tired. Late night, huh?" I said, my gaze catching the movement of a squirrel in the branch of a tree outside the window. "Mr. Banker must be more exciting than he looks."

"Wilhelmina! Obviously, California living hasn't improved your manners. Andrew was a true gentleman. He took me to the Symphony and afterward to a very nice restaurant. We have a lot in common and we talked until two in the morning. I couldn't believe it. I haven't stayed up that late in years and years." Her voice sounded tired but happy.

I smiled against the phone, picturing my mother up late enough for her makeup to fade and her hair to grow limp, entertaining a man with her knowledge of dinner party etiquette and the perfect mulch for a rose garden. "Sounds lovely. Are you going to see him again?" I asked, and took another bite of bagel.

Mother cleared her throat and I heard the sound of the mattress creaking as she shifted on the bed. "I see him every month when I take my check to the bank."

"Now you're being evasive. When's the last time you went out with a man and talked until two in the morning? I think bellbottom jeans were in style the last time you went on a real date. Oh yeah -- they're back in style again."

"Very funny. I'll have you know I went out just last month."

"Right. I'd forgotten." I picked up my coffee mug and took a sip. Morning conversations with Mother were always entertaining. "As I recall, you met him at church. He said he was a widower, lonely for female companionship since his wife's death in a boating accident."

"Laughing at your elders is disrespectful." Now she sounded peeved. "I know I taught you better, but for the life of me can't seem to see the results."

I laughed out loud, unable to keep it in,

remembering her righteous anger when she found out the man was hopping from church to church, parading his grief around to trap lonely widows and divorcees into an affair with him, while his wife was home, very much alive. "I'm sorry, Mother. But I did warn you about believing every sob story you hear. Con men are known to frequent churches as well as bars. Remember Judas?"

"Well, lucky for me Jo Martin had already heard of him at St Christ Lutheran and gave me the low down before I lost anything more than my pride."

"Yes, thank God," I said, my thoughts turning serious. "You deserve someone wonderful, Mother. I hope you find him." I rubbed my finger absently around the rim of my cup, thinking of the years she'd stayed home to be with me and Adam after our father died, not venturing out on a life of her own, but taking care of our needs. Living on social security and the small check she got each month from working part-time at a local florist, we didn't have a lot, but we had each other. She was always there whenever I had a track meet or volleyball game, cheering me on.

She chuckled softly. "I don't know about that. I kind of like my independence. Besides, if I got married again I'd have to share my bed. It took me half a dozen years to get used to sleeping alone and now that I've learned to spread out and fill up the empty space I don't know that I want to go back. There is freedom in being a bed hog."

"I know what you mean. Sometimes the small things are the hardest to give up." I sat in a chair at the table, loneliness suddenly overwhelming me. Last night's conversation with Handel in the vineyard, my nightmare, and the miles separating me from the only family I had, were bringing me down to a place I didn't want to be. "That's why divorcing couples fight over the silliest things," I said, trying to keep my voice light. "They'll often give up the house or child, but go round and round over who gets the matchbook collection or the record player, although nobody smokes or plays records anymore."

"Then my name must be nobody. I may not smoke but I do own a record player. In fact, Andrew and I listened to some records last night."

"Really? Nat King Cole and Frank Sinatra?" I asked, a nostalgic note in my voice, remembering winter nights at home when I was a teenager, sitting by the fireplace playing cards with my mother and brother, listening to a stack of records and singing along.

"Yes, and of course my favorite -- Doris Day," she said, ending with a pleased sigh.

I smiled. "Sounds cozy. And you say he stayed until two?"

"Don't be impertinent, Billie! I'm still your mother."

"Yes you are. Thanks for reminding me. I wish you were here so you could make me a proper breakfast. I can't even seem to toast a bagel as well as you do."

"Billie, are you all right? You sound a little down."

I shook my head, wondering how she could do that across thousands of miles. "I'm good. Just tired I guess. I didn't sleep very well last night." I tried to sound upbeat but knew I failed to pass the test of sound with my mother when she didn't answer immediately with the suggestion of an herbal tea or some such sleep aid.

"It's the nightmares, isn't it? You're having them again."

I sighed heavily, and propped my head on my hand at the table. I knew there was no use lying about it. She would know and worry even more. "Yes. I did have the nightmare. But you don't need to worry. I'm not going to fall apart and seek out the nearest psychiatrist. I worked through this years ago, and came out the other side. I'm not going to let it take over my life like it did before. This was a one time thing."

My positive attitude hung over the kitchen like a shroud of insecurity. I wished I believed the words I spouted, but was afraid that when night fell I would be staring wide-eyed into the darkness, unable to let myself sleep for fear of the dream pulling me in.

"Honey, I'll be there by this evening. Adam doesn't have classes this morning. He can drive me to the airport and I'll take the first flight out." I heard the bed creak again and imagined her hurrying to dress and pack so she could come take care of me.

I stood up and went to the window over the sink, my thoughts as heavy as the rain clouds gathering overhead again. "I can't let you do that, Mom."

"Why not? That's what mothers do. We love our children until the day we die, and we won't take no for an answer." I heard dresser drawers being opened and shut and knew she was already in the process of packing.

"No," I said, my voice firm with resolve. "I have to deal with this myself. I'm an adult now, not a teenager. You were there when I needed you, but now I need to find my own strength. I don't know why it started again. I do know it's going to end. I'm not afraid of Paul anymore, and I won't endure this dream as penance for past sins."

"You have nothing to do penance for, Honey. I'm so sorry I left. I should have stayed to support you instead of rushing home when you needed me," she said, her voice choked with tears.

"Mom, you didn't desert me. I told you to go home.

This has nothing to do with you leaving. It has to do with my own unresolved issues. Funny thing though - I didn't know they were unresolved." I bit my lip and watched as fat raindrops began to pelt the windowpane, a soft pinging melody playing on the glass.

"I should have known after our dinner with Handel. You brought up the incident with Paul as though you were talking about someone else. So flippant and casual, and yet I knew it hurt you to speak of it."

I closed my eyes and breathed deeply, refusing to give in to emotion. It was easier to shut down that side of my brain and deal with things logically as I did at work. "I don't know if that had anything to do with the nightmare coming back. But I do know that Paul can't hurt me anymore and that's why I was flippant. He doesn't scare me. He never really did. I was angry, furious at his lies, but not really afraid. That's why I don't understand the dream. In the dream I'm terrified of my attacker."

Mother's silence accompanied my statement like a seeing-eye dog. She finally spoke, her voice reserved as though she were holding back. "All right," she said. "I'll stay home for now. But if you need me, I'll be there."

"I know," I said, wiping my eyes. "You always have."

Chapter Seven

Sometime after closing, when Charlie's pickup finally disappeared down the gravel drive, I slipped into the winery. Flipping lights on as I passed through different sections, I reached the door to Uncle Jack's cellar some ten minutes later. After getting turned around a couple of times I now felt I knew the winery well enough to navigate it in the dark. Of course, I wasn't about to shut off the lights and test my theory.

I stood before the door, key in hand, wishing I'd let Charlie in on my plan. Why had I ever thought going down there alone was a good idea? I pressed my ear flat against the oak panel of the door and listened. For what? Jack's ghost? There was no sound, other than the buzzing of fluorescent lights above my head. It was now or never.

I turned the key in the lock. The deadbolt slid back easily, leaving me without an excuse to hesitate any longer. Ignoring the shaking in my hands, I turned the knob and opened the door. Darkness confronted me, stairs receding down into a black hole. I reached out and flipped the light switch. The bare bulb in the stairwell flashed and sparked out.

"You weren't going to explore without me, were you?"

I jerked around, dropping the key from my hand. It clattered against the stone floor, the metallic clink sounding like a crashing cymbal in the quietness of the winery. I bent to retrieve it, hiding the sudden relief I felt at Handel's presence. "What are you doing here?" I asked, feigning a fair amount of annoyance in the lift of my brows as I stood and faced him.

He smiled and shrugged. "I'm a sucker for punishment I guess."

I pushed the key into the pocket of my jeans. "If you think being around me is insufferable than why don't you stay away?" I turned toward the stairs and started down, anger replacing trepidation quicker than oil floating to the top of water.

He hesitated at the head of the stairs and cleared his throat. "I find your rejection of me appealing in a strange way."

"Fine," I said, hiding a smile, "then tag along."

"I believe I will, since you asked so nicely."

We descended stone steps to another door that creaked upon its hinges as I swung it open. The room beyond lay cloaked in darkness. My heart sped up, the rapid bu-bump filling my hearing to the exclusion of all other sounds. I groped for a light switch along the inside wall but couldn't find one within reach. I felt Handel's hand on the small of my back as he paused behind me.

"You want me to get a flashlight?" he asked, his mouth close to my ear.

The thought of his deserting me even for a minute filled my heart with dread. I half turned and grasped his arm. "No, don't go."

"Are you all right?"

I nodded and released his arm, embarrassed at my clinging. "I'm sure Uncle Jack wouldn't have worked down here all the time without electricity. I just need to let my eyes adjust for a minute and I'll find it."

Handel stepped around me and entered the room, his tall form quickly blending into the shadows. I felt something drop onto my shoulder and barely contained a shriek before jerkily brushing the small spider to the floor and stomping it to death in my fear.

"Serves you right," I muttered.

"Did you say something?"

I looked up just as the light came on. Handel stood in the middle of the room where a string dangled from a naked bulb. I quickly shook my head and he turned away to investigate.

Strangely enough the room did not divulge long-held secrets merely by stepping inside its walls. But it did send a chill down my spine and along my forearms. The temperature had dropped as we descended the stairs and inside the stone room it felt even colder. I rubbed my arms as goose bumps appeared, and followed Handel across the room. Stacks of cardboard boxes leaned haphazardly here and there, as well as old machinery, crates, and odds and ends that I couldn't identify.

"What do you think this is?" he asked, stopping before a long-forgotten machine rusting away in the corner.

"Too far gone to be worth anything."

He raised his brows. "I didn't come along just to search for treasure, you know. I came for moral support."

"Really." I pulled open the top drawer of an old file cabinet and flipped through the mostly empty folders lined up inside. I didn't know what I was looking for, but it was simpler than facing Handel's wide-eyed innocent look. "Moral support for whom?"

"Billie. You don't have to pretend with me." Handel's voice softened and he stepped closer. "You're looking for answers. I want to help you find them. I don't know what significance this winery and vineyard have for you, but the past affects all of us in one way or another."

"I don't know what you're talking about. Uncle Jack left me a key to a secret cellar. Anyone with a lick of curiosity would find that hard to resist." I slammed the drawer shut and opened the next one down. "What's the past got to do with it?"

"Fine," he said, putting up his hands in mock surrender, "if that's how you want to play it." He turned away, whistling the classic Tina Turner hit, *What's love got to do with it.*

I tried to ignore Handel as I finished going through the drawer, not finding anything of interest beyond a few ancient purchase tickets and sales receipts. The bottom drawer was bent and required the use of muscle to pull it open a mere six inches. I peered inside. It looked as though the back of the drawer was missing. Perhaps the mice had run off with the contents because as far as I could tell it was empty.

A low counter ran along an entire wall, racks of wine bottles stored beneath it, layered in dust and cobwebs. I bent and pulled one out, lifting it to the light. The label was the same as the bottle in Uncle Jack's video, although up close I could see the hands of the clock as well. They were set at six o'clock. Was the hour significant or just a child's passing whimsy? The amber colored bottle glowed with a life of its own, the liquid within dark and seductive. I couldn't take my eyes from it.

"Find something interesting?" Handel appeared at my side again and for some strange reason his presence felt reassuring.

I set the bottle on the table and stuck my hands in the back pockets of my jeans. "I guess this is the wine my uncle and I made. The bottle's dated and numbered."

Handel tilted it back to read the label better. "It says number 24 of 25. He must have expected his wine to be worth a lot someday." He grinned. "Well, there you have it. Your fortune is made. At a million dollars a bottle you've got yourself quite a little nest egg down here."

I sighed, my mood suddenly changing to resignation. I don't know what I expected to find in Uncle Jack's lair, but now with the simple truth staring me in the face I could stop imagining. "I won't hold my breath - but you never know. Maybe it is worth something." I waved a hand at the full racks along the wall under the counter. "There has to be at least three hundred bottles under there. Maybe he really did hit upon a wine to revolutionize the world."

"Well, we won't know until we try it," Handel said. He reached under the counter and randomly chose two bottles from different years, and set them beside the first. "You don't have a corkscrew on you, do you?"

I shook my head, a small smile curving my lips. "Sorry, haven't carried a corkscrew in years."

"This place is kind of creepy, don't you think?" He glanced over his shoulder as though expecting a spook to pop up from between the old crates and barrels stacked in the corner.

"Oh, I don't know. It has a special ambiance. Sort of pre-American Revolution. If I added some shag carpet, a pool table, and a disco ball, I'm sure you'd be right at home."

I picked up one of the bottles and started for the door, eager to be out of here as much, if not more, than Handel was. He grabbed the other two bottles and followed, managing to pull the string for the light and swing the door closed before trudging up the stairs behind me.

The bright fluorescent lights of the winery seemed welcoming as I reached the open door at the head of the stairs. After the intense quiet of the cellar I was happy to hear water dripping, the electric hum of generators, and the faraway sound of a train whistle. Life was meant to be spent above ground, and I wondered why Uncle Jack had spent so much of his below.

Handel breathed a sigh of relief behind me as he emerged from the stairwell. "Ahh! Fresh air."

I pulled the key from my pocket and locked the door again, feeling a silly satisfaction in knowing I controlled the comings and goings to my wine cellar.

"Don't want anyone to know about your secret treasure, huh?"

"Something like that."

After securing the building once again for the night, we walked back to the house. I held the screen door open, but he hung back. "I better take off. I've got to be in court in the morning. Still have a bit of preparation to do." He held the bottles toward me. "Give me a rain check?"

"Sure," I said, trying to hide my disappointment. I tucked the bottles under my arms and went inside, kicking the door shut with my foot. A minute later I heard the sound of Handel's car retreating down the driveway.

Drinking alone was not something I wanted to get in the habit of doing but I'd already waited well past the legal drinking age to taste the wine I'd made, albeit subconsciously, and I didn't think I could wait any longer. I lined the bottles up on the kitchen table and rummaged through the drawers for a corkscrew.

My interest lay entirely with the bottle of wine my uncle and I made together. I popped the cork and let it breathe as I selected a water glass from the cupboard. Any crystal goblets Uncle Jack once owned had obviously gone the way of the furniture. With the opened bottle and glass in hand, I wandered back to the bedroom. Perhaps this wine would serve two purposes tonight, to tell me whether or not I had any business in the winemaking world and to help me sleep without dreaming.

I climbed up on the tall bed and stretched out, leaning back against a stack of pillows as I poured the wine into my glass. Perhaps once a deep chardonnay, the color had faded over the years to a tawny brown. I swirled the liquid lightly around the sides of the glass to let the alcohol evaporate and breathed in the heady bouquet. A nutty, toasty sensation was followed with the underlying hint of something floral. Roses perhaps. I closed my eyes and took a sip, letting it linger on my tongue. The wine had mellowed to a very enjoyable full-bodied weightiness. I smiled as I drained the glass. Perhaps my uncle had made a wine to revolutionize the world. At least my small corner of the world. Feeling more relaxed and tired enough to sleep through the night, I poured myself another glass and got up to change into pajamas.

"Wait a minute." I stared at my reflection in the bathroom mirror, my brows knit in question. I had all kinds of information bubbling around in my head that wasn't there ten minutes ago. How tannins can cause a young wine to taste bitter. Why a fruity wine is not necessarily sweet, and how the things around the vineyard and in the soil give the wine so many extra qualities, tastes, and smells. Sure, I could have read these things somewhere, but I didn't think so.

A voice from the past played in my head. *"Wine is the nectar of God, Princess. And we are God's winemakers. Creators of something that will stand the test of time."* Who else but Uncle Jack would have said such a thing to an eight-year-old child? A little over-zealous perhaps, but certainly excited to pass on the family business secrets.

In a pink tank top and cotton shorts, I climbed back up onto the bed and poured a third glass. I relaxed my head against the pillows and closed my eyes, trying to remember something else from that week. Images of my recent visit to the cellar swirled together with images from a past I thought was long gone.

The cellar was lit with a naked bulb, a glowing eye that cast enough light around the room to accentuate the shadows still lurking in the corners and under things. A round clock hung on the wall above my head, its steady ticking a testament to life going on above ground. Dark, sun-ripened grapes filled a crate on the countertop. I lifted a cluster and brought it to my nose, breathing in the pungently sweet aroma. The feel of the plump orbs in my hands was tantalizing, heady, like embarking on a new adventure. I squeezed one between my fingers and let the juice run down my hand and wind its way around my skinny arm until it dripped on the stone floor.

"Wine is the nectar of God, Princess," I heard my uncle say, and I turned to meet his smiling gaze across the room where he stood with an empty bottle held out in each hand. "And we are God's winemakers. Creators of something that will stand the test of time." He laughed, his voice floating to me on the edges of my consciousness. "You and I will fill these bottles with a wine that will make the world beg for more!"

The sound of breaking glass pulled me from my stupor. I jerked upright and looked wildly about the room. I was alone, and the lamp was still shining brightly. I looked down and expelled a sharp breath. The glass I'd been holding had fallen and hit the bedside table, shattering with the impact. The rest of the wine had sloshed down the side of the table, and spattered the bedspread and carpet.

"Damn," I muttered as I climbed from the bed and made my way slowly to the bathroom for a damp towel. After wiping up the mess the best I could, I covered the spot with a dry towel and climbed back in bed. My eyes were heavy and I felt a comfortable weariness descend upon me, seeping into my brain and draining down to my toes. I found the movement of my arm to turn off the lamp a nearly impossible task, but as I snuggled deeper into the blankets my last waking thought was that I had remembered something. Something important. But I couldn't bring myself to ponder it long enough to recall what it was.

Chapter Eight

The doorbell rang. I lay with my eyes closed, not yet ready to face the world or whoever was outside on the front steps. The chime sounded again and then someone decided to try the old-fashioned version of asking for admittance, pounding on the door with a fist.

I groaned and pushed the blankets back, my tolerance for banging sounds at an all time low. Daylight streamed between the blinds and the room seemed stuffy when I slipped out of bed and hit the floor with a soft thud, twisting my ankle.

"Ouch!"

I limped through the house, favoring my right leg, as the doorbell sounded once again. "All right already!"

The steps were unoccupied when I yanked open the door and squinted into the bright sun. I looked around, expelled an exasperated breath, and finally pushed the door closed hard enough to make the pane of glass rattle. I stood there for a minute, wondering if I was going crazy, when the sound of knocking started on the back door.

By the time I limped to the kitchen and unlocked

the door my uninvited guest was already running across the flagstones toward the tire swing. The sight of Handel's nephew brightened my mood and I watched him stuff his upper body through the tire and begin to swing.

"Hey, Davy!" I called when he glanced my way. "Were you looking for me?"

He grinned and swung higher. "You sure sleep a long time."

I grimaced. "Not as long as I would have if you hadn't woke me up."

He showed no remorse but continued to climb higher, his legs pumping and his blonde hair lifting with the breeze each time he swung forward. I watched him for a minute, then went back in and shut the door. Unaccustomed to children and their individual quirks, I had no idea what he wanted from me. Perhaps just to see if I was awake.

After starting the coffee maker I went to take a quick shower and change. Fifteen minutes later, wearing jeans and a tank top, my hair pulled back into a damp ponytail, I strolled into the kitchen and found Davy sitting at the table with a cup of my coffee, eating a piece of toast slathered with a half inch of peanut butter.

"What are you doing drinking coffee, kid? Don't you know it'll turn your feet black?" I asked as I poured myself a cup.

He smirked and shook his head. "Your feet aren't black," he said with a mouthful of toast.

"Nope." I looked down at my bare feet and wiggled my toes. "But I'm an adult. Only kid's feet turn black. You have to be over twenty-one to drink java safely. Didn't your mother tell you?"

He bit at his lower lip before pushing the coffee

cup to the middle of the table. "Do ya got any milk?" he asked, his face a mask of seriousness.

I nodded and went to the refrigerator. I'd purchased a few items the day before at the little gas & grocery a mile down the road, half a gallon of fat-free milk, corn flakes, coffee, bread, and peanut butter; the staples of life.

After rinsing out his cup and refilling it with milk, I sat across from him at the table and watched him eat his toast. He licked a trail through the peanut butter with his tongue before taking another bite, then set it down to take a drink.

"So," I said, raising one eyebrow, "do you make a habit of coming in and having breakfast in other peoples homes?"

He drained his cup before shaking his head. "Just at Jack's house. He said I could come in anytime."

"Really? Well, did you know this house is mine now? That makes Uncle Jack's invitation obsolete. If you know a good criminal lawyer, you might want to call him. I could have you arrested for breaking and entering."

His eyebrows shot up and his eyes went wide, sudden panic filling his face. "You're not going to tell my mom, are ya? You can call Uncle Handel. He's a lawyer."

Guilt washed over me. I was not adept at handling children, but I certainly hadn't intended to scare him to death. I reached out and patted his hand. "It's all right. I was just kidding. I wouldn't really have you arrested. Besides, I'm glad you dropped by for breakfast. Now we have the opportunity to get to know one another better."

He didn't respond other than to bite at his bottom lip, and I had the feeling he wasn't so sure he wanted to get to know me.

I picked up my cup and took a sip. "What did you and Jack talk about when you came for breakfast?" I asked, trying to break the newly formed ice.

The boy could certainly win a stare down with those wide blue eyes, nearly pupiless in the dim light of the kitchen. He never blinked, his hands still on the edge of the table, his upper teeth pressed into the soft skin of his bottom lip, as though in a trance.

"Don't want to tell me?" I shrugged. "Fine. I can live with that. Just thought maybe he shared his winemaking secrets with you. When I was a little girl he shared a few with me. We made a special wine together one summer when I was here for a visit."

The glacial blue of his eyes seemed to melt and he blinked. "He told me," he said, crossing his arms and leaning back on the legs of his chair, a small version of his uncle Handel. I hoped he didn't fall as well. He'd probably hold that against me too.

"Is that right? He mentioned me?"

He nodded and nearly lost his balance, but quickly set the chair down and leaned forward, elbows on the table. "He said you were a fast learner for a girl."

"Oh really. For a girl, huh?"

"Uh huh. He talked about you a lot."

I frowned down at the scarred tabletop. Sometimes loneliness was a cruel master. Had Uncle Jack obsessed over me because he never had a family of his own? I drained the coffee in my cup and stood up. "Okay, so what's the plan for the day?"

Davy licked his lips, his eyes wide with eagerness. "You want to play hide and seek? I know some great places to hide around here."

"I bet you do. But I think that game might be a little one-sided. You don't want to be stuck hiding all day, do you? I might never find you," I said, turning off the coffee maker. "Why don't we explore together and you can show me places I haven't seen yet?"

"Okay." He stuffed the rest of the toast in his mouth and tried to chew, his cheeks bulging with the effort, peanut butter coating his lips.

I shook my head and handed him a napkin. He set it down and used his tongue instead. The phone rang and I went to pick it up. "Hello?"

"Ms. Fredrickson? This is Charlie. I think there may be a problem over here."

"A problem?" I asked. Why in the world would Charlie call me about a problem in the winery? I was still a blank page when it came to running things.

"You know the locked cellar you were interested in? Well, it's been broke into. One of the guys noticed scrapes in the door and around the lock. Someone took a crowbar to it, I guess." The puzzlement in his voice was clear. He didn't think there was anything down there worth breaking and entering for.

"Was there damage anywhere else in the winery? Anything at all missing?" I asked. The cellar had been locked for as long as Uncle Jack owned the place. Why would anyone want to break into that room when there were plenty of things to steal above ground?

"Not that we've found. I had a couple of the guys take a careful look around but nothing seems out of place or missing. Do you want me to call the police? I couldn't say for sure if anything valuable was stored there. I went down and checked it out but I can't imagine Jack hiding anything down there worth a dime. Unless someone wanted to steal that secret formula he was always joking about. There were quite a few bottles of wine. Could have taken a few of those, I guess. But why wouldn't they just steal wine from up here?"

I bit at my bottom lip. Should I tell the man I'd

already been in the cellar and cause him to wonder why he hadn't been informed, or let him think he was the first? I didn't think there was anything down there worth stealing either, but someone had obviously believed otherwise. Although, calling the police seemed a bit drastic as nothing appeared to be missing. And I really didn't want to go into the whole key inheritance thing.

"No, Charlie, don't call the police. It was probably just a prank of some kind. Kids on a dare or something. I'll be over in a bit and check out the cellar myself, but I wouldn't worry about it."

"I'm sure you're right. I hate to involve the police and get one of the neighbor kids in trouble for something so petty, but if they could get in the winery when it's locked up at night, they could really do some damage if they had a mind to."

"You're right. Maybe we should look into a new security system. You did make mention the other day that it was outdated."

"Yeah. Antiquated is a better term. But Jack didn't want to spend the money on security. He said if we tightened things up it would just make someone think there was something special worth stealing."

Charlie's sarcastic tone made me laugh into the phone. "I see. Good security gives the burglars incentive, something to strive for, huh?"

"I guess so."

"Well, call around and price it out. I'd like to have it done right away if we could. No sense putting it off any longer."

"Will do," Charlie said, clearly agreeable.

"Thanks, Charlie. Oh yeah -- could you have them price the house too? I'd feel better if there were a security system over here as well."

"You bet."

I hung up and turned around to find that Davy had disappeared from the room after dutifully placing his cup and plate in the sink. I rubbed the kink in my neck. I must have slept on it at a funny angle or something. A run would loosen things up but I'd promised to explore with Davy and now to check out the cellar. Well, the two could be combined and everyone would be happy.

"Davy!" I called, as I headed toward the front of the house. "Where'd you go?"

The living room was empty but I heard creaking coming from one of the bedrooms. I followed the sound and found the boy jumping on the master bed, his arms held out at his sides as he bounced. Luckily he'd taken his shoes off or I'd really have had something to scream about. The kid was driving me crazy.

"Did Jack let you jump on the beds, too?" I asked, hands on my hips. I caught a glimpse of myself in the dresser mirror and nearly died from shock, the look on my face so like my Mother when she was about to let loose with one of her tirades. They say that once you have kids, you turn into your mother, but I just had to be around a kid for a few minutes. Frightening.

He came to a sudden stop, and plopped on his bottom, the look of a burgeoning trial lawyer in his eyes. "Nope. But you didn't say I couldn't."

"Great -- semantics from a six-year-old," I said, crossing the room and standing over him. "Has Uncle Handel already been instructing you in the nuances of the law?"

He pushed blonde hair back from his forehead and glared up at me. "I'm eight, not six!"

"All right then. And I suppose eight-year-olds are immune from prosecution because their brain cells haven't yet matured to the point of knowing the difference between jumping on their own beds and jumping on a neighbor's."

"Uncle Handel likes you," he stated in a singsong voice and then ran from the room, leaving me standing there like a kite knocked from the sky, impotent against the teasing wind. Boys were obviously an unknown species even before they turned into men. I picked up his tennis shoes and trudged after him.

*****

With Davy at my heels, I followed Charlie through the winery. The rubber soles of his worn work boots made very little sound but the corduroy pants he had on whistled with each step, causing Davy to break out in uncontrollable giggles. I turned to put a finger to my lips as we stopped before the cellar door.

"I'm sorry this happened Ms. Fredrickson. I really don't know how the rascals even got into the winery. The other locks are fine." He scratched his head, his eyes scrunched up in thought. "There is a back window that can be pushed open if you climb up a ladder, but it seems like a lot of trouble to go to just to break in here."

I nodded, a commiserating smile on my lips. "It's not your fault, Charlie. And once the new security system is up and running, we won't have to worry about it happening again."

Charlie bent and ran a hand over the scraped up wood of the door. "You want me to have someone replace this lock and sand down the door?" he asked.

I bit at my thumbnail as disappointment flooded through me. This cellar would no longer be my personal secret. Others would go down to check out Jack's subterranean exploits, marvel at the eccentricity of his life underground, and cough on the same dust particles I had privately harbored away just yesterday. Giving up my private cellar felt wrong somehow. Possessing the only key was like pulling up the rope ladder on a childhood fort, running the show, being the boss of something. I needed that. Between managing a law office, and controlling my own television remote, my life still felt contrived. I didn't really run anything, decide anything, or control anything. I became a lawyer because my mother thought I would be good at it. And I was, but that didn't change anything. I watched the history channel and PBS because I wanted to sound intelligent when I went to parties. And last but certainly not least, I was here because an uncle I barely remembered was manipulating me from the grave.

"Ms. Fredrickson?"

Charlie's voice intruded on my thoughts. "Sorry, I was thinking. Umm, yes, have the door repaired and a new lock put on. And I'll hold a copy of the key, if you don't mind." I stepped around Charlie and pushed the broken door open. "Davy and I are going to explore. See if any Leprechauns buried a pot o'gold down here," I said in my best Irish brogue.

Charlie chuckled and patted Davy on the top of his blonde head. "Have at it. Maybe you have the luck of the Irish. All I found down there was a pot o' junk."

I smiled. "Its all in the eyes of the beholder, Charlie. I bet Davy and I will find us a treasure."

Davy clomped down the stairs, eagerly leading the way. "It's dark down here, Billie," he called up from the bottom. Now we were on a first name basis. When did that happen?

"I'll get the light, kid. There's a string, but you probably can't reach it," I said, before I realized my innocent statement was actually a sort of confession.

Charlie's brows drew together in a frown, but he didn't call me on it, just turned and walked away, his cords whistling briskly with the rhythm. I hurried down the stairs. Davy stood making popping sounds with his lips as he waited, a pent-up bundle of energy.

I pushed open the door to the cellar, tried to delete the creepy-crawly phobia from my brain, and carefully made my way to the middle of the room where I knew the cord to be. The darkness seemed to shift and ebb as my pupils dilated. I raised my arm and blindly grasped for the string, giving it a yank when it came in contact with my fingers.

"Wow!" Davy said from the doorway as the light illuminated the room with its decades-old, dust-covered shelves and boxes. "This is cool!"

"Yeah, I guess it is." I turned around and surveyed the room through the eyes of my inner child. The objects I'd casually referred to as junk when I'd been with Handel, suddenly seemed mysterious, full of promise, and absolutely cool. Way cool, in fact. "Hey," I said, pointing across the room. "Why don't you take that side and I'll take this side. The first one to find treasure has to run up and get us both a soda from the machine in the office."

Davy grinned so wide I thought his face would split. "One, two, three, go!" he yelled, before I had time to set any ground rules. He dropped to his knees and started squeezing through a space no bigger than a few inches, scurrying like a rat in a maze to find cheese.

I shifted objects aside, climbing carefully around a rusty machine to get to a shelf that looked promising. A stack of dusty books leaned haphazardly, hardbacks covering topics of wine production and sales, mingled with paperbacks dealing in harvesting, marketing, and insecticides. I glanced at the covers as I rearranged them in a neater pile and set a couple aside to look through later.

Stacks of boxes filled the corner. Two more lay

open on the floor, the contents tumbled out as though someone had been interrupted in the middle of a search. I didn't remember the boxes being open before or rifled through. I bent down and picked up a keychain that lay in the midst of the junk. A little emblem dangled from the end with the words, City of Lights, San Francisco. The back was engraved with the initials, SP. A tarnished key was attached to the ring. I turned it over in my palm and frowned, then reached in my pocket and drew out the key to the front doors of the winery. I pressed them together. They matched.

"Well now we know how they got in the winery," I mumbled under my breath.

"I found something!" Davy yelled from across the room, not five minutes later, his voice muffled as though he were talking through one of those string and tin can telephones.

I turned around and caught sight of legs sticking out from behind the old file cabinets in the corner. He had managed to squeeze his head between the cabinet and the wall, no doubt restricting his brain capacity. As I watched, he wiggled backward and stood up, his cheeks red and raw looking as though they'd been in a vise. And I guess they had. In his hands he held a metal tin, the kind hard candy used to come in. He held it up over his head and waved it like a flag.

"Look what I found! Now you have to go get the sodas." His grin was contagious, and I found myself making my way back across the room with a matching grin on my face.

"Did you really find that back there?" I asked. I was sure the cabinets were set too close to the wall for anything that size to slide between.

He nodded, sitting down cross-legged on the stone floor to open the tin. "There's a hole back there," he explained absently, his attention focused on the can. The lid was slightly dented in one corner but it popped off without too much fuss, revealing a thick crumpled envelope nestled inside. He pulled it out and looked beneath at the empty container, disappointment filling his face. "There's nothing in here 'cept a bunch o' papers," he grumbled with evident disgust.

"I'm sorry to hear that," I said, bending down to pick up the discarded envelope. "But the tin is kind of cool. Maybe you could use it to put rocks in or something," I suggested. I pulled the flap open and found myself staring at what appeared to be a stack of photographs, the top one marred with fingerprints and smudges from lots of handling, but the images shockingly familiar.

"Can I get the sodas, Billie? I'm thirsty." Davy stood up, rubbing his nose with dirty fingers.

Unable to speak, I just nodded.

"What kind ya want?" he asked, heading to the door.

"Whatever you like," I said numbly. I didn't want him to see my face. I could feel it hardening, like damp clay left to bake in the sun, the outer layer brittle and beginning to crack.

The clumping of his shoes up the stairs faded away. I stood transfixed to the spot, my gaze on the yellowed envelope in my shaking hands. I pressed my back against the wall and slowly lowered myself to the floor, hugging my knees against my chest as I tried to breathe normally. A feeling of panic filled me as it had in Handel's office the day of the funeral, and I wondered vaguely if I would black out again. Would I wake up to Davy's wide, blue eyes peering down at me with childish fear? I couldn't let that happen. After sucking in a gasping breath, I closed my eyes for just a moment and leaned my head against the wall, trying to calm my agitated spirit.

"Billie!" Davy called to me from the top of the stairs, bringing my head up and my eyes wide open. "Mom says I have to go home now."

I struggled to my feet, tucked the envelope inside the back waistband of my shorts and pulled my shirt down over the edge. "I'll be right there," I called.

The past intrudes in so many ways. People you never want to see again, places you hated living, regret that rears an ugly head. Guilt, hidden and obtuse, suddenly unpacked from the mothballs of the mind, becomes acutely painful, nearly unbearable.

I pulled the string and shut off the light.

Chapter Nine

Davy left with his mother, clutching the old tin container to his chest and arguing about what constituted leaving home without permission. Margaret shook her head and pulled him along by the hand, clearly frustrated by his prolific imagination when it came to excuses.

The envelope pressed uncomfortably at the small of my back, my forgotten past, like a word erased, basically gone from sight but still smudging the page. I hurried back to the house, not even saying goodbye to Charlie. I couldn't face anyone, least of all myself, glancing deliberately away from the hallway mirror as I shut the front door. The house was quieter than usual, or maybe it was just me, needing noise, music, something to throw off the direction my thoughts were going.

Without conscious thought, I fled to the bedroom. I shoved the envelope hurriedly in the top drawer of the bureau. Beneath crew socks and t-shirts it smoldered, a packet of latent truth ready to burst into an inferno.

The truth will set you free. My therapist had made

me believe those words at one time, and I'd repeated them like a mantra when it hurt to speak the truth, but now such rhetoric seemed like blasphemy. How could the truth set me free when it was crushing my soul, incising my heart, and bringing me to my knees with condemnation? I didn't know if I could live with the truth.

I turned on the shower, let it run until the steam began to fill the bathroom, stripped off my clothes and stepped in. I didn't want to think. Thinking would just bring more pain. The hot water pounded against my body, dulling my senses, lulling my brain into weariness. Ten minutes later I stepped out, toweled off, and crawled beneath the blankets on the bed. Sleep is what I needed. Obscure peaceful oblivion.

Sometime later, the ringing of the telephone nudged me awake, insistent and annoying like a mosquito buzzing round my head. I pressed the pillow against my ears and settled back into a restless slumber, fragmented dreams vying for attention.

The only light in the room was the faint glow of a nightlight shining under the door of the hallway bathroom. I yawned and sat up, letting my bare feet sink into the thick shag carpet. I loved to feel it between my toes. Our carpet at home was short and rough. Mom said it wore well, whatever that meant. I wouldn't want to wear it. It was scratchy.

I went to the window and looked out. I could see the tire hanging from the tree, patiently waiting for daylight, so Handy could turn it into a magical ride to the clouds. I squinted into the trees expecting to see something else, someone else, but all was quiet and still.

Moving quickly, as silent as a mouse, I changed out of my pajamas into jeans and a sweatshirt. My long hair was a mess but I didn't care. I pulled it back with a stretchy band and headed for the door, impatient to be out and about. I tiptoed down the hall and through the living room, my senses alert to every creak of the floor, fearful that someone would wake and order me to go back to bed. The back door opened silently and I peeked out at the moon still glowing brightly in the sky, reminding me of cheese and the fact that I was hungry. I grabbed a banana off the counter and hurried out, closing the door softly.

The sweet scent of roses greeted me as I rounded the end of the house and I stopped to press my nose into one of the flowers, the petals, soft and smooth against my skin. I plopped cross-legged on the grass beneath the bushes, the perfect breakfast table, and peeled my banana.

The crunch of tires on gravel alerted me to the passing of time. Someone was already coming up the long drive. The morning sun would soon light up the world and my special quiet time would be over. The workers at the winery would start arriving, carrying lunch boxes and newspapers, shuffling in the front door like dairy cattle at milking time. I finished the fruit and buried the peel beneath the loose dirt in the rose beds, then stood up and stretched. The silvery light of dawn was already busy turning black objects to gray.

I ran across the gravel drive, scooted around the side of the building, and pushed through the door in the back that I knew was left open. The winery hummed with a sound all its own. Perhaps the grapes buzzed with energy as they changed into wine. I didn't know, but I liked it. The pull of the cellar was magnetic and I found myself waiting by the door, hoping Uncle Jack would rise early and meet me here.

A hand gripped my shoulder and I turned, a smile on my face, my eyes wide. I froze - my heart began to *pound with fear, and I opened my mouth to scream...*

I sat straight up in bed, gasping for breath, my heart pounding in my ears like a jungle drum. The empty echo of a scream filled my mind and my eyes strained against the darkness of the room. I turned toward the window. No light showed through the slats in the blinds. A feeling of despair weighed me down, twisting my insides. My dream had changed and yet the same faceless enemy stalked the corridors of my mind.

I pushed the hair out of my face, trying to focus on not falling as I climbed from bed. A cool breeze blew in the window and a million hairs rose over my bare skin. I fumbled through the bottom drawer of the dresser for a sweatshirt and jeans, then struggled into them in the confining darkness, a sense of déjà vu in the simple task.

My feet took me toward the kitchen, where I finally thought to flip a light switch. But the room remained shadowed. I flipped the toggle up and down, as they always do in bad horror movies, an inadequate action much like pushing the little disconnect button in and out on an old rotary phone and saying, 'hello, hello,' with the same result. Nothing.

"Great," I muttered as I headed toward the dark hulking shape of the refrigerator. The leg of a kitchen chair caught my big toe and I yelped, stumbled the remaining steps, and leaned haphazardly against the solid appliance while holding my injured foot with one hand, swearing under my breath. My cell phone, across the room on the kitchen counter where I'd left it sitting, took that opportune moment to begin playing a light-hearted rendition of *Yankee Doodle*. The little light flashed as it played, giving me the help I needed to maneuver safely around the table and pick it up. I noticed the display had chalked up 10 unanswered calls throughout the day. Someone was persistent.

"Hello," I answered breathlessly, "House of horrors. Can I help you?" I leaned against the counter, still babying my injured foot.

"Billie? Are you all right?" a familiar voice asked.

I squinted into the dark, my brain still fuzzy with the dream. Who would call in the middle of the night just to ask if I was all right? That was a silly question. My brother, of course. Adam could be sadistic at times, waking me from a deep sleep to inform me that there was a tornado warning and we had to go down to the basement. Only, I was so groggy with sleep that I didn't realize until I carried my pillow and blanket downstairs and stood shivering on the cement floor with bare feet, that Adam and Mom were not joining me and all was quiet aboveground. Not to say that he couldn't be kind and empathetic at times, but he was my brother after all. It was his job to annoy, tease, and cajole me, depending on the circumstances.

"Adam. What's up?" I asked. I pulled the door open on the cupboard behind my head and reached in for a water glass. I could hear laughter and talking in the background. Sounded like a frat party and I hoped Adam wasn't making a habit of staying up till all hours every night.

"What's up with you?" He sounded slightly perturbed, which made me smile for some reason. "I've been calling all day and you never picked up. This is a fine time to answer the phone. Where have you been? Mom is worried out of her head. She made me take her to the airport to fly back out there."

"What? You didn't really," I said on a groan, closing my eyes and hoping he would laugh and say, gotcha. But I knew this time my brother was serious.

"She's on her way, Sis. She wouldn't tell me why she's so worried, just that you needed her. As usual, I'm out of the loop. Apparently, its that girls-only ESP thing again." He was silent for a moment and I bit nervously at my lip, not knowing what to tell him. "Look," he said, his voice low as though afraid of being overheard by his college friends. "I know I'm just the kid brother, but if there's something I can do..."

I rubbed the sleep out of my eyes before answering. "Thanks, Adam. But the best thing you can do is keep your grades up or she'll be after you. What time is her flight scheduled to arrive?"

"Ten in the morning, but she was planning on surprising you, taking a cab or ..." A loud crash, followed by raucous laughter, drowned out the rest of my brother's words.

"Adam? What's going on there? Don't you guys ever sleep?" The big sister in me couldn't stay quiet any longer. "Mom will nail your hide to the wall if you don't keep your grades up. You'll be living at home, with a curfew again," I warned.

"Yeah, whatever. You're the one who was out all day and night. And you never did say where you've been."

"I haven't been anywhere. I was asleep. So, I didn't answer the phone. What's the big deal?" I went to the sink and filled the glass with water. Now if I just had a couple sleeping pills. But if my mother came and found me on a sleeping binge, I would never get rid of her. Old habits and all.

"Sleeping, huh? Yeah, well, you've tried that one. It doesn't work. You better think of something else before she gets there." The thumping bass of a stereo turned up to hearing loss proportions nearly drowned out his next words. "I'm not a kid anymore, Billie. You can count on me -- you know?"

"I know. I love you too." I flipped the phone closed

and stood staring out the kitchen window into the night. The trees nearly obscured the sky from this vantage point but the moon still glowed brightly through the branches.

A shadowed figure separated from beneath the trees, moving stealthily along the side of the house toward the garage. I leaned closer to the windowpane, squinting into the yard. Was someone out there, nosing around, perhaps the same someone who broke into the cellar?

I picked up my cell phone to call 911, but thought better of it. If a neighbor kid were out doing mischief, I would take care of it myself. I'd dealt with far scarier situations in my line of work, individuals harboring malicious intent rather than simple destruction of property. It would do me good to get into lawyer mode, with my, I'm in charge attitude. That way I could distance myself from the things I couldn't control, like dreams of a past best left forgotten.

After pushing my bare feet into the running shoes I'd left by the back door, I slipped outside and followed the direction I'd seen the prowler move just moments before, around the side of the house. As I paused in the shadow of the garage, my gaze moved slowly over the winery and outbuildings, looking for movement or a subtle change in landscape. The sky began to lighten, but not enough to see clearly. Dark shapes loomed everywhere: crates, a stack of firewood, tree stumps, something covered with a tarp against the shed. Someone could be hiding ten yards away and I wouldn't know.

I took a deep breath and slowly released it, screwing up my courage for the walk across the open area. A hand grasped my shoulder and I spun around, my fist making contact with the man's face a split second before my knee did damage to his lower regions. A grunt and groan of pain told me I'd hit pay dirt even before he dropped to the ground, curled into a ball. Those self-defense classes were definitely worth every cent.

"What did you do that for?" he asked, his voice abnormally high and breathless.

"Handel?" I bent over him, concern vying with my consternation at his sudden appearance. "What are you doing here?!"

He struggled to his knees and tried to breathe normally, dawn's light etching the pain in his face like charcoal on paper. "Looking for you." Tentatively, he reached up and touched his bleeding nose. "Guess I found you."

I straightened up and glared down at him, shaking my head. "I'd say I'm sorry, but you did sneak up on me -- in the dark, I might add. Not a wise decision, after all."

"No." He grimaced as he tried to stand. "And that's the last time I do a favor for anyone."

I reached out and helped him to his feet. His nose was still bleeding and I used the edge of my sleeve to wipe it gently away. His eyes narrowed suspiciously at my ministrations but he stood still until I was done.

"Thanks," he said, his voice soft and surprisingly free of sarcasm.

"You're welcome." I stepped back and glanced around for his car. "By the way, what are you doing here and who are you performing this favor for? Surely not me, because I don't remember asking you for anything." The tail end of his car peeked out from the other side of the garage. Did he choose that spot in order to be hidden from view?

He gave a short laugh. "You never change, Billie. You're the same stubborn, I can handle things myself, cuss you were at eight."

"Okay," I said, my interest now piqued. "What does that have to do with why you're here?"

He began brushing the dirt off his jeans, avoiding eye contact. "Your mother called a couple hours ago and asked if I would come out and check on you. She said she was worried because you hadn't answered your phone all day."

"What? What else did she say? It must have been something good or you wouldn't have made a trip all the way out here in the wee hours of the morning. I'm sure even you have been known to ignore the phone at times; let the answering machine pick up."

He bent down and picked up the baseball cap he'd dropped, adjusting it carefully on his head. "She said you might be suffering from depression," he said. His gaze drifted slightly over my left shoulder.

"Depression? Why would she think I was suffering from depression just because I didn't answer the damn phone?" The tiny fragment of truth in that presumption did not give her an excuse to broadcast my past inclinations to a man I hardly knew. Mother would get a piece of my mind when she got here.

He shook his head, his gaze still wandering. "I don't know."

"What are you looking at?" Exasperated, I turned around and stared at the buildings behind me.

"I thought I saw something move, but it must have been the trees blowing."

"Were you walking around behind the house a little while ago?" I asked, suddenly wanting everything to be a big misunderstanding. I could go back in, forget about protecting the winery from vandals, and pack my bags for home. I was tired.

His brows drew together and he shook his head. "I

drove up, went to the front door, saw you standing here and came over." He tentatively touched his sore nose. "I think you know the rest."

"Well, I saw someone sneaking around back there. That's why I came outside. Thought I might thwart another break-in to the winery. Charlie told you about that, didn't he?" I pushed the sleeves up on my sweatshirt and placed my hands on my hips. "You wouldn't happen to know any kids around here that fall into the trouble category, would you? Besides Davy, that is."

"Neighbors?" He shook his head slowly, the lines at the corners of his eyes more pronounced when he was frowning in thought. "Nope. But the question should be: what the hell were you thinking, coming out here to confront a prowler instead of calling the police?"

"Thanks for your concern, but I'm quite capable of taking care of myself." I tilted my head and smiled sweetly. "I took care of you, didn't I?"

He expelled a frustrated breath. "Sure, but I wasn't fighting back, and most important, I'm not the intruder!"

His anger cut me to the core. "You sound pretty intrusive to me. You and my mother." I started to walk away, intent on cocooning myself back inside the house, hiding from Handel, my mother, and life in general. I no longer knew why I was here or even cared.

"Are you running away, Billie?"

I stopped. Handel's baiting struck a chord within me. Was I willing to run away? From everything? Go back to the way it was, practice law, pretend none of this had ever happened, assured that my past was dead and couldn't catch up? Was I so fearful of the truth? And what exactly was the truth? If I left now, I probably would never know.

Streaks of pink colored the horizon as the sun began its ascent, to illuminate the world and perhaps my soul, with startling clarity that I couldn't look away from. I turned around and met Handel's gaze, a dare to be taken.

"Fredricksons don't run away from anything," I said, and I meant it.

He looked pleased. "Good. Then let's go check out the winery."

"What about the police?"

He shrugged. "Who needs the police when I've got you?"

*****

The winery appeared locked up tight, no sign of breaking and entering, or doors left open to fate. We walked around the outbuildings and through the trees behind the house, but found no trace of a prowler even in the growing light of morning.

I told Handel about the key I'd found in the cellar after the break-in. He frowned thoughtfully. "Are you sure it wasn't already down there? Maybe it fell out of one of the boxes."

I shrugged. "That's possible I guess. You don't think it may have been a disgruntled employee, maybe someone Jack fired from the winery?"

"I don't think Jack ever fired anyone in his life," he said with a shake of his head.

Handel smiled when we stopped by the tire swing. He put a hand on either side and held it steady. "Get in. I'll send you to the clouds."

"Now that sounds familiar," I said, returning his smile.

"It should. You took a lot of trips there."

I pulled myself up to sit in the curve of the tire. "Not as comfortable as I remember though."

He laughed and began to push me, higher and higher, until my head did feel as though it might touch the clouds. I closed my eyes and leaned back, feeling the rush of air against my face as I flew upward. The euphoria of childhood is hard to recapture, but for a moment I could swear we were back there. When I opened my eyes I was sure that Handel would be standing in his overalls, bare-chested, his skin as brown as a Mexican migrant worker.

I didn't think childhood friendship could spark such feelings of intimacy. What was it about Handel that always brought my emotions to the surface so readily? Anger, attraction, frustration, happiness; all feelings I'd experienced in passing, but with Handel they were more intense, like being influenced by a powerful drug.

I opened my eyes, only slightly disappointed that Handel was no longer ten-years-old. He had matured rather well and wasn't half bad to look at, when I wasn't angry with him. He stepped back and watched as the swing slowly lost altitude, his hands in the front pockets of his jeans, and a crooked smile on his lips.

"Where'd ja go?" he asked, a perfect imitation of his boyhood slang.

I looked up and pointed. "You see that cloud? The one that looks like a rhinoceros? I landed up there." I slipped out of the swing and stood facing him. "Thanks for the ride, Handy."

"Any time."

Later I would blame my actions on feelings of nostalgia or the romantic way the sky reflected in his eyes, but at that moment I didn't need an excuse. I just drew his head down and kissed him. Not a quick thank you kiss, or a hasty goodbye kiss, but a long, deep, soul-searching, can't catch my breath kiss. And then I ran into the house to hide.

Chapter Ten

Handel must have been just as confused by my actions as I was because he didn't follow me. In fact, a couple minutes after I ensconced myself back in the bedroom, I heard his car spin out in the gravel drive as he fled the scene. I went into the bathroom and stood staring in the mirror for several minutes, unable to decide whether I enjoyed making a fool of myself or just came by it naturally. Then I noticed Handel's blood on my sweatshirt. This I could handle. I put it in the sink to soak and went to get a clean t-shirt.

As I pulled open the top drawer I remembered the envelope hidden there, but it was too late. It peeked out from under my clothes, daring me to accept the past, the pain, the reality of the unknown.

My fingers tightened on the envelope and I drew it out. Sometimes life feels as if it moves in slow motion, like watching the progression of the minute hand on a watch. I stared at the envelope in my hand for what seemed an eternity before climbing up in the middle of the bed, sitting cross-legged, and opening the flap.

The top photograph shocked me as it had in the

cellar, familiar faces, younger and more vibrant, uttering their secrets without ever saying a word. My mother, her long hair shining down her back, her face bright and smiling, as beautiful as any model on the cover of Glamour magazine, being held possessively in the arms of a handsome young man. A man that was not my father.

I was afraid to look at the other photographs, because I knew they would be more of the same. Pictures of Jack and my mother -- in love. Pictures that told a story, and in the wrong hands could spawn a whirlwind of trouble. I was afraid they already had.

Handel's story of my father beating Jack within an inch of his life suddenly took on new meaning. Was I the catalyst that spawned the whirlwind? Memory swirled in my mind, bits and pieces of the day I found the photographs in Uncle Jack's desk, stared at each one with eyes of confusion, anger, and fear. The pictures brought out a protective instinct in me, a need to shield my father from the truth. I hid them in the hole behind the file cabinets, a place I'd discovered when Jack left me alone in the cellar one day, and hoped they would never be found again. I didn't remember showing them to my father, but then my ability to recall was something other than exemplary.

I dumped them out on the bed and spread them around me, snapshots of my mother and uncle kissing, embracing, and posing for the camera like young lovers on their honeymoon. I couldn't remember my parents ever acting that way in front of me. Perhaps my father was a private person, incapable of demonstrative actions, keeping his lovemaking strictly for the bedroom. Obviously, mother had no such compunctions. Or was she only this way with Jack, the adventurer, the man who wasn't afraid of taking chances? Did she take chances when she was with him? What happened to make her settle for good, old, dependable Dad?

My eyes misted over and I sniffed away the moment. Feeling sorry for myself because my parent's marriage had been a sham was a useless endeavor. Every child wants to feel that they were conceived in love. Mother said she loved Dad until the day he died and whether or not it was the kind of passion I could clearly see in these photographs, my parent's love for one another was real enough. A sturdy, faithful, forgiving love that accepted life for what it was. At least that's what I chose to believe.

I scooped up the photographs and stuffed them back into the envelope. These were other people's memories, not mine. I was a mature, levelheaded woman. I could accept that my mother had lived a life at one time totally separate from my own. She may have had affairs with ten different men before she married my father. It didn't matter to me as long as my memories were safe. But were they?

*****

Mother arrived like a Midwest tornado, heralded by Adam's alarm but still surprising in her ability to annihilate my self-esteem by taking over my life. Handel was her mode of transportation, the trunk of his car barely able to contain all of her luggage. Perhaps his flight from the house earlier wasn't precipitated by my actions but rather the need to get to the airport on time. Now I had to reevaluate my conclusions as to what, if any, impact my kiss had on the man.

I stood stoically by the front door of the house, watching as Handel swept past me, carrying Mother's things, intentionally avoiding my gaze. Mother followed, clasping the handles of her purse and carry-on bag in one hand, the other stretched forth to pull me into an embrace. She hugged me and then pulled back to look directly into my eyes.

"How are you, Darling?" she asked overdramatically, as though she were playing the part of Joan Crawford in *Mommy Dearest*. She held my hand in hers and squeezed it slightly.

I squeezed back, just to let her know I could play the game too. "I'm swell, Mother, now that you're here. I'm sure I don't know what I would have done without you."

"Now Wilhelmina, there is no use in trying to pretend with me. You needed me and now I'm here. It's as simple as that." She released my hand and brushed my bangs away from my face, the way she always did when I was a little girl. Messy hair was a blot on her mothering skills and I mustn't let people think she let me out of the house un-groomed.

"Why is it, Mother, that the more complicated you make my life, the simpler it is for you?" I turned and followed Handel into the house, not waiting for her reply.

Handel had stopped in the living room, and stood with his arms crossed, waiting, with the bags at his feet. I approached him warily; afraid he would say or do something that would transmit to my mother as a budding relationship. We certainly had nothing of the kind. One kiss. That's all it was. Nothing to write home about, and definitely, nothing to tell my mother about.

"You can put those in the guest room. I already moved into the master bedroom," I informed Handel needlessly, as though he might care which bedroom I now occupied. I turned to leave.

"Where are you going, honey?" Mother asked from the doorway.

"To the kitchen, to commit suicide with a

corkscrew."

I heard Handel's soft laugh behind me as I fled the room.

I opened the remaining bottle of wine left on the counter and poured a glass for myself. It wasn't the same full-bodied chardonnay as before but certainly capable of taking the edge off my nerves. Uncle Jack may have had a few flaws in his character but he made a good bottle of wine, and in the winemaking industry that's all that really matters. Who was I to besmirch his person with past history?

I sat in a chair at the table and put my feet up on the chair across from me, slouched low on my tailbone with my head leaned back, and stared up at the ceiling. My mother was here and there was no getting rid of her, at least not in the foreseeable future. She had decided I needed her and she would not be dissuaded.

Mother and Handel joined me moments later, she tugging him along by the arm against his will, perhaps a tad worried about my reaction to her showing up unannounced. "But you must stay for a bit, Handel. Billie hasn't even had time to thank you properly for picking me up at the airport."

"Yes," I said, glaring at him over the rim of my glass, "Thanks so much, Handel. Of course, if anyone had informed me that Mother was coming I might have been able to prepare a more elaborate welcome." I waved them to the table. "But please, join me in a glass of wine."

"Isn't it a little early to be drinking?" Mother asked, her brows knit with worry. She picked up the bottle and eyed the label with suspicion. "Is this from Jack's private cellar? I've never seen this design before. It looks rather childish."

"Very private, Mother. But then you would know

what a secretive person Jack could be, wouldn't you?"
The words sounded bitter and I wished I could take
them back, but once out, words have a life of their own.

My mother stared at me for a long moment, clearly
rattled, then set the bottle down and left the room.
Handel released a pent-up sigh but didn't say a word.
He went to the cupboard for another glass, filled it from
the bottle, and took a seat across from me at the table.

"Can I ask what that was about?" he asked finally.

"No. It's none of your business."

I sat up and leaned with my elbows on the table,
staring him down. Daring him to flinch and back off, but
he just smiled and sipped his wine. "If you say so."

I finished the first glass and poured another. "You
don't have to stick around, you know. You've performed
admirably as Mother's chauffeur and now you can buzz
off."

"Holding grudges again, I see." He drained his
glass in one gulp and stood up. His blonde hair fell
across his forehead as he braced his palms flat on the
tabletop and leaned across the space that separated us,
his face mere inches from my own. "I liked you better
when you were eight. At least then you cared about
someone other than yourself."

He didn't wait for a response, just turned away
and exited through the back door. I sat there for a long
time staring at the wine in my glass, trying to work up a
feeling of righteous anger at his words, but nothing
came to mind other than a touch of remorse. I felt
drained like the bottle before me, emptied out and
unable to replenish myself. Was my mother right? Was I
falling into a dangerous depression?

*****

Mother appeared back in the kitchen sometime
after Handel left. She had freshened her makeup and

changed into a summer top and walking shorts. She tried to pretend nothing was wrong, that my words had not wounded her, but the pasted on smile was not convincing. "One of those suitcases was for you," she informed me. "I went by your place and picked up a few outfits. Thought you might be tired of the few you brought."

"Thanks," I said, fiddling with the empty glass on the table.

"Those long flights are debilitating with the seats so close together. I think I'll go for a walk and stretch my legs." No suggestion of my going along. "Do you have a pair of crew socks I can borrow? I packed tennis shoes but seem to have forgotten socks."

I stood up quickly and felt my legs go wobbly. Mother's look of concern was enough to straighten me out though. "Sure. I'll get them for you."

She put out a hand to restrain me. "Don't bother. I can find them. Why don't you lie down on the couch and rest? You look tired."

"They're in the top drawer, right hand side," I called after her as she started away.

Taking my mother's advice, I went to the living room and stretched out on the couch. Velvety darkness quickly enveloped my brain and I let it suck me deeper still. The next thing I knew, Mother was bending over me, shaking me awake, an expression of shock mingled with a touch of anger in her eyes.

"Billie, where did you get these?" she demanded, holding the envelope of photographs over my face and waving it back and forth.

Fully awake now, the sluggishness of sleep completely evaporated, I sat up and combed my hair back with my fingers. Mother was physically shaken with the discovery, more so than I had been. I wondered what other secrets she harbored and whether I'd ever really known the woman she truly was.

"Well?" She looked desperate, driven, like someone who will do anything to bury the past.

I bit at my bottom lip before answering. "In Jack's cellar."

"No," she shook her head. "Jack wouldn't leave something like this just lying around waiting to be found. He promised me." She paced to the fireplace and back, looking down at the envelope in her hands as though by sheer will power she could make it disappear.

"He promised you what, Mother? Not to tell Dad about your affair?" I stood up, blocking her retreat. "What kind of woman pits one brother against another, using love as a weapon?"

Her mouth trembled and her eyes filled with tears, but I didn't back down, unable to let go of my own guilt, I wished to share the pain. She shook her head and two tears coursed down her cheeks leaving a pale trail in her foundation.

"It wasn't like that," she said, her voice quiet, introspective. "I met Jack first. He was older, and a little wild. Impetuous. Exciting. I thought that's what I wanted; thought I loved him." She met the accusations in my eyes and released a heavy sigh. "But things didn't work out, and then I met your father. He was the opposite of Jack. He thought things out, took responsibility seriously, and believed marriage was forever. I tried to be what he needed. Sometimes I failed." She wiped the tears away with her fingertips and sniffed.

"That's what you call it -- failure to be what Dad needed? What about fidelity? Or plain old loyalty?"

The slap of her palm against my cheek shook me

to the core. I couldn't remember her ever hitting me. Not like that. She was usually so restrained, so civilized. My words had unleashed something in her, something tucked away for many years. Guilt?

"Don't you dare speak to me that way. I am still your mother and you have no business accusing me of something you know nothing about," she ground out in measured tones.

I snatched the envelope from her hand, ripping it apart, and scattering the contents across the wood floor, the intimate portraits testifying to Mother's carnality like witnesses for the prosecution. "I know two things," I said, before my brain had time to catch up with my mouth. "I found these the first time when I was eight. The same week that Dad beat Jack to a pulp. What I don't know is whether or not I told him about the pictures. I can't remember that part." My lips trembled and I swallowed, the lump in my throat making it hard to speak. "I think maybe I did, and he held it against me. That's why he changed toward me, pulled away. Why he quit loving me."

"Oh, Honey, he never quit loving you." My mother wrapped her arms around my stiff body and pulled me close, forgetting her own anger at the sight of my tears. She smoothed my hair and whispered those comforting indecipherable words that mothers always do, and I felt a small part of my heart begin to mend. Blame shifting was simply reflex. In fact, I wondered if my childish actions so many years ago had caused a rift in my parent's marriage. She pulled back, holding me at arms length and shook her head. "Billie, you're not thinking clearly. You're taking something that happened when you were eight-years-old and trying to make it fit with the way your father treated you when you were fifteen. I don't believe the one had anything to do with the other."

I sucked in a shaky breath and nodded. "You're probably right."

"Of course I am. I'm your mother."

I absently rubbed the side of my face, still feeling the sting of her slap.

She reached out and put her hand over mine. "I'm sorry, honey. I shouldn't have hit you. It was uncalled for."

I sniffed, smiling weakly through my tears. "No, you shouldn't have. But it was called for."

Mother's gaze strayed to the photographs at our feet and she looked slightly embarrassed, the heightened color in her cheeks a telltale sign. I knelt down and began picking them up, turning them facedown in a pile.

"That was a long time ago. I was a different person." Mother let out a short laugh tinged with bitterness. "People always say that when their past sneaks up and bites them in the ass." She sat on the edge of the couch, elbows on her knees and her head in her hands. "I want you to know the whole story, Billie. Maybe then you'll understand. Discovering that your parents lived a whole other life before you were born must be confusing."

I tapped the remaining pictures into a neat pile and looked up. "You don't have to explain anything, Mother. I should have left the pictures where they were, hidden in that hole in the cellar, and put them out of my memory as I've put everything else from that time."

She shook her head. "No. Its time we dealt with things instead of shoving them under the carpet. Your father liked to pretend everything was fine, even when it wasn't. He couldn't deal with controversy."

"You mean he didn't want to deal with it."

"Perhaps. He liked things simple, on time, and unchanged. He may have been set in his ways but he could also be loving and kind, generous, and endearingly faithful."

"Not like Jack."

"No," she said softly, "not like Jack."

We talked on for an hour or more, Mother's eyes lighting up at certain points in her story, dissolving into tears at others. I sat at one end of the couch and she sat on the other, our legs curled beneath us.

"When I realized I was pregnant, Jack scoffed, said I couldn't be. One time wasn't enough to get me knocked up. He refused to believe it was his. Actually accused me of seeing other men." Mother's voice wavered and I felt her withdraw into the pain of her past. She gazed out the window as though reliving the scene in her mind's eye.

I wanted to hold her, comfort her somehow, but the subject was so far beyond what I'd imagined, infringing upon my reality with surprising repercussions. My earlier shock at discovering my mother's secret past was nothing compared to the freefall my heart did now, plummeting to the sharp rocks of despair. Was I ever Daddy's little girl or only a changeling usurping the place of a true daughter? Was Uncle Jack my father? A man who didn't want anything to do with me and then out of guilt tried to make up for it by spending a few weeks of his precious time one summer making wine with an eight-year-old girl? It certainly cleared up any questions of my inheriting the winery.

Mother was silent for several moments, leaning her head against the back of the couch as though too exhausted to hold it up any longer, her eyes closed to further scrutiny. Perhaps my gaze was too intrusive, my interest too personal. I stared at her, the lines around her eyes, the droop of her jaw, the thinning lips, and imagined her as she once was, before me, before my father, before we aged her with the burden of our love. But I couldn't stay quiet for long. The need to know, to understand how she could hide this side of my identity from me for so long, was overwhelming in its intensity.

"Mother -- why didn't you tell me that Jack was my father?" I asked, my voice rough with feelings trying to break free. I tried to think the whole thing through logically, with reason, distancing myself from the circumstances as though I were trying a case in court, but my heart would have none of it.

"What?" She raised her head and stared at me, her expression aghast at my suggestion. Did she think I would listen to the story of her life and not draw any conclusions? She was pregnant. Jack wouldn't accept responsibility. And along comes James, the good brother. I certainly didn't need a photograph to fill in the details to that scenario.

"I know Dad was my father in every way that counts and always will be, but I should have been told about Jack. I had a right to know," I persisted.

Mother's mouth dropped open. Finally she released a pent up breath and I could see her shoulders slump as if the last of her secrets had been expelled. Then she leaned forward across the couch and looked me directly in the eyes. "Jack was not your father," she said, her voice taking on that patient tone she used when I was small, helping me to understand something beyond my cognitive ability. "Jack was your uncle, that's all."

My brows drew into a frown of frustration and I took mother's hand in my own, needing her to connect with me physically as well as emotionally, to understand how hearing the words out loud would shatter their power over both of us. "Why can't you just admit the truth? Dad's dead. Jack's dead. There is no reason to pretend any longer. I can take it. I'm a big girl."

She sighed and shook her head, her lips curved in a patient smile but untold sadness in her eyes. "Billie, I am telling you the truth. Jack was not your father. The baby..." she paused and swallowed hard. "I had a miscarriage in my third trimester. I lost the baby, and Jack and I never saw each other again -- in that way."

I drew back, slowly releasing her hand. Relief swept over me from head to toe, and I suddenly realized how very much I'd wanted to be wrong. My father was not perfect, but he was the only father I ever knew and I couldn't imagine replacing him in my mind with anyone else.

"Did Dad know?" I asked.

"Of course," she said. "I wouldn't have married him otherwise. I told you about my pregnancy to help you understand the huge difference between your father and Jack. Jack could be very generous when it came to things, but he wasn't so giving with his heart. James, on the other hand, seemed frugal at times, saving, scrimping, worrying about finances, but he gave his heart to me without holding anything back."

"Then what happened to him?" I asked. I remembered two fathers. The father I had as a child was exactly what she described, but the one who appeared after the night Paul attacked me was someone else. I couldn't reconcile the two. People didn't just change for no reason, and I always believed I was that reason.

"I don't know. He wouldn't talk about it." She glanced out the window and swiped at her eyes with the tips of her fingers. "I couldn't remember him being so

closed down since... well, since that time we spent here.
When we left and went home, your father fell into a
depression of some sort. He wouldn't talk about it then
either. After about a month or so he seemed to shake
himself out of it. I hoped it had nothing to do with my
past relationship with Jack, because when we married,
James swore it was a new start and nothing that came
before would come between us. He kept his word too
and never brought it up in anger. But after hearing
Handel's version of their fight that summer... what else
can I believe?"

I reached down and picked up the discarded stack
of photographs. "Why do you think Jack kept these,
Mom? Was he still in love with you or did he just want
something to hurt Dad with?"

She closed her eyes and wearily shook her head. I
could tell she was emotionally drained from our
conversation. Perhaps now would be a good time for
her to take that walk. I didn't want her to hurt anymore.
My carelessness had brought back memories that she
obviously never fully dealt with.

The past would always hold unanswered
questions, secrets left hidden, hearts left broken, love
lost to pride or indecision. Why don't we ask the
important things while there is still time? *If only* could
drive a person to second-guess their way through life. I
was slowly finding that out for myself.

She finally looked up and smiled, strengthened
once again from some inner place. "Jack used to collect
mementos when he traveled," she said, "to remember
his experiences. Sort of a period at the end of a sentence
in his life. Perhaps the photos were just that -- a period
at the end of our love affair." She stood and reached out
her hand for the photographs, her lips set in a firm line.

I reluctantly handed them to her, the lawyer in me

silently crying out to preserve the evidence. I didn't think any of the photos would turn up in the family photo album. But shouldn't there be some record of the tiny life that culminated from their affair, a baby instantly heaven-bound, but still indelibly printed on my mother's heart, and perhaps Jack's?

"Mom?" I said as she headed for the front door. She stopped and turned. I swallowed and asked the question that now burned in my mind. "What was the baby's name?"

"Henrietta."

I grinned. "Then she would have been Henry. Billie and Henry. I think you secretly always wanted boys."

She laughed and shook her head. "No. You wanted to be a boy. Wilhelmina is a beautiful, old-fashioned name. It was my great-grandmother's. But you chopped a masculine nickname from it and refused to be called by anything else. Now you have to live with the consequences."

"What consequences?"

"Gender confusion," she called over her shoulder as she opened the door, then turned to point a finger at me. "By the way, I haven't forgotten why I'm here. Next session is about you."

After she left, I stretched out on the couch and stared up at the ceiling, one arm thrown carelessly across my forehead as the photographs flashed through my minds-eye once again. I saw them in a different light now. Like an ill-fated love story on a Hollywood screen, they projected sadness, hopes dashed, love lost. My mother was the beautiful heroine and Uncle Jack the handsome but self-centered young man that dangles love and snatches it away. Dad's quiet, unassuming friendship must have been a breath of fresh air after such a tumultuous relationship. She would have fallen for him slowly, not realizing the cloth of love was being woven around them, binding them together with strong threads of mutual respect, kindness, caring, and trust.

I blinked and the ceiling came back into view. Who was I kidding? If my father trusted my mother, then he wouldn't have beat Jack to a pulp twenty years ago. Would he? Or did that have anything to do with the photographs? Would I ever know?

Chapter Eleven

Two days of Mother roaming the house, watching me surreptitiously from across the room, waiting for me to fall apart, was almost enough to give me a breakdown in and of itself. But I did have other things to occupy my time. The Breckinridge Security Company descended upon the house and winery, installing a system that would deter the most seasoned burglar. And Davy showed up again, sneaking across the south vineyards to avoid the busy road, and his mother's watchful eye.

He knocked at the back door about ten in the morning, startling me from my catatonic perusal of the newspaper. Before he arrived my eyes were drooping, and I was nearly asleep where I sat. Sleeping less at night, as though I could stay the dreams by not giving them enough time to materialize, I walked the floors and grazed from the refrigerator at three in the morning. I would either find a way to stop my nightmares in a healthy way or become an obese insomniac.

"Hello, Davy. What's up?" I yawned, folded the paper and pushed it to the side, as he joined me at the table.

"Nothin'. Just wanted to see what those trucks were doing here." He eyed my cold toast with interest and I slid my plate toward him.

I nodded. "They're wiring the house and winery so that no one can break in again. If anyone tries to get through the doors or windows without the code, the alarm goes off and the police show up," I said as I watched him chew.

"Cool. Can I try it?" he asked, obviously eager to make the local boys in blue work for their donuts.

"Does your mother know where you are? Because she didn't seem too happy about you walking over here before without telling her." I enjoyed Davy's company, for the most part, but I didn't want to get in the middle of a parent/child tug of war. If Margaret didn't want him roaming the neighborhood alone, I certainly wouldn't argue.

He put down the toast, ignoring my question. "Is your grandma visiting again? Uncle Handel said your old lady would straighten ya out. What's that mean?" he asked, squinting at me in the semblance of a frown.

"It means your uncle needs to stay out of other people's business," I said with a tad too much vehemence. Davy scooted back in his chair and looked ready to take flight.

"Who is a grandma?" Mother demanded as she entered the room, her hair and makeup perfect as always, without a jowl in sight, fit and trim as though she still did an hour of aerobics every morning. How could anyone mistake my mother for a grandmother? But to an eight-year-old, everyone over twenty-five looks ancient. I remembered thinking the same thing when I was that age.

"Davy, you remember my mother, Mrs.

Fredrickson," I said, winking companionably at the boy across from me.

"Yes, we met at the funeral," Mother added, as she poured herself a cup of coffee. "But unless my daughter gets married soon and has a lovely baby, I will not allow anyone to call me Grandma." She patted Davy on the shoulder and smiled. "You may call me Sabrina, young man."

He looked up at her unblinkingly and then nodded. "Okay, but Mom doesn't like me to call old people by their first names."

Mother let out a burst of laughter tinged with irony. "I can't win, can I?"

"Don't even try," I said shaking my head.

Davy got up and went to the refrigerator. He took out the milk carton and set it on the counter before turning belatedly to me, a half grin on his lips. "Can I have some milk?"

"Of course you can. A growing boy needs lots of calcium," Mother said, stepping in and taking a glass out of the cupboard. She set it beside the carton and let him pour it himself. "Strong teeth and bones and all that."

"That's what Mom says."

I stood up and stretched, yawning widely, afraid if I stayed still much longer I'd fall asleep. I looked out the window. The brightness of the day contrasted sharply with my inner turmoil, the edge of depression, as yet undefined in relation to its root cause. I originally thought it had to do with Mother's secret, but after hearing the details of her first love, the repercussions of that unwise alliance, and the pact she made with my father to let go of the past, I no longer deemed it worthy of continued guilt on my part. If my father let his jealousy get away with him and took it out on his brother one fine summer afternoon, who was I to take the blame for that? I was only an eight-year-old child at the time.

Soft, white, puffs of cloud broke up the expanse of blue sky outside and I felt the need to walk beneath them. Clouds always amazed me with their ability to float weightlessly in the heavens. Even gray and filled with rain, they hung above the world, heavier, but still suspended, not giving in to the gravity of earth, until finally letting loose their load, releasing it like so many bad memories, never to be carried again. "I'm going for a walk. Why don't you and Sabrina play a game of hide and seek?" I suggested. Not giving either of them a chance to protest, I hurried out through the back door.

My feet kicked up a tiny cloud of dust as I walked down the row of grapevines, my white tennis shoes turning a murky gray with the settling film. I squinted up into the sun, remembering the same path by moonlight the other night with Handel. The image of Handel and I as children, running through the vineyards at night, had stayed with me, and I could only conclude that the memory was significant. My therapist said that we pick and choose the memories we need to remember, not necessarily the most important ones, but those useful to our continued wellbeing. How was Handel important to my continued wellbeing?

I stopped to inspect the vines and clusters of inconspicuous blooms that would soon turn into small, hard, green, acid berries, growing and ripening eventually into plump, hardy grapes. The petals fell away at my touch and I saw the hardened nubs pushing through. It was hard to believe the rocky soil at my feet was so conducive to growing the best wine berries. Minnesota farmers complained loudly when the rains weren't as heavy as normal, the land green and fertile, or the soil dark and moist. But they were usually growing corn or beans, pumpkins, or golf courses.

I heard the crunch of a boot on gravel before my eye caught the movement of someone walking in the next row over. I held perfectly still and waited, but obviously I'd been spotted as well. Handel bent and peered through an opening in the vines, his blonde hair hanging over his forehead as usual.

"Hey. I thought I saw someone out here," he said, beginning to make his way through to my side, careful not to damage the vines. "Out for a walk? Or are you delving into your new position as owner of Fredrickson Vineyard?" He straightened up and smiled, his teeth gleaming brightly in the California sun like a Hollywood movie star on vacation.

"A little of both, I guess. I needed to get out of the house, get some exercise, clear my mind." I started walking again and he fell into step with me, moving away from the house and winery.

"You haven't seen Davy by any chance?" he asked, peering back at the house in the distance, as though just remembering he was on a mission. "Margaret's been looking for him again. I told her he was probably over here; she shouldn't worry. But you know moms."

"There is no need to worry. I left him in good hands. The old lady's." I laughed softly. "Boy, are you in the doghouse. And she liked you too."

Handel had the good sense to appear chagrined. He cleared his throat. "Great. That kid is going to be the death of me. He repeats everything he hears. He'd make a terrific witness for the prosecution."

We walked another hundred yards or so before he tugged on my arm to stop. "Hold up, will you?"

I turned and looked up at him, at his blue eyes, the blonde thatch of hair falling over his forehead, the tanned skin showing in the open V-neck of his cotton sweater, and although I was still peeved with his earlier attitude toward me, I desperately wanted him to kiss me. Desperation doesn't always show on a person's face though, but rather, charges through their veins at the speed of light, giving an extra bump to the heart muscle.

He stared at the ground a moment before raising his gaze to my face, seemingly oblivious to my elevated blood pressure. "I'm glad I caught you out here. It seems an appropriate place to talk." He shrugged, a wistful smile on his handsome face. "At least it used to be. We could tell each other anything."

"Did you want to tell me something?" I pushed my hands nervously in the front pockets of my jeans. I hoped he wouldn't bring up the kiss, remind me that I initiated it, and tell me he just wanted to be friends. Rejection was not something I took well.

But he said none of that. Instead, he drew my hands out and pulled me slowly toward him, then lowered his head and kissed me. Not an I'm sorry kiss, or let's just be friends kiss, but a deep, heart-searing, mind-melding lip-lock that took my breath away.

"You're not going to run away this time, are you?" he asked, once we came up for air.

I shook my head, unable to think of anything witty to say and he kissed me again. Finally, I pulled away and stepped back. "Wow," I breathed.

He grinned. "We're in agreement then."

He took my hand in his and we continued our walk to the end of the field. My earlier inspection of the vines was forgotten in the heady intoxication of romance. Thoughts, of whether I was ready for a budding relationship, bounced through my head. The fact that I still harbored resentment against most of the men I'd dated was a very real point against trying again, but there was something different about Handel. Sure he was male, arrogantly accustomed to getting his own way, and he came with a mini-me nephew. But he'd also been there more than once when I needed him, past and present.

He seemed to realize I desired time to acclimate to our new level of friendship, keeping the conversation neutral on our return to the house. Outwardly, I listened intently as Handel explained the attempted murder case he was working on, but inside I was jumping up and down like a little girl who now had Ken to go with Barbie.

"How's it going with your mother?" he asked, after a lengthy pause in the conversation.

I smiled. "You mean has she committed me yet?"

He chuckled as we slowed to a stop outside the kitchen door. "No. I mean -- are you getting along or should I drive her back to the airport and send her off?"

"You'd do that for me? Risk the wrath of Mother just to please me?" I asked, facing him squarely, hands on my hips.

Handel's fingertips were warm against my skin as he reached out and stroked my cheek, his gaze steady. "I'd even risk the wrath of zombies for you."

"Thanks, but zombies have nothing on Mother."

He shrugged. "She's a surprisingly strong woman. Much like her daughter."

"I'm not that strong," I admitted with a small shake of my head. "I fall apart quite easily. Why do you think she came?"

"Because she loves you. But you're stronger than you think. Look how you were ready to take on a burglar single-handedly the other night."

"That was mere stupidity. Besides, a burglar is easy compared to nightmares." I bit at my lip, my gaze straying to the tire swing, reminding me of childhood and how quickly things change.

"What kind of nightmares?"

I sighed. "Nothing really. Still getting used to the time change I guess."

He didn't appear convinced but before he could question me further, the back door opened and Davy stuck his head out. "Hey, Uncle Handel!"

"Hey, Davy." Handel grinned. "Your mom is looking for you. You'd better run home as fast as you can."

"Aw, shoot! Can't I stay here with you, Uncle Handel? Sabrina and me were just gonna play hide and seek. She's in the bedroom counting. I gotta hide."

"Sabrina?"

"You know - Billie's old lady."

Handel made a choked sound and covered his mouth with his hand. "I wouldn't call her that if I were you," he warned. "Women don't like the word old."

I laughed. "It's not the word, it's the connotation," I said. I put my arm around Davy, who squinted up at us in confusion. "Don't worry. I'll let Sabrina know you had to leave. She can find you another time."

"You heard the lady. Now get moving." Handel prodded the boy along by giving him a light push toward the field. "Your mother wants you home for lunch."

"All right," Davy mumbled, head down, shoulders sagging, as he shuffled away.

"He sure knows how to play the mentally-wounded nephew, doesn't he?" Handel kept his gaze on the boy until he was out of sight between the rows of vines.

I smiled. "I'm sure he learned from the best."

Inside the kitchen the smell of burnt coffee, left to sit on the warmer for too long, permeated the air. I poured the sludge down the sink and put on a fresh pot. Handel leaned against the counter watching me; absently folding the corner of a towel left lying there.

"Are you nervous about something?" I asked.

He frowned. "I don't think so. Why?"

I shrugged. "Not even a little afraid to come face to face with Mother?"

"Thanks for reminding me," he said, his tone caustic. "Actually, I was thinking about something else. But now that you mention it, perhaps I should run home too."

I shook my head and pushed him toward a chair. "No way. You're not escaping that easily. Besides, Mother probably fell asleep on the bed while she was counting to a hundred. That always happened when she played hide and seek with Adam."

He eyed the chair in question. "Are you sure it's safe? You didn't give me the broken one again, did you?"

"I didn't give you a broken one last time," I said, laughing. "You're the one that broke it."

"If you say so."

I poured two cups of coffee and sat across from him. "So, what were you thinking?

He leaned forward on one elbow, his chin in his hand. "About you mainly. What you must have been like growing up. As a teenager. In college. The years I've missed between eight and now." He grinned. "I won't use the word old, but I like the way you've aged."

I felt my face flush with embarrassment. "Matured might be a better choice. Aged is right up there with old." I sipped my coffee, trying not to look as uncomfortable as I felt. In court I had no problem being the center of attention, sort of like starring in community theatre, but otherwise I preferred to blend in. Handel's direct scrutiny of me as an individual was disconcerting. Was this why my relationships always failed? I had a fear of sharing my thoughts and feelings?

"So, what were you like?"

"Pretty much the same -- only shorter."

"Sounds intriguing."

"Oh yeah. A short, smart-mouthed, pimply girl is always intriguing to the opposite sex." I batted my eyelashes at him. "And you thought I never had a date because I was violent."

His brows drew down in a frown. "I thought we were past that."

"Sorry. Old habits."

"I see you two have made up and are playing nice again," Mother said as she breezed into the room. Her entrance couldn't have come at a worse time. I didn't want her fostering the idea that Handel and I were a couple. After all, it took more than a few kisses to change life patterns. But her mind wasn't as focused on us as I imagined. She poured a cup of coffee and opened the back door. "Did either of you notice which direction Davy took off in?" she asked, stepping out to glance around the tree-lined yard. She appeared less than eager to go in search of the eight-year-old boy.

Handel smiled at me across the table, his cup cradled between his palms. "You don't have to worry, Sabrina. I sent him home to his mother."

She stepped back in and closed the door, her eyes narrowed in thought. "I'm not expected to find him there, am I?" she asked.

"I don't think so."

"You'll have to play hide-and-seek with Davy another time," I said, amused by the seriousness with which she took the game. "Margaret wanted him home for lunch."

She nodded. "Oh, that's good. I fell asleep when I

was supposed to be counting."

"Imagine that."

My teasing tone brought a smile to Mother's lips. "You think you're pretty smart, don't you, young lady?"

"I just know you."

"Really?"

Handel cleared his throat. "Well, Billie did suggest that you might have fallen asleep."

Mother turned her gaze on him then, blistering in accusation. "I have something to discuss with you, young man."

He slid down in his chair as though trying to disappear under the floorboards. "I was afraid of that. You know, Davy has a wild imagination. I wouldn't take anything he says seriously."

She glared down at him for a moment. "Do I look old to you?" she asked finally, her tone leaving no option other than a resounding no.

Handel shook his head and gave her one of those slow smiles I liked so much, the corners of his mouth turning up ever so slightly, his eyes sparkling with admiration. "You definitely don't look like an old lady to me. In fact, my friend at Antonio's asked for your number. He thought you were hot."

Mother laughed lightly, and patted his cheek, eating up Handel's flattery like a kitten lapping cream. "You mean that dark-haired man at the front desk? He was quite attractive, but he seemed a bit old for me."

Handel nodded, playing along. "I think he's forty-two, but I'm sure you could liven him up. Want me to give him the okay?"

"Why not?"

I set my cup down with a thump. Coffee sloshed out over the table, but I was too appalled by the conversation to worry about it. "Mother! I can't believe you would go out with a perfect stranger. You don't even know his name." My mother dating a sweet, widowed banker was one thing, but an Italian Stallion was quite another. I remembered the man too and the way he'd ogled us both. At twenty-one she may have been naïve enough to get involved with a man like Jack, but at fifty she ought to have a little common sense.

"Actually, his name's Antonio. He owns the restaurant," Handel informed us.

"I thought you were friends with the chef," I said with a scowl.

"The chef is his brother, Carl. We went to school together."

Mother patted my cheek as though I were two. "I didn't say I'd go out with him, honey, I only said he could call. What are you so worried about?"

"I'm not worried."

"Good." She put her cup in the sink, and leaned against the counter, minutely examining her nails. "I really need a manicure. Do you think we could go into town today? It would be nice to get out for awhile." She looked up, her gaze resting on me. "Maybe you could have your hair done too," she said, the unspoken criticism pricking my soft underside.

Handel rose, ready to take flight. As most men, unwilling to get in the middle of a confrontation, he knew when to disappear. "I better get going. Margaret will be sending Davy to look for me next." His gaze locked with mine and I knew he was going to bend down and kiss me goodbye, telegraphing our changing relationship with a bold stroke.

"Handel," Mother said, interrupting his intent. "Your father worked at the winery twenty years ago. Is he still around or did he retire?" she asked.

The random question surprised me, although

many times I'd thought of asking the same thing myself, but didn't want to broach a painful subject. I assumed Handel had no relationship with his father and was happy with the status quo. If I weren't so very interested in the answer I might not have picked up on his discomfort. He hid it well. A slight stiffening of his shoulders the only clue. "My father disappeared soon after you folks went back to Minnesota. No one was really surprised or searched too hard for him. He was an alcoholic and had a history of running off. Only this time he didn't return." Handel's voice held no resentment at the fact, but rather acceptance, and if I wasn't reading more into it than was there, it also held satisfaction. His father was mean and abusive and Handel didn't miss him. I couldn't blame him for that.

"I'm sorry," Mother said simply, and squeezed his arm comfortingly.

"Thank you, but it was a long time ago."

I cleared my throat to catch Mother's attention. "Shouldn't you touch up your makeup if we're going to town?" I knew even a subtle hint that something appeared less than perfect on her face would get her out of the room.

"Oh. Why yes. I better get ready," she said meeting my gaze, surprised by my easy capitulation. She usually had to work a while to get me to a salon. I was not a beauty shop kind of girl. I even chopped at my own hair on occasion just to postpone the inevitable. She gave Handel a charming smile. "Don't be a stranger around here. I think you're good for my daughter. I don't know the last time I was able to talk her into doing something for herself. A bit of pampering goes a long way toward renewing the spirit, you know."

"Mother, I'm right here. Don't talk about me as though I've left the room."

"Sorry," she said, eyes wide with innocence.

When she was gone, Handel pulled me into his arms, a comforting embrace without any strings. Finally, he pressed a kiss against my forehead. "I'll call you," he promised.

*****

The salon was booked and Mother couldn't get in until Friday. She made an appointment, obviously planning to stick around, and we got back in the car. The heat from the afternoon sun filled the vehicle, a blazing furnace on wheels. I flipped on the air-conditioning before pulling into traffic.

"Well, what now?" I asked. We were already out and about and might as well make the most of it. There were things I wanted to purchase for the house, small items that would make it my own. Uncle Jack's taste in décor went South of the border often times and I preferred soft, muted, relaxing colors. Call me a boring, Midwestern traditionalist, but I found it much easier to fall asleep in a room painted a soothing shade of eggshell than in Jack's master bedroom painted brick red with black trim. Luckily, he neglected to hang any of the abstracts in there, but I still felt as though I had fallen into hell's waiting room when I lay on the bed.

"Might as well get a feel for your new town. Maybe do some shopping?" Mother gazed raptly out the window, her built-in radar buzzing away as she waited for it to hone in on a sale. She loved to shop.

"That's what I was thinking, believe it or not."

She patted my knee. "I knew you'd turn out right sooner or later."

"Don't get all excited. I'm not turning into you," I said. "My aversion to shopping is just overshadowed by my tremendous dislike for Jack's decorating choices."

Mother pulled down the visor mirror and fluffed

her hair. "His taste does seem a bit eccentric. In the old days I would have said eclectic, but obviously he changed quite a lot in twenty years." She reapplied her lipstick before flipping up the visor; worry lines etched between her brows as she turned toward me. "Do you think he may have gone a bit crazy in his last years? I mean -- he painted excruciating things on canvas, gave away all his beautiful furniture, and willed you his estate."

"Are you saying he wasn't judicious in his choice of an heir?"

Mother's radar must have lit up. She pointed for me to turn at the next right. A large furniture store sprawled on the corner. Next to that a paint and carpet store. Just what I needed. I parked the car between a little convertible and a huge SUV and shut off the ignition.

"Honey, his judgment was as sound as a newly tuned piano," she reassured me. Smiling, she snapped her purse shut and opened the door of the car.

"For a crazy man," I added under my breath.

*****

After two hours, and endless arguing over what I wanted and what Mother thought I should want, I ordered a camel leather couch and recliner to match, a new butcher block kitchen table set, and a lovely landscape to hang above the fireplace. I wasn't so impressed with the frame, but thought it might be the same size as the fancy one on Jack's giant abstract and I could trade off. Delivery wouldn't be for three or four days, and that gave me just enough time to get the walls painted.

By the time we went next door to the paint store I was too tired to fight over degrees of white. I allowed Mother to choose the perfect shade for my bedroom and kitchen while I gathered brushes, rollers and drop cloths for the job. I enjoyed painting. The simple chore was an inexpensive form of therapy for me, relaxing my mind and giving me something to focus on besides the usual suspects.

A young man helped carry all the things to our car. Mother waited as I thanked him and shut the trunk, then pointed across the street to a fancy coffee shop with outdoor seating. "Let's sit a minute and relax. The striped umbrellas over the tables look inviting. And I bet they have those chocolate muffins you like so much," she added, as though that would clinch the deal.

After shopping I needed a jolt of caffeine and wasn't about to shoot down the best idea she'd had in hours. I ordered espresso but Mother decided to have a blended coffee, saying it made her feel so very Californian. We sat at one of the tables sipping our drinks and watching passerby, the camaraderie of fellow shoppers after a successful mission warming our hearts.

"Don't you find it strange that Handel's father disappeared and never returned?" Mother asked, as she stirred her drink, slowly mixing in the whipped cream and drizzled chocolate. She took a sip before meeting my curious gaze.

"What are you getting at? There are people all over the country that walk out on their families and never come back." I shrugged. "Besides which, he was an alcoholic. He could have wandered off and fallen in a canal for all we know, been swept out to sea and eaten by little fishes."

Mother didn't smile at my joke, but pressed her lips in a straight line. "An *abusive* alcoholic - isn't that right?" She nodded at my look of surprise. "I saw the bruises on Handel when he was a boy."

I leaned forward, intent on the conversation. "Then why didn't you do something?"

Mother folded her hands on the table and stared into her glass. "You know it's not that simple. I didn't know for sure and by the time I met his father and realized the truth, we were leaving."

"You met his father?" I asked. My eyes narrowed with interest. "What was he like?"

"Very attractive, a dark-haired version of his son, only he had a harder edge to him, probably due to the drink. He was polite enough and friendly when approached, but there was something about him..."

"Meanness?" I finished for her, my spirit ready to champion Handel even when he no longer needed it.

She shook her head. "No. Secretive. That's the word I would use to describe him. A man not to be trusted."

"Well, I'm glad he disappeared and Handel and Margaret won't ever have to see him again." I picked up my cup and swallowed the last of the strong brew.

"That's the problem." Mother held my gaze steadily across the table. "I saw a man lurking out behind the winery the other day. He was older and definitely worse for wear, but I'm pretty sure it was Sean Parker."

"What?" I demanded. Several people at the nearby tables turned to look in our direction. I leaned forward, barely able to restrain my voice. "Why didn't you tell me?"

"You were in the winery following Charlie around that day and I'd forgotten all about it by the time I saw you. When Handel showed up this morning, the incident suddenly popped into my mind."

I bit at my bottom lip, wondering how this would affect Handel and his sister. Would they be relieved to realize their father was alive after all, or resentful of his survival when their mother had gone to an early grave. I knew how bad childhood experiences often follow us into adulthood, not letting go, but clinging to the back of our minds with razor sharp claws. Whether Handel admitted it or not, the abuse from his father and subsequent disappearance continued to influence him. Time doesn't always heal all wounds.

Mother glanced across the street, her gaze following a man walking a very large German shepherd. They turned the corner and disappeared from sight before she spoke again. "I have a bad feeling about this," she said, her voice low but vibrant enough to be heard above the street noise, like a seer with her sights set on a future time and place.

I was beginning to feel a little creeped out myself by the way she was acting, but I wasn't about to let on. Even if Handel's father had come back to town, what did that prove? That even a bum comes home to roost? I stood up and threw my paper cup in the nearby trashcan.

"Ready to go?"

"Aren't you even worried about Handel's reaction?" Mother asked, as she followed me across the street to the car. "You are going to tell him, aren't you?"

I unlocked the doors and slid behind the wheel. "You don't even know for sure that the man you saw was Sean Parker," I said, turning the key in the ignition and glancing in the rearview mirror. "And if so, why did he show up at the winery and not his own home? The Parker's live in the same house they did twenty years ago."

She nodded. "That's a good question. Perhaps he was looking for Jack. I understood they were friends as teenagers. That's why Jack was letting Sean work at the winery even though he'd been fired from multiple jobs because of his drinking." She secured her seatbelt as I pulled into the street.

"So, he thought after a twenty year coffee break he would be welcomed back with open arms? That must have been some friendship." I shook my head, and snorted a laugh. "I guess he realized with Jack out of the picture his chances of employment here were pretty slim, so he took off again. I admit Handel would be angry if he knew that his father had been skulking around, but I'm sure there is nothing to worry about. Sean Parker, or whoever the man was, is probably long gone. Don't you think?"

Mother's silence filled the hot car.

Silence from Mother was usually not a good sign. She was telling me something by not telling me something. The trouble being that I wasn't clairvoyant. I'd passed through the fire of silence more than once as a kid and come out the other side, learning a valuable lesson by Mother withholding the gift of her voice. Adam and I would rather be yelled at than get the silent treatment. But I knew this time her silence wasn't intended as a reprimand but rather because she didn't have an answer.

We were turning onto the gravel drive when she reached out and brushed my cheek with the backs of her fingers. "Maybe it's time to go home, Billie," she said. "There are so many problems to deal with here. Are you sure you're ready to take them on?"

My answer was sharp. "You were the one who said I should stay. You said being a divorce attorney was depressing. I thought you wanted me to make the change."

Mother pulled her hand back as though I'd slapped her. "I only want what's best for you. Since you've been here you haven't been sleeping, your nightmares have returned, you seem unsettled. Now you've taken up with Handel, a man with enough problems of his own."

I pulled into the garage and shut off the engine, my temper flaring as hot as the black metal hood of the car. "Whoa! This is starting to sound a lot like meddling. I know you came back because you were worried about me, but I'm fine. And I don't know what you mean by "taken up with", but I can assure you that Handel and I are just friends. Not that I need your permission." I jerked open the door, climbed out, and slammed it behind me.

Chapter Twelve

Plastic sheets covered the countertops and floor of the empty kitchen, splattered with droplets of Dovetail white paint. Mother stood on the third rung of a ladder, touching up the edge of the ceiling with a tiny brush, her movements meticulous and sure. She didn't turn or acknowledge my entrance, although the crinkling of the plastic under my feet was like a trumpet proclamation.

Like an unspoken agreement we began painting walls this morning, Mother in the kitchen, and I in the bedroom. The atmosphere in the house had begun to feel pressurized. I was afraid the roof would blow off any minute.

The paths we trod throughout the house remained separate, not stepping into a room already occupied by the other. Except for the DJ on the radio, yapping in between sets of country music, no words had been spoken since yesterday afternoon. My foray into the kitchen now was out of desperation. I needed a soda.

The refrigerator was also draped with plastic and I awkwardly held it up and away to get the door open. The coolness inside was enough to make me yearn for a

Minnesota snowstorm. Paint fumes gave me a headache, so I thought keeping the windows open and the air flowing through the house would counteract that. But instead I had a headache from the heat. I reached behind the milk carton and a container of cottage cheese and pulled out a can of cola.

"This is beyond silly, you know," Mother said, one hand holding the wet brush in mid-air, the other grasping the side of the ladder for balance. "I ought to be able to say what's on my mind without you getting all bent out of shape and giving me the silent treatment."

I popped the top of the can and took a long swallow, not meeting her gaze, feeling the power of silence. My mother could always win an argument simply by saying nothing. Now I was in control, not responding, letting her brew in her own juices, as I dealt in payback.

"The only reason I said anything was because I heard you talking in your sleep again night before last. I'm frightened for you, honey. You seemed so desperate." She stepped down from the ladder and set the brush on the edge of an empty paint can.

I pushed the door closed and found my way out of the plastic sheeting. Holding a grudge against my mother because she cared about me was ridiculously foolish. My lips curved up mischievously as I held out the can. "Want a drink?" I asked. Mother had germaphobia, or at least that's what Adam and I called it. She would never drink from the same glass as someone else and warned us against the dangers of sharing with our friends. Adam had, on occasions, drank from her glass when she wasn't looking, just to see if her dire predictions would come true.

She narrowed her eyes, the better to hide her amusement. "No, thank you. I think I'll have a glass of water." She stepped past me and tried to get into the cupboard for a cup. Finally, she just pulled the whole sheet down and wadded it into the corner of the room. "Well, I'm about done in here anyway," she said.

"You did a great job, Mom," I said, looking slowly around the room. The kitchen walls reflected the light from outdoors, making everything bright and shiny. "I thought maybe a paint called Dovetail would be a little dingy, like dirty sheets, but no." I grinned. "It's as white as fresh bird droppings hitting a pane of glass."

"Funny girl." Mother made a face. "That's the last time I help you choose paint."

"Promise?" I lifted one brow and held out a hand to shake on it.

"Get out of here and finish your bedroom while you still have the best light. If I don't get this kitchen cleaned up we won't be having lunch any time soon." She swatted me on the seat of my pants as I turned to leave. All was forgiven.

*****

"Charlie, what in the world is this?" I asked, pointing to a column in the Cost of Sales report. I leaned back in my chair as he stood beside me and ran a finger slowly down the page, clicking his tongue at each entry.

Finally, he cleared his throat and shrugged his shoulders, a sheepish look on his face. "I don't know. That's what we have an accountant for, isn't it?"

"This is going well," I muttered. I stood up from the rectangular conference table and pushed my chair in. "Obviously, Fredrickson's is not always running in the black, and one of the many reasons is that the head doesn't know what the hand is doing and the hand doesn't know what the foot is doing."

"Huh?" he scratched his chin and glanced toward the door, his attention divided between me boring him to death and waiting expectantly for the pizza we'd ordered to be delivered for lunch.

"If you don't know what this amount is for, neither does the accountant. An accountant only uses the numbers you give him, unless he's got a creative streak and that could end badly with a long prison sentence."

"Well, I can't remember everything. Jack was overseer; I'm best at managing people and keeping things running. Loren does most of the ordering and Sally manages the office."

I closed my eyes and tried to imagine a calm sea, but instead saw only crashing waves as my patience neared its end. "Never mind," I said, shaking my head. "I appreciate your help but I need to set up an appointment with our accountant. What's his name?"

"Becker," he said after a moment's hesitation.

"Thank you." I gathered the papers on the table and tapped my pen against the stack. "Once I get a handle on things around here, we can decide what needs to be changed."

"Changed? Then you've decided to stay and run the place?" he asked, surprise showing in his face.

"I haven't really made a decision yet, but whether I go or stay, I still want to see that the winery is profitable."

He pressed his lips firmly together and squared his shoulders before meeting my gaze. "I'll step down if you want to hire a more qualified manager, Ms. Fredrickson. I always knew I wasn't really management material, but Jack put me in the position anyway."

I nodded. "I understand that Charlie, but I don't want to replace you. You are a good manager in many ways. We just need to train you properly in the areas you lack."

He didn't appear convinced of his own abilities. "I

don't know if that's possible. Teaching an old dog new tricks and all."

I smiled. "It's possible."

The door opened and Sally stuck her head in, glancing first at Charlie and then me. "There's a man out here. He says he wants to talk to the boss."

Charlie sat down in a chair and folded his arms, deferring to my authority. "I'll wait for the pizza," he said.

I followed Sally out into the winery office. A man stood leaning against a file cabinet, his hands in the front pockets of his jeans. He wore a pair of battered work boots, a flannel shirt worn so thin it looked as though moths had been feeding on it, and a stained and faded baseball cap.

"Hello. I'm Ms. Fredrickson. And you are?" I asked, extending my hand.

He slowly straightened, ignored my outstretched hand, and pulled his cap off. His long hair was liberally streaked with grey and tied back from his face with a leather shoestring. "The name's Parker. Sean Parker." Standing taller than his son, and quite a bit thinner, he appeared to be all sharp angles, his skin like damp leather left to dry in the sun. "I'm looking for a job," he said simply.

I couldn't help but feel sorry for him, a man down on his luck with no one to care, but then I thought of the pain he'd inflicted on his family, on Handel, and I pushed aside mercy. "We don't have any openings right now," I said, my voice firm and final.

"Jack Fredrickson was a good friend of mine once upon a time," he said, by way of explanation. "I didn't realize he'd passed. I'm sorry to have bothered you." His eyes may once have been as blue as his son's but now they were faded, as though light and hope had gone out of them. He gave a little nod, replaced his cap and walked out.

Sally sat quietly at her desk through this exchange, but now stood up and followed him to the doorway. She gazed after the man as he departed the building. "So, that's Handel and Margaret Parker's father. Looks like he's had a lot of visits from the wrinkle fairy."

"I guess he's lived a hard life," I said. "Would you get our accountant on the phone please?"

Sally nodded and went to her desk where she flipped through the Rolodex. "Do you want to speak to her or just set up an appointment?" she asked, her hand poised over the buttons of the telephone.

"Her?"

Sally smiled. "Alexandra Becker. Didn't Charlie tell you?"

"No. Wrong assumption, that's all. Set up a time when she can come out. Thanks." I stepped into the hallway and hurried to the front door of the winery in time to catch a glimpse of Sean Parker walking slowly down the gravel drive toward the highway before the dust from the incoming pizza delivery truck bellowed up and obscured him from view.

"Having second thoughts?" Sally asked, suddenly appearing at my side.

I took the slip of pink notepad paper she held toward me, ignoring her insightfulness. "Tomorrow at two?"

She nodded. "If you want Alex to come here. Otherwise, she has four o'clock open today, but can't leave her office."

"Tomorrow is fine."

I held open the door for the pizza man. He struggled to balance ten boxes as he followed Sally to the conference room where everyone would soon gather for lunch. One hundred twenty dollars worth of pizza was a small price to pay for happy employees. Besides - was it a crime to buy your employees' trust and allegiance?

*****

"Ms. Becker, my uncle left this winery to me, but I'm afraid he didn't leave a set of instructions." I smiled at the woman across the desk from me. Her short, dark hair and black-rimmed glasses made me think of a female Buddy Holly. I leaned forward and folded my hands on the desktop. "My manager, Charlie Simpson, is teaching me the basics, but he appears to be lacking where the lead meets the page." She seemed flustered at my mention of Charlie, clasping her hands in her lap and glancing away. I continued. "The bottom line, the numbers end of this business is a blur to me right now. I would appreciate any insight you can give."

She opened her briefcase and pulled out a thick file. "I brought a copy of last year's tax return, among other things. I'll try to guide you through it. I also do the payroll for the winery. But Mr. Simpson signs the checks." I'd never heard anyone call Charlie Mr. around the winery. The formal use of his name sounded derogatory. She pulled nervously at one earlobe as she watched me glance over the first page. "I heard you were a divorce attorney," she said, undisguised disdain in her voice.

I looked up. She seemed ill at ease, sitting stiffly in the chair facing me. I wasn't sure what she was uptight about. "Yes."

"Were you thinking of opening a practice here in California? Not that there is a shortage of attorneys in our fair state," she said, a frown of disapproval curling her lip. I had the clear impression that she didn't like lawyers very much. I wondered how she got along with

Handel.

I shook my head. "I'm afraid I have enough to keep me busy right now. I'm neglecting my practice in Minnesota as it is. I haven't actually decided whether I'm moving here. I may just fly out every so often to check up on things."

Her brows drew together and down. "I was led to believe you'd already made that decision."

"Really? Led by whom?" I asked, meeting her gaze a little defiantly. I didn't like to feel that I was on trial without knowing the charge. "I don't remember discussing it with anyone."

"Jack, of course." She shuffled through her briefcase again before pulling out a small manila envelope, sealed and taped across the end. She hesitated, holding it in her lap for a moment. "Jack left this for you. He said you would know what to do with it."

I narrowed my gaze on Ms. Becker's face as she handed me the envelope. Was that relief I sensed, as though taking care of a nasty IOU? I asked, "Jack told you I was coming here to stay? How could he know that?"

"Look." She reached across the desk, and tapped the corner of the envelope where someone had penciled the date. "Jack came to my office two days before he died. He handed me that package, and asked me to give it to you when you came. He said you were going to live here and run the winery while he was gone." She paused, letting the information sink in. "Handel Parker normally had power of attorney when Jack was out of the country, and made sure everything was running properly. I didn't understand why Jack would bring someone new into the mix, an outsider, but he was adamant that you would take over. "

"Really? And what was different this time?"

She shrugged. "I don't know. I assumed he was going out of the country again, perhaps on an extended trip to some exotic place.

"A very exotic place," I murmured. Jack either had the ability to see the future or he planned his own death. Either way, I didn't like it. Why did he want me here? Why all the mystery? And why did he leave all these sealed envelopes around town for me to open? I felt like I was in a game of Clue.

"Aren't you going to open it?" Ms. Becker asked, trying to appear nonchalant. She took her glasses off and wiped them on the edge of her skirt. Without them she appeared even younger than the twenties I'd assigned her at first sight.

"Why don't we save time and you tell me what this is all about?" I leaned forward with my elbows on the desk, and my hands folded under my chin, giving her the look my third grade teacher perfected on me.

She shifted nervously in her seat. "What do you mean?"

"How long have you been an accountant?" I countered, watching her squirm.

"Four years."

"And before that?" If my assumptions were right, Jack's philanthropic tendencies favored those who worked for him in the past, people he could use for his own purposes when the need arose and their gratefulness would blind them. He had a lawyer and an accountant in his pocket. How many more were there?

"I went to Southern Cal."

"And I'll bet you had a full scholarship through Fredrickson Winery, am I right?"

Her silence was damning enough.

"So, what exactly did you do for my uncle?

Besides, taxes and bookkeeping, that is." I leaned back in my chair, the springs creaking on the swivel base, and crossed my arms.

Her look of astonishment, followed quickly by anger, was too real to be faked. She glared across the desk at me. "Jack was a good man. He would never ask me to do anything improper, if that's what you're getting at."

I raised my brows but didn't interrupt.

"He brought that package to my office, just like I said. He told me you were coming to run the winery, and that I should help you in any way I could." Alex Becker was clearly rattled but I wasn't so sure it had as much to do with my uncle's secrets as my accusations.

"May I call you Alex?" I asked, trying to put her at ease. When she nodded reluctantly, I smiled. "What job did you have at the winery before you went away to college?"

"I worked in the office mostly. I was always good with numbers. Sometimes Jack asked me to help clean up after a tour group came through." She stared down at her hands clasped tightly in her lap, then looked up, her gaze candid. "He was like a father to me. I miss him a lot."

The simple admission sent a chill down my spine. Jack, the man that wouldn't accept responsibility for his own child, was a father figure to young people? Had he reformed in later years or was he a master manipulator, as I was beginning to suspect.

"Why did Jack want me here? What was he planning?" I asked, hoping to catch Alex off guard. Jack must have divulged something to someone, trusted them enough to share his secrets, his plans for the future.

Alex Becker shook her head. "I don't know what

you're talking about. The only confidences he shared with me were the stocks he invested in. I'm his accountant, not his counselor." The woman's vehemence was genuine. She shoved her glasses back on her face, closed her briefcase with a click, and rose. "If you don't have any more business questions, I'll be on my way. I have other appointments today."

I grinned up at her, imagining her as a little girl, getting angry with her friends, taking her doll and going home. Alex didn't return my smile. "Thank you for coming out," I said, unwilling to concede at this point that I might be wrong about her.

"If you have any more questions perhaps you should email them to me and I'll try to respond as soon as possible."

She shook my proffered hand and hurried away, leaving me still unsure of my uncle's intentions, but positive that I would be receiving a hefty bill in the mail.

I stared down at the taped envelope and sighed. "Here we go again."

Chapter Thirteen

"Hello, Billie." Handel stood in the doorway to my office not three minutes later. Alex and he must have passed one another on the road. "Are you busy?" he asked, one hand on the doorframe.

"For you? Never." I smiled, set the letter opener down, and pushed the unopened package out of sight in the drawer of my desk. "Don't you have to be in court this afternoon?" I asked, as I slipped out of my chair to greet him.

"Already been there. Judge called a recess until the jury gets back on their collective feet." He glanced out toward Sally's desk before closing the door behind him.

"What happened?"

He made a face. "The flu happened. There were so many jurors out sick today, Judge Reynolds inquired whether the Rapture had taken place, although he was sure if it had, he would have been taken as well." Handel pulled me into his arms, a move that startled me momentarily by the intimacy he seemed to take for granted. He continued, his chin atop my head. "Instead of bringing in the alternates, he decided to wait it out."

I pulled back and looked into his eyes, sensing that something wasn't right. Gone was the teasing light, replaced by something dark. He dipped his head and kissed me lightly on the lips before letting go. "What's the matter?" I asked, hoping it didn't involve the subject of his father.

He dropped heavily into the chair Alex Becker had recently vacated, sighed, and released the buttons on his double-breasted suit coat before answering. "It seems there have been sightings of a man long thought to be dead. And it isn't Elvis."

To anyone who didn't know Handel well, his cryptic message may have sounded glib, but I knew he was hurting. I couldn't withhold information from him any longer. I took the chair beside him and reached out to run my hand down his arm. "Your father. I know. He was here yesterday looking for a job."

Handel pulled away at my touch, his expression thunderous. "You spoke with him and didn't bother to notify me? The man deserves prison, not welcomed back with open arms."

His words were harsh but not surprising. He couldn't even bring himself to call the man his father. "I certainly didn't welcome him," I said, shaking my head and trying to control my temper at the accusation. "I didn't even know who he was until he introduced himself. He looks old, worn down. He wanted work and I told him we weren't hiring."

Handel blew out a frustrated breath, leaned forward and held his head in his hands, as though the world had suddenly fallen on his shoulders. Sean Parker was still alive and well and able to hurt his family merely by showing up.

"Did he stop at the house?" I asked, wondering how the news traveled so quickly. I didn't think Mother would dare interfere after our conversation. But there were others at the winery who had seen him.

Handel shook his head, his words muffled as he continued to stare at the floor. "I got a call from a friend of mine at the sheriff's department. A Sean Parker was picked up for vagrancy in town and released. I was hoping it was a case of mistaken identity. A different Sean Parker," he said, his voice rough with anger.

He didn't rebuff me when I leaned over and rubbed circles over his back, relaxing the tension, trying to convey my support through the heat of my fingers. There were no words to make the situation better. Handel's pain wouldn't go away until he dealt with his father face to face, told him what he thought of him and tried to come to terms with the past. Something I would never be able to do.

Finally he straightened, his expression grim. "I suppose I better tell Margaret. She's never cared much for surprises."

"I'm sorry, Handel. I had this silly notion that I was protecting you."

He stood up and made as though to leave. "What was Alex doing here? I was surprised to see her talking to Charlie out by the car," he said, ignoring my apology.

I followed him to the door. Now was not the time to go into Jack's scholarship program or deal with the muddy waters of Jack's life. Handel had enough to deal with. My reply was vague. "Answering questions. Charlie doesn't seem to have a clue about the financial side of things."

He nodded. "Well, if you need me to mediate, let me know."

"Sure." I pressed my lips firmly together.

He stood there a moment with his hand on the doorknob, not saying anything.

Entangled

I reached out and pulled his coat together, buttoned it. "Come over for a walk tonight?" I offered, my fingers lingering along his lapels.
One side of his mouth lifted in a crooked smile. "We'll see," he said as he pulled open the door. "I'll call you."
I dropped my hands and turned back to the desk. This afternoon was made for discovery, Handel's father surfacing after a twenty-year disappearing act, and now my mystery envelope to open from Uncle Jack. Jack apparently was a man of many faces: my mother's ex-lover, my benefactor, and as far as I could tell, a lousy businessman. I wondered what other faces would emerge as I learned more.

*****

I called Minneapolis to discuss the immediate needs of my remaining clients, and any problems Jody might have dealing with them. She kept me on the phone for an hour talking about her daughter's report cards, the gray local weather forecast, and how much everyone missed me at the office building's spring party. After that, I decided to call it a day. My thoughts weren't on the business of the winery anyway, but scattered about like buckshot, flitting from the return of Handel's father, to the question of what Jack was planning before his untimely death, to Alex Becker and her relationship with my uncle.
I cleared my desk, grabbed the envelope out of the drawer, and hurried out. "I'm going home, Sally."
She looked up from the file drawer she was rifling through and nodded. "Sounds good to me. Wish I were the boss." She selected a folder and took it to her desk. "Did you get everything you wanted from Alex?" she asked, pretending to be absorbed in the papers at hand.
I paused, a puzzled smile on my lips. "I guess so.

What did you think I wanted from her?" I asked, sensing an underlying question in her words.

Insecurity flitted across Sally's face, as though she knew she'd asked a question that could get her into trouble, replaced with a beet red color that clashed harshly with her auburn hair. She shrugged. "Oh, nothing."

I raised my brows and set my hip on the edge of her desk, not quite ready to leave now that we'd gotten down to office dynamics. "Tell me. What do you know about Alex Becker that might interest me?"

Sally's mouth fell open and then she laughed. "I can't believe you asked me that. Alex is a nice girl." She lowered her voice and looked toward the open door. "Only -- I just wondered if you knew she and Handel used to be an item."

"Really?" Now it was my turn to play coy. "Why do you think that would interest me?" I asked, fiddling with the etched-glass paperweight on her desk.

"I've seen the way he looks at you." She grinned. "You don't have anything to worry about."

"That's good to know. By the way, what was the relationship between Alex and my uncle?"

She clued in to the change in my tone, shuffling papers around before answering. "Jack treated Alex like a daughter. I know he helped pay her way through college. Alex was so grateful she would have scrubbed toilets for the man if he'd asked. Charlie moved out of the house when she was ten. A rough divorce, from what I've heard. I don't think she ever got over it."

"Charlie is Alex' father?" I gasped.

My tone must have held a twinge of annoyance because Sally held up her hands in defensive mode. "Don't shoot the messenger. I didn't think it was my place to tell you. Sorry."

"Right. Is she married? What's with the name Becker?"

Sally ran a hand through her red tresses. "No, not married. I think she just took her mother's maiden name after she was of age."

"Well, no wonder she acted the way she did. I don't think any kid ever gets over their parents divorcing." I stood up, a little more enlightened as to Alex Becker's attitude. She wanted to follow my uncle's wishes and yet couldn't understand the man's choice in me, one of the hated family-dissolvers. "She seems nice enough, but I don't believe she holds divorce attorneys in very high esteem."

Sally's smile was confident as she crossed her legs and leaned back in her chair. "Well, I know for a fact Handel Parker is very attracted to attorneys."

"Is that right?" I stepped into the hall. "Likes to look at himself in the mirror a lot, huh?"

I heard her laugh behind me as I pushed open the outside door and ran smack into Sean Parker. He had obviously been waiting for a while, standing in the shadow of the building smoking, four more butts discarded at his feet.

"Excuse me," I said, an automatic reflex before I noticed he didn't move aside.

His tall, grizzled frame filled my path as the door swung shut behind me. "I need to talk to you, Billie," he said. Smoke drifted from his nostrils, like an aging dragon unable to render a flame. He dropped his cigarette and crushed it beneath the toe of his boot, his gray eyes never leaving my face.

My first instinct was to run. And then I mentally shook myself. The man was a transient, had wasted his life and no doubt destroyed his liver, but he wasn't a threat to me. A lack of manners did not indicate a criminal mind, as my mother had always implied it did. More than anything, he was to be pitied. His family didn't want anything to do with him, and their lack of love was well deserved.

"How do you know my name?" I asked, wondering if in his alcohol-fogged brain he could remember a little girl from twenty years ago. Although, he didn't seem inebriated at the moment.

He sniffed and wiped his nose on the sleeve of his shirt, reminding me of Davy. "You're Jack's niece, aren't you? I heard about you."

"Jack Fredrickson was my uncle," I confirmed, then stepped around him and headed across the gravel parking lot toward the house.

Worn out and decrepit though he appeared, he kept up with me, staying by my side until I stopped a few yards from my front door. I faced him down, hands on my hips, assuming the look of a tough-as-nails businesswoman. He didn't appear intimidated at all. I'd have to work on that.

"What is it that you want, Mr. Parker?"

He slipped his hands in the back pockets of his jeans and stared at a point somewhere over my left shoulder when he spoke. "I know I asked you before, but I really need a job." I started to interrupt and he shook his head. "I asked all over the county. Nobody has anything right now. Least not for me. I understand folks being leery. I've never been what you call stable. But the wine business is what I know."

"I'm sorry, but we don't have any positions open at the winery."

"I'll do anything. Fetch and carry, wash cars, clean, paint, whatever. You name it."

His desperation frightened me. A man without hope was a man without scruples. He might be inclined to do anything, and that anything could be a hundred times more dangerous than giving him temporary work.

"Mr. Parker, have you contacted your family?"

He licked his lips, dry and cracked from the elements. "I don't got a family," he said. "I just got me. And whether or not I'm worthy to be included in the human race, I still need to eat."

"I understand that. I just don't know what to tell you." I reached in my pocket and pulled out a ten-dollar bill. "Here. Buy yourself some dinner."

He glared at me; jaw working as he ground his teeth angrily. "I don't need charity, I need work."

I snatched the bill back. "Fine. Talk to your son. If it's okay with Handel, I'll give you a temporary job, otherwise you're out of luck." Knowing I was probably sinking my relationship with Handel simply by suggesting I give his father a job, I felt as if I'd gone far enough out on a limb. Talk about torpedoing my relationships.

"What does Handel have to do with anything? I thought you owned this winery now." He took a step closer, eyes narrowed, hands loose at his sides. I forced myself not to back up.

"Mr. Parker, I believe my daughter gave you her answer," my mother interrupted from the steps of the house. She stared him down, a lioness protecting her cub.

Sean Parker squinted up at her, the lines deepening around his eyes into crevices. "Mrs. Fredrickson. Nice to see you again," he said, giving a little nod of recognition. "How's your husband?" he asked, his mouth twisting up into the semblance of a smile, which was even scarier than his frown.

My mother ignored the last. "Wish I could say the same, but once every twenty years is more than I want

to see you. Now, my daughter suggested you speak with
your son. But whether or not you decide to do that, you
will leave this property right now or I will have the
police here in five minutes." I noticed belatedly that she
held the cordless phone in her left hand, her weapon of
choice.

"Now there's no need to do that. I was just
leaving." He looked my way again, bitter and
unrepentant, and I felt the hairs on the back of my neck
tingle. Before I had time to react, he snatched the ten-
dollar bill out of my hand, smirked, and trudged away
down the drive.

My mouth dropped open, and I stared after him,
willing him to stub his toe or trip on something, but he
kept walking without mishap. I joined my mother at the
front door. She clasped my hand and pulled me into the
house.

"That man has a lot of gumption, coming back here
after everything," she said. She strode to the front
window and peeked through the sheers, making sure he
kept right on going. "He didn't threaten you, did he?"
She looked back at me.

I shook my head. "No, no threats. But he is a bit
intimidating. I think I know why hobos rarely failed to
get handouts during the depression. People didn't feel
sorry for them so much as they wanted them to leave
and be on their way."

Mother let the curtain fall back into place. "Well,
he's gone now. But from the look in his eye, I doubt it
will be the last time we see him."

The phone rang in my mother's hand and she was
so startled she nearly dropped it. She put a hand to her
chest and laughed self-consciously, then pushed the
receive button after the second ring. "Hello?" She
listened a moment and held the phone toward me. "It's

for you."

I sat in my new recliner and dropped the envelope on the floor at my feet. "This is Billie."

"Hi, it's me. Mind if I come over in a bit? I think I need that walk in the vineyard." Handel sounded down. I hoped after he heard about my confrontation with his father he wouldn't run straight home again. The boy from my childhood had been hurt a lot. Because of his father's disappearance he was never able to have closure on that part of his life. Now he was in a position to shut the door on his father, and never look back. Would he be able to do that or would familial ties bind him to a man capable of inflicting further damage to his heart and soul?

"It's not even dark yet," I said, keeping my voice soft. "The vineyard in the moonlight is much more conducive to confidences and ...other things." Mother was across the room straining to hear every word.

"Don't worry, I have to run to the store for Margaret before dinner. And when I get back I think I'll spend an hour in the weight room. How about eightish."

I leaned my head against the soft leather chair and closed my eyes, relieved by this small reprieve. "Sounds good. I'll meet you by the swing."

I set the phone on the arm of the chair and looked up, but Mother had left the room. "What? No opinions this time?" I muttered under my breath. I kicked the footrest down and went to my room.

Chapter Fourteen

The rope creaked against the tree limb with the burden of my weight. I leaned back, my hands gripping the sides of the tire and gazed up at the sky. Leafy branches obscured much of my view, but stars were already filling up the darkening expanse, producing a vibrancy never seen within city limits. There, streetlights and neon signs seemed to be at war for attention, blocking out the beauty of nature with a brilliant façade. But one person's tattoo was another person's masterpiece. I used to be one of those people that preferred rush hour traffic and crowded malls to two-lane highways and corner stores. But after the last few weeks my brain no longer buzzed with impatience or stressed about unfinished business. I could sit in my backyard and gaze at the sky, not worrying about anything. Except for what Handel would think when he heard what I told his father. And that was a pretty big *except for.*

"Been waiting long?"

Startled by his sudden appearance, I lost my grip on the tire and fell backwards, my legs sticking stiffly up in the air like a plastic doll. Handel laughed and helped me up and out of the tire. The smile stayed on his face even after my feet were back on the ground.

"You shouldn't sneak up on me like that," I reminded him, glad for the cover of night so he wouldn't see the flustered color in my cheeks.

"I'm just glad you didn't hit me in my privates again."

I couldn't help but smile at the grim look he made in retrospect. "I told you I was sorry for that."

He stroked his chin. "Actually, you didn't."

"Well, I'm sorry."

He smiled and took my hand as we walked toward the vineyard. The swish of our feet in the tall grass reminded me that I needed to mow back here. A handyman would be nice, someone to keep the yard up, paint the sheds, install a new garage door opener. Sean Parker came to mind, but I quickly banished him from my thoughts. Handel would never approve of helping his father stay in town by giving him a job. He wanted nothing more than for his quick departure.

The First Quarter Moon shone the best it could at half strength, the dark side mysteriously shadowed, a bicameral orb containing both light and dark. I felt that way myself at times, holding to what I knew to be right and yet in a separate compartment of my heart planning the overthrow of my scruples. Good and evil, humanity's age-old struggle.

The rows of vines along each side of our path grew thick and lush with grape leaves, which Charlie told me was a good thing, for the vines' sucrose would be translocated in low concentration from leaf to fruit during ripening. I looked forward to seeing the process all the way through. Uncle Jack taught me the rudiments of winemaking but Charlie said you had to experience the entire growth period of the vines, from spring leaves to winter dormancy, to really appreciate what went into the art of wine. I'd convinced him he was an artist, and I was now his star pupil.

"You seem happier," Handel said, breaking in on my random thoughts, his voice soft so as not to disturb the ambiance of the vineyard. He squeezed my fingers slightly and then released them to pull a candy bar from his back pocket.

"Happier?" I asked, with a glance at his darkened profile.

"Happier than when you got here. Like you've finally accepted this place as your own." He offered the bar to me, but I shook my head. He took a bite and chewed around his words. "You've been learning the business, painting the house, buying furniture, and kissing your uncle's attorney. I rest my case."

I smiled in the dark. "Oh yeah? I would call that circumstantial evidence. Happiness cannot be bought with things, or so I've been told."

He stuffed the rest of the candy in his mouth, leaving nothing but the wrapper in his hand and the hint of chocolate in the air. The tug of his hand on my arm brought me to a stop. I slowly turned, seeing his features by the glow of the moon, shining darkly as though made of onyx.

"You are going to stay, aren't you?" he asked, his fingers clasped warmly around my forearms.

"For now," I said, unsure of what the future held. Handel seemed to want more than I could give at this time. At least, more than I was ready to give. The attraction between us was undeniable but attraction could also be immaterial when it came to a lasting relationship.

He nodded. "I guess that will have to do."

"By the way," I said, curiosity overriding my better judgment, "what's your story with Ms. Alex Becker? I heard you two were an item."

I felt his grip tighten almost imperceptibly and then he dropped his hands to his sides. "What do you mean?"

Counter a question with a question, an old male ploy. I laughed softly. "I wasn't asking for intimate details, Handy, just wondering if you're still seeing her."

The hum of a low flying plane thrummed above us, the sound cheerily out of place. I glanced up and caught the twinkle of lights before it disappeared over the house and oak trees, heading south. Handel glanced up as well. He seemed startled.

"Where did you get that information?" he finally asked, his tone obviously annoyed. He started walking back toward the house and I fell into step with him, not willing to let him cut our conversation short by leaving early.

"Are you still seeing her?" My bulldog mentality had served me well in court but with men it often proved destructive. I would continue to question even when commonsense prodded me to stop, coming to the startling conclusion that men did not enjoy being grilled.

"We went out a couple of times last year, but no. We're just friends."

As we approached the house, the warm glow of the porch light stretched forth to meet us. Mother must have turned it on after we left. Something in the set of his mouth gave me pause. Was his relationship with Alex over or just postponed? Sadness showed in the droop of his shoulders, the slowness of his step. I wished I'd never brought the woman's name up. I bit at my bottom lip, unsure how to respond.

He stopped when we stepped onto the flagstone path. I could see him clearly now and sensed that his soul was about to be bared to me as well. He pushed the hair back from his forehead and met my gaze. "I went to high school with Alex' older sister. Sarah was the reason I made it through my junior year. I was ready to drop out. I'd had enough of school, teachers, people telling me what to do. My mother was dying from cancer and Margaret and I were just trying to hang on. I felt as though a hidden current was pulling me under."

His eyes shimmered with dark pools of sadness. I held my breath waiting for him to go on and yet unsure if I wanted to know the depth of his feelings for another woman.

He continued, his gaze straying from mine. "Sarah was in my English Lit class. She wrote beautiful, haunting poetry, full of pain and sadness. Words that grew from something ugly in her life that she would never talk about. I fell in love with her. Everything about her. Her lisp. Her dark curls. The way her eyes lit up at the sight of her cat. And I hate cats," he admitted with a bittersweet smile. "I dreamed all year of kissing her, but she just wanted to be friends." He swallowed hard and pushed his hands in the front pockets of his jeans. "The first day of summer vacation we went to a movie together. She cried all the way through it. I can't even remember what we saw; I watched her instead of the screen." He fell silent.

I waited, knowing when he was ready he would continue. The neighbor's dog barked in the distance.

Handel drew a deep breath and slowly released it. "I drove her home and she said goodnight. I knew something was wrong, but I didn't know what to ask. I just turned around and left." He looked up and I saw anguish in his eyes.

"What happened?" I asked, my voice a mere whisper of sound.

"She killed herself the next day. Jumped into the canal and drowned. It wasn't an accident," he said, his voice choked with tears. "She didn't know how to swim. I'd promised to teach her that summer."

"I'm so sorry." I wrapped my arms around him and leaned my head against his chest, trying to give him comfort while the steady beat of his heart held me there.

The back door opened and shut and we drew apart, the moment shattered by the force of my Mother's curiosity. She stood under the porch light, squinting across the yard toward us. "Handel? Your sister called. She wants you to come home. Your father is there."

Handel's shoulders stiffened. He turned back to me but his attention had already deserted. "I have to go." He didn't wait for an answer but sprinted toward his car out front. Before I could catch up with him, he'd already spun the Porsche around and was driving away, the back tires kicking up gravel and dust. I stared after the car's taillights and hoped he wouldn't do something foolish in a moment of anger.

"You didn't tell him, did you?" Mother joined me, gazing down the dark, dust-filled drive. She slipped an arm around my waist.

"I had every intention of telling him, but the conversation took another direction and then he –"

"And then it was too late," Mother finished for me. There was no reprimand in her words but only commiseration. "Well, to be honest, Margaret sounded rather happy about her father's return. So perhaps everything will be fine."

"I doubt Margaret really remembers Sean's

brutality. Handel said she was only four-years-old when he disappeared."

"That explains a lot. It's much easier to forgive and forget things you can't remember." She gently tugged me toward the house. "Let's go inside, honey. I'm sure Handel will call if he needs to talk."

I followed her inside, my insecurities tagging along behind. Handel had just opened himself to me, recounted a moment from his past that still caused him pain, and although I felt blessed with the knowledge that he trusted me with his secrets, I also felt guilt that I caused him more pain with my suggestion to his father. Sean Parker's fortuitous return had put a damper on everything.

*****

The tasting room overflowed with customers, a busload of already tipsy people, hopefully at the end of their tour for the day. I glanced at my watch and was happy to see we would be closing in another hour. An amorous young couple, obviously newlyweds, sat in a corner of the room, their lips tasting each other's as much if not more than the wine. The remaining group consisted of mostly retirement age couples, and four single men ranging in age between thirty and forty. I moved among them, greeted each one, and gave a little history behind Fredrickson's.

An elderly man swirled his wine and stared pointedly at me over the rim. "You seem awfully young to be a wine vintner, Ms. Fredrickson. Your husband must run the business end of it and you do the entertaining, huh?"

I smiled and tried not to take his comment personally. There were still men my own age that thought women incapable of managing a business. I wouldn't hold it against someone who grew up in a different era and was taught no better. "I haven't been a vintner for very long, Mr. James." I pointed to the historical black and white prints hanging on the wall across the room. "Those pictures tell the history of Fredrickson's. My uncle was the vintner here before me. I'm not married, but he seemed quite confident that I could run the place just fine on my own."

The admission of my unattached status brought two of the single men my way. They hovered and asked inane questions, while trying to prove their expertise at wine tasting. I made small talk until the driver of the bus informed his passengers that he would leave in five minutes whether they were on board or not. Then he went outside to wait behind the wheel. One by one the room cleared out, those who had already paid for a case of our wine were met at the bus with their purchase.

The room fell silent as the newlyweds, the last to leave, exited the building, still touching and caressing even as they walked, as though unable to get enough of one another. I shook my head and turned back to the tables, now in complete disorder, spilled wine and overturned crystal marring the once immaculate tablecloths. Instead of the formal presentation our guests were met with, the room now lounged in dishabille. As soon as our guests were out of sight, Alice and Benny, the cleanup crew for the tasting room, began stacking wine glasses in a plastic container to be washed, and throwing the soiled linens into a laundry sack on wheels. They worked together like synchronized swimmers, emptying glasses, stripping tables, dumping the wine spittoons.

My services no longer needed, I found my attention drawn toward the framed history on the wall. I stepped closer, my reflection staring back at me on the surface of the protective glass. I'd pointed out the collection to those customers that professed interest in the history of Fredrickson's, but hadn't really examined them thoroughly myself except for the brief glance upon my arrival in California.

In the oldest photograph, a tall, spare built man leaned in the doorway of the winery, a common farmer in overalls and a long-sleeved shirt. A droopy, felt hat shielded most of his face from the lens of the camera. Parked nearby was a wagon filled with sun-ripened grapes, and a small boy in the midst, his head peeking out between stacks of overflowing crates. The winery looked much different than now, and smaller, a glorified barn really, complete with hayloft doors and chickens scratching at the ground near the man's feet.

"Holy moly. What are you still doing here?" Sally asked, suddenly popping up at my elbow. She had a habit of surprise attacks and when I teased her about it she admitted being sneaky as a child.

"Not much." I inclined my head toward the pair working behind me. "They seem to have everything under control."

"It's what they do and they do it well," she said, her eyes alight with humor. "What are you looking at?" A slow grin turned up the sides of her mouth when I pointed out the picture. "Getting an idea of what he'll look like in a dozen more years?"

I narrowed my eyes, frowning. "He who? I'm not following."

She tapped the glass over the face of the man. "Handel Parker. This is his grandfather, the original H.P. Didn't you know?" she asked, stepping back to let me take a closer look.

I shook my head, completely baffled by the news. Handel never said a word about his family ties to this place. He had to know, living here his entire life, and perhaps clinging to the belief that it would all be his again one day. Was that the resentment I'd felt from him upon my arrival at the winery?

"How long ago was this?" I asked, facing Sally.

She bit at her bottom lip and tilted her head, her eyes rolled upward in thought. "He lost the winery in the 1950's, so I suppose this picture was taken late 40's."

"What happened?"

Sally shrugged, a movement that usually meant *I don't know*, but with her meant *well, it's like this*. "A few years in a row of a poor yield, not enough rain. Then with the war, there was a shortage of employees. All the young, working-age men took off for Europe with dreams of killing Nazi's and returning home as conquering heroes. What they finally returned to was being unemployed. Factories and businesses shut down in their absence, and women had replaced them in those that didn't. The Parkers struggled on for a few years, but finally Handel's grandfather couldn't afford to make the mortgage payments and ended up selling to these folks." She pointed to the next picture in the series.

A couple surrounded by five children, stood huddled in front of the winery. Above them over the doors hung a new sign with the name, *Wines of Sanchez*. Dark-haired and stout, with pleased toothy smiles, they all faced the camera except for the father, who with arm raised pointed proudly toward the sign, and was frozen in time.

"And where is the Sanchez family now?" I asked, my eyes moving to the next picture, also taken during the Mexican family's reign. Mr. Sanchez and his eldest son held bottles of new wine for the photographer to record into history, while workers scurried in the background loading a truck with cases of the same.

Sally reached out and straightened a picture that hung slightly off kilter. "Jack told me the Sanchez family wanted to move back to Mexico. They thought our country was too materialistic." She laughed and shook her head. "So, they were happy to accept Jack's offer to buy them out. That was during the height of hippies and flower power, so maybe the whole bell-bottom, fringed-vest, thing scared'em off."

I couldn't help but smile at her suggestion. "You're probably right."

The cleanup crew had already left the room and I looked around at the bare tables. Tomorrow morning everything would once again be prepared for our guests, spotless linens, sparkling crystal, and the best of Fredrickson's wine set out for their enjoyment. I felt a sense of pride in the small accomplishment.

Sally also gazed about the now quite empty room. "I better go as well. I've got a date tonight." She fluttered her lashes and grinned. "I need to recoup and reapply the war paint."

"Have fun. See you tomorrow," I called as she headed out.

I took another look at Handel's grandfather. With knowledge comes recognition. Now I could see a family resemblance. Sean Parker had the same lanky, rawboned form, the same grim set to his mouth and jaw. The little boy on the wagon was obviously Handel's father, his tow-headed appearance so like Davy. It made me smile.

But I was also curious as to why Handel felt it necessary to keep silent about his family's connection to the winery. Why withhold the information? I would have better understood his proprietary air about the place and perhaps even his earlier suspicious attitude toward me if I'd known. But now I felt deceived. Did he purposely divert the conversation and my attention away from the pictures the day he gave me a tour of the tasting room?

I took another glance about the room, shut off the lights, stepped out and closed the door. I went toward the offices. The outer rooms were dark, but a light had been left on in the conference room; the door stood ajar as though someone might still be around.

"Charlie?" I called, pushing the door open and glancing about. But the room was unoccupied. I absently straightened the chairs around the table; a silly habit picked up from my job as desk monitor in third grade. At the door I looked around once more and then flipped the light off.

A man's stocky frame suddenly blocked my exit from the room, a menacing shadow close enough to suck the air from my lungs. I would have screamed if I'd had the breath to do so. Charlie's voice pulled me from the void. "Did you call me?"

My heart raced like a favored long shot pounding toward the finish line. I took an involuntary step back. I couldn't catch my breath and probably looked like a fish on dry land, floundering about.

"Ms. Fredrickson, are you all right?" Charlie asked, and he reached out and flipped the light back on. The look on his face reminded me of someone doing an impersonation of Richard Nixon, blustery and puffed up, eyes bulging as he stated, "I am not a criminal," but Charlie's expression was obviously only worry for me.

I nodded, still unable to speak and pulled out a chair at the table. My legs were shaking so badly I thought it would be prudent to sit before I fell. Charlie watched me from the doorway, a man consumed by guilt but unable to fathom what he did. I tried to smile through my anxiety attack.

"I'm fine." I finally managed to gasp out.

"I'm real sorry for scaring you. I didn't know anyone was back here. I was going to shut off the lights when I heard you call."

I shook my head and took a deep breath as my heart slowed its frenetic pace. "It's all right, Charlie. I shouldn't have stayed up and watched that horror movie last night." I tried to laugh it off. "I don't usually fall apart so easily. But you are rather scary in the dark."

He chuckled, his head bobbing up and down. "That's what my wife used to tell me."

His comment reminded me of the estrangement between him and Alex and I wondered if their damaged relationship had anything to do with his elder daughter's suicide. Death often pulls family members apart rather than strengthening the bonds. But now was not the time to question. I stood up and stepped past him, letting him get the lights and close the door. "Goodnight, Charlie."

"Goodnight, Ms. Fredrickson."

Chapter Fifteen

I awoke screaming in the night three times, the nightmare descending upon me with ferocious intensity. I don't know whether the small scare with Charlie in the offices set them off or my mind was just teetering on the brink of collapse but real sleep eluded me. Perhaps my mother was learning to sleep through the commotion because she never came to my bedside, or more likely, my screams were only imagined, lingering flotsam floating to the surface of my mind.

Finally at three a.m., unable to take anymore, I climbed from bed and wandered to the kitchen, exhaustion weighing me down. Not wanting to wake Mother -- she had the nose of a Beagle -- I took a can of diet cola from the fridge instead of brewing a pot of coffee. After satisfying my thirst, I slipped on my shoes, unlocked the back door and stepped out into the night. A gentle breeze blew through the trees, a cool caress upon my heated cheeks. I was glad I'd pulled on jeans with my t-shirt after waking, as the night temperature sent a shiver along my arms.

I walked slowly around the house and toward the

road, trying to clear my head of the dream's haunting memories: groping hands, stifling darkness, clinging vines that held me down as panic swelled my chest. The recurring nightmare clung like spider web, clouding my clarity with a film of dread. It seemed the world had gone deathly quiet, but soon I realized the night sang a melody all its own. A low hum of energy, pervasive and soothing, punctuated by the crescendo of a cricket's chirp, filled the grass on every side. The starry hosts gazed down, reverent observers, a million celestial eyes watching earth's nightly orchestrated performance in God's theatre.

I continued toward the highway, keeping my step light so as not to disturb the stirring repertoire of the night. The crickets paused in their song as I passed, as though an invisible conductor motioned them to stop, and then resumed when I was further along.

Caution brought me to a standstill at the end of the drive. The black ribbon of highway melted away in both directions, the white lines dissolving into the night. I could still feel the heat of the day emanating from the pavement, drawing creatures to its warmth. A siren call to death. I knew how they felt, yearning for peace and a place to lay their head, to rest from the cacophony of life.

The low hum of a motor dragged me from my reverie. Whether an early morning commuter heading to the city or a lonesome trucker crossing the country with a full load, the sound was a wake-up call to my senses. I turned away from the road and started back the way I'd come. Headlights pierced the darkness, flashed around a curve in the road and lit up my small section of the world for one brief moment, before rushing by at sixty miles an hour.

I didn't remember leaving even one light on, but

now the house was aglow, quite possibly outshining the San Pablo Casino thirty or forty miles away. Mother sat on the front steps, huddled in her sleepwear, clutching the phone in one hand and holding the front of her robe together with the other. She looked like the outcast at a sleepover party, the girl that gets locked out of the house as a prank. Hair drooped around her face, the curl nearly gone, as artificial light leeched its color, giving her a vapid appearance. I hadn't seen my mother without makeup for many years. She seemed much older and more fragile. I wanted to wrap my arms around her thin shoulders, to protect her. Until she spotted me and opened her mouth to speak.

"Where have you been?" she demanded, leaping from her perch on the top step and hurrying toward me. "I was ready to call the police. I thought perhaps you'd gone sleepwalking and been forced into a car by a serial killer. This is California after all." She ran out of words by the time she reached me and instead of continuing her tirade, threw her arms around me and wouldn't let go.

"Mom, I'm fine." I finally drew back and managed a smile. "I couldn't sleep so I went for a walk. Completely awake, I might add."

"Honey," she said, her voice quiet now but resonating alarm. She cupped my cheek with her free hand, her palm vibrantly warm against my cool skin. "You've got to get some help. This can't go on."

I didn't argue; my insides twisted at the thought of the nightmare winning. I knew the ten years of relative peace I'd had was over. The dream had returned full-force and I could no longer ignore the implications. My past struggles were not dead and gone, or peacefully in repose, but on walkabout, satiated by my fear.

We went back inside. She tucked me into bed the

way she had dozens of other nights so long ago, smoothing the hair back from my forehead and replacing it with a kiss. But instead of leaving, she climbed into bed with me and held my hand until I fell asleep.

*****

Charlie showed up at the door of my office the next morning around nine. He appeared reluctant to step inside, hovering there with his hands in his pockets. I waved him in and pointed to a chair.

"Please sit, Charlie. I won't be comfortable sitting here if you're standing way over there."

He sat down and gripped the arms of the chair as though afraid it might lift off the ground. "Ms. Fredrickson, I need to tell you something," he said.

I hoped he wasn't quitting. Charlie was not the most qualified manager in the world but he was honest and hard working. I had enough to deal with right now without finding a replacement. I bit my bottom lip and waited.

He cleared his throat. "I haven't exactly been forthright with you," he said, a hint of defiance in his words even as our eyes met. "Alex Becker is my daughter."

I nodded, my expression unchanged. "Yes, I know."

He licked his lips, his eyes narrowed in thought. "You knew? Did Alex tell you?" he asked. Bright expectation filled his face and I wished I didn't have to dispel it.

"No. Sally told me."

"Oh." He frowned down at the surface of my desk, the lines around his eyes deepening into a sunburst of age as he tried to hide his disappointment. Then he drew a deep breath and looked up again. "There's something else, ma'am. Something I'm ashamed of."

I had no idea what he was referring to and couldn't imagine anything he would be ashamed of. Everyone loved the man. His slow and steady wins the race attitude might annoy me at times but he was a cuddly, warm-hearted character I couldn't dislike.

His front teeth protruded over his lower lip as he hesitated, and he shifted in the chair. "I'm the one that broke into the cellar. I had to know what Jack was doing down there. Something isn't right about this place. My daughter..." He stopped and shook his head, unable to go on.

My mouth fell open at his admission. "You broke into the cellar?" I asked, shock replacing my earlier skepticism. His alarmed phone call to me about an intruder in the winery during the night and subsequent installation of a very pricy security system rankled in the forefront of my mind. "Why would you do that? If you wanted to know what Jack did down there, why didn't you ever ask him?"

Charlie rubbed a hand over his face, a weary gesture. "I guess I was afraid of what I wouldn't find. But with Jack gone, I couldn't wait any longer. I had to know if my thoughts were just crazy nonsense."

I leaned back in my chair, and studied the man before me. Charlie always came across as stable, levelheaded, sometimes too practical for business growth, but never unrealistic or one cent short of a dollar. Obviously, he hid his crazy side better than most.

"And were they?" I asked, not sure what his thoughts entailed but still rankled that my private cellar had been infringed upon.

Charlie released a sound heavy with resignation. "I didn't find anything."

"What exactly were you looking for, Charlie? And what does it have to do with your daughter?"

The denim shirt he wore today was faded and softened with time and washings to a blue so pale it appeared almost white. The cuffs rolled up to his elbows, revealed an abundance of curling, dark hair along his forearms that matched the thick mass tumbling over his wide forehead. I couldn't imagine him fathering the petite woman who sat in my office just the other day. They both had dark hair but otherwise I saw no resemblance. Alex must take after her mother.

Charlie shook his head slowly, as he stared at the portrait behind me, impotent anger turning his face a blustery red. Jack's abstracts were bold, designed to shock the observer out of their humdrum world and into Jack's world of frenzied unease. In contrast, his self-portrait, for that's what it was, soothed the onlooker with muted color, and soft, blurred lines, in a somnolent sort of way. Jack's features were undefined and yet you could see the personality of a man satisfied with life and at peace with who he was.

"I've lost two daughters. I blame Jack for both of them. He thought giving me this job would make up for everything, but it only made me more suspicious."

"Now I'm really confused," I said, turning to look at the portrait that had his attention, but couldn't see what angered him other than the way Jack airbrushed himself to look handsomer than he actually was. Alex had obviously shifted her affection for her father to Jack sometime after her parent's divorce, but what connection did Jack have to Sarah? I was afraid to ask, reluctant to admit to Charlie that I'd discussed his family's personal lives.

He shook his head and stood up, his gaze still fixated on Jack's painted image. "It doesn't matter anymore. Jack's dead. Hell will have to suffice. It's out of my hands." He pulled an envelope from his back pocket and handed it to me across the desk. "I'm sorry about this, Ms. Fredrickson. I know you don't have anything to do with the past around here, but I still live with it each and every day." He cleared his throat before continuing. "This is my resignation. I hope that's all right, I can't afford to be fired at my age."

Without another word he turned and hurried toward my office door. I stood up, put my fingers to my lips, and gave a loud blast of a whistle that nearly sent him into a tailspin. "Charlie! I'm not finished with you yet," I stated loud enough for Sally to hear as she listened outside the door. "Sit!" I demanded, pointing to the chair recently vacated.

Still stunned by my amazing ability to whistle, he obeyed like a docile child, sat and folded his hands in his lap. I moved out from behind the desk and took the seat beside him. "Look. I'm not condoning what you did. In fact, I expect you to pay for the cost of repairing the door and replacing the lock. But -- ." I held up the envelope and ripped it in two. "I have no intention of firing you or letting you resign. I need you to run this place, Charlie. I can't do it without you. Please stay."

Charlie's face lit up, his toothy grin wide and contagious. He nodded again and again until I thought he was going to neigh with glee, but he started laughing instead, a hee-haw sort of laugh that forever changed my horsy image of him.

"What is so funny?" I asked.

He pointed to the torn envelope in my lap. "I put cash in there to pay for the door and you just tore it up."

*****

Handel called and asked if I could meet him for lunch in town. He wanted to speak with me alone, without the threat of interruption. After his abrupt departure the last time I'd seen him, I was curious to know the outcome of his father's visit and whether my name came up in the conversation. I also wanted to ask him about his grandfather and the fact that he neglected to mention his family's connection to the winery.

I left the office at eleven, ran to the house to primp and change clothes, and pulled up to the bistro half an hour later, right on time. Handel's red Porsche was nowhere in sight, so I sat in the car and waited.

A sharp rap against my window woke me from the first real sleep I'd had in days. I jerked upright, my vision blurred against the bright afternoon sun. Handel stood outside my door, leaning down to peer in at me, wearing a curious look of concern. I glanced in the rearview mirror, checking for any embarrassing sign of drool, but luckily my makeup appeared unmarred. I opened the door and he stepped back to let me out.

"Have a nice nap?" he asked, reaching out to take my arm. His grin was more than teasing; it pulled me in with warmth. His eyes crinkled slightly at the corners and a small line creased his left cheek, small signs of his advanced age, two whole years past me. At thirty, his male attraction meter was just nearing the peak, whereas, I assumed mine was sliding down the backside of the hill.

"Yes, thanks. Nice that you could show up," I said, not willing to let his tardiness go unspoken. He had asked me here in the first place.

We walked into the bistro and soon had a small table for two in a snug corner beside a potted fig tree. After ordering, we sipped iced teas and listened to a man perched on a stool strum an acoustic guitar. The bistro was vibrantly busy, the sound of voices rose and fell, laughter burst out unexpectedly here and there, and a waiter sent a glass crashing to the floor. But our table was an oasis in the midst of churning life, the hubbub simply white noise, calming my nerves as I sat across from Handel. Small talk floated between us, words of ease and insignificance, when all the while I wished to reach out and touch his cheek, ask him if he still loved her, whether he could ever love me. I don't know where those thoughts came from. I certainly had not been consciously entertaining them.

"My father mentioned that he spoke with you again." Handel's statement tore my gaze away from the man playing on stage and back to him, my secret thoughts fluttering away. "You didn't mention it the other night," he said, his voice a reprimand, sounding hurt rather than anger.

I licked my lips. "I'm sorry. I meant to, but you left so abruptly." I didn't bring up the fact that our conversation had taken a left turn that night and wandered into the past. The subject of Sean Parker didn't seem noteworthy after hearing Handel's confession of love for Sarah Simpson.

He nodded, his hands absently folding the napkin before him, a telltale sign that he wasn't anymore in control than I. "I guess I did." He reached out and touched the back of my hand and I released the grip on my glass and laced my fingers with his. The connection gave me hope, a tentative grasp on his affection.

The waiter brought our food and I pulled back, folding my hands in my lap as serving dishes were placed before us. The sizzling platter of thinly sliced beef, onions and peppers gave off a spicy cloud of steam. Handel offered me the container of warm tortillas and we prepared our fajitas, my appetite suddenly taking precedence.

The sensual, thrumming melodies played on stage filled any uncomfortable silences we may have had, allowing us to eat and drink without self-consciousness.

I noted Handel's hearty appetite and was encouraged. He couldn't be mad at me if he was hungry, could he?

"How is everything?" The waiter asked, bending over our table with a pleasant smile on his face. "Can I get you anything else right now?"

Handel and I shook our heads, our mouths too full to respond politely, and the man moved on to another table.

"I'm stuffed," I said twenty minutes later as I pushed my plate away. "I can't eat another bite." I lifted my glass and took a sip, watching Handel over the rim.

He finished the last of his third fajita before answering. "I could probably pack one more in but I'd regret it later." He laughed and threw his napkin on his plate. "Are you up for dessert?"

I shook my head, my eyes wide with amazement. "Not me, but go right ahead. I'll watch in awe."

"I better not. Just have to work out harder later."

We sipped our drinks, our glances straying toward the stage. Handel leaned across the table and touched my arm, getting my attention and sending a jolt through my veins. His touch was light, lingering moments after I met his gaze.

"I need to clear up some things with you, Billie."

I nodded, giving him the go ahead, as though he were the only one unclear and I had all the answers.

"I told you about Sarah because I wanted you to know that I wasn't taking your feelings lightly."

I narrowed my gaze. "My feelings?"

He exhaled and started again, his voice patronizingly patient as though I were a child. "You asked about Alex and whether I was still seeing her, even though I've blatantly been pursuing you. Alex is just a friend."

"Does she know that?" I asked, annoyed by my

feelings for the man, and the jealousy I reluctantly acknowledged to myself.

"Of course. In fact, I'm pretty sure she's been seeing someone else for the last few months. But she wouldn't talk about it when I asked. I hope he's not married."

"And why are you so worried about it? She's not your responsibility." I didn't like the idea that he was at another woman's beck and call.

"I've tried to be there for her whenever I could. She's as much a sister to me as Margaret." He reached out and tried to take my hand in his, upsetting my glass in the process as I pulled abruptly away. The cold liquid ran across the tabletop and into his lap. He yelped, then jumped up and slapped at his slacks, trying to keep the tea from soaking in.

I laughed, and covered my mouth with my hand as the waiter miraculously arrived with a towel and began cleaning the spill. After he left, I leaned back, the grin still on my face. "I'm sorry."

Handel stared at me across the table and slowly shook his head. "You are the craziest woman I've ever met," he said in all seriousness. "I don't know why I find that so attractive."

I burst into laughter again; catching the attention of many in the small restaurant as the musician ended his song on a plaintive note and stepped off the stage for a break. I'd been called crazy before, but never with such angst-filled sentiment. Finally, after catching my breath, I pushed our drinks deliberately to the side and reached across the expanse of the table, my fingers open and inviting. "Maybe because you're just a little bit crazy too," I said.

He hesitated, and I worried that I'd gone too far, pushing away another man I cared for out of nebulous fear. Then he laced his fingers with mine. He leaned forward halfway and I leaned in to meet him across the tabletop, our lips coming together in a simple kiss of truce.

He pulled back and stared down at our linked hands for a moment. "My father said you offered him a job." My expression must have been horrified because he quickly shook his head. "I'm not angry with you. He explained that you wouldn't help him unless he spoke with me first."

"He was very persistent," I said, squeezing Handel's fingers in a plea to understand. "I was more or less trying to get rid of him. Mother even threatened to call the police if he didn't leave."

"Was he violent?" he asked, his features stiffening into a mask of anger.

I quickly shook my head to reassure him. "No, no. Nothing like that. Mother just overreacted, that's all."

He released my hands and sat back, crossing his arms, as though putting up a defense against emotions he didn't know how to deal with. "Margaret and I talked with him the other night. He gave some song and dance about leaving twenty years ago because he didn't want to hurt us anymore. Said he came back because he was a changed man and hoped we would give him a second chance. I didn't believe a word he said, but Margaret did. At least she wanted to, bad enough to fight for Davy's right to know his grandfather. I couldn't very well win against my sister's arguments. She's always been a woman with a mind of her own. I just hope she isn't sorry in the end. I've never wanted to be wrong so badly in my life."

The longing in his tone was surprising, and I didn't believe he was thinking only of Margaret. I assumed he'd given up completely on his father, wished for nothing more than to never see him again. But a little boy peeked out from behind his eyes, desperately needing to feel the love of his dad.

"So, what are you going to do?"

He cleared his throat. "I was hoping you could help me with that."

The waiter took the rest of our dishes and left the check. I propped my elbow on the table with my chin in my hand. "What can I do?" I asked.

"Margaret invited him to stay at the house. He wants to find a job to pay his own way, which is great, only he insists on working at the winery. Says it's the only thing he knows. I told him I'd help him get a job in town. There's even an opening at my office building for a custodian. Someone to clean after hours." Handel rubbed a hand over his face, and shook his head. "It was like talking to a brick wall. Finally, Margaret suggested I speak with you."

"Do you want me to give him a job?"

He hesitated, staring down at the tabletop. His shoulders slumped as though the decision weighed more than he was ready for. "I don't want you to do anything you're not comfortable with," he finally said, meeting my gaze.

I had strong reservations against doing any such thing, but those blue, dark-lashed eyes were impossible to say no to. "I have a lot of small fixit jobs around the place, and taking care of the grounds. If he doesn't mind working in that capacity, I could use the help." He wouldn't actually be working in the winery, and hopefully the odd jobs would peter out quickly, leaving him with nothing to do but disappear again.

One side of Handel's mouth pulled up in the semblance of a smile but it didn't reach his eyes. "Thanks. I'll tell him. Whether he's interested or not, at least I can assure Margaret that I tried."

"If that's what counts."

He glanced at his watch and frowned. "Aww, I have an appointment in fifteen minutes. I really wanted to talk to you about something other than my family problems, but it looks like it will have to be another time." The musician stepped up on stage again and prepared to entertain the bistro crowd. Handel inclined his head toward the man. "You seem to like music. I have tickets to the symphony later this week. Would you go with me?"

"A night out would be nice. Not that I don't appreciate Mother's attentiveness to my every move, but I feel as though I'm in adult day-care."

"Try living with a sister," he countered with a grin. He straightened and picked up the check as though ready to depart the restaurant.

"Hold on. I have a few questions for you," I said.

His eyes narrowed with a spark of interest as he settled back into his seat, but I could tell his mind was already on his coming appointment. "What would you like to know?"

"Why didn't you tell me your grandfather once owned the winery? And why was Sally the one to tell me that those pictures on the wall of the tasting room link your family to mine? Did you think I'd feel threatened in some way?"

He frowned and leaned with his arms on the table. "To be honest, I didn't really think about it much at all. That was a long time ago. Way before I was born. Why should the knowledge threaten you?"

I licked my lips nervously, afraid I'd once again misread the man. "I don't know. Perhaps you have an evil plan to take back ownership through litigation."

"You shouldn't do that," he said, staring pointedly

at my mouth.

"What?"

"Lick your lips when you're talking. I have no idea what you just said."

I reached out and punched him in the shoulder. "I said get over it, the winery's mine now!"

He laughed and stood up. "Shall we go?"

I slid out of my chair and he took my hand.

Chapter Sixteen

Sean Parker showed up at the winery the next day asking for me. Sally pointed him toward my office. Only half past eight in the morning, I still wasn't working on all cylinders. Three cups of coffee had only succeeded in keeping me awake enough to make frequent visits to the restroom. The shades on the window were drawn but the florescent light still penetrated my half-closed eyes and aggressively fed the migraine I nursed. I looked up and tried to smile a welcome when he tapped on the open door.

"Hello, Mr. Parker. Come in."

He wore a collared shirt, pressed and starched if the stiffness with the way he moved was any indication. Margaret probably wanted him to make a good impression even though his employment was already a given. He hesitated before dropping into a chair, his glance moving about the room and then stalling on the portrait of Jack hanging above me. His evident interest narrowed into a near-sighted squint.

I leaned forward, my arms folded on the desk. "I see you're eager to get started. Can I ask you what you find so appealing about working here, Mr. Parker?"

His eyes were hooded like an old cobra. He shrugged, his shoulders lifting and falling within the starched shirt, bones of discontent eager to be free. "I'm sure you know my father owned this place once upon a time," he said, the raspiness of his voice giving testimony to years of smoke inhalation. "I've worked here most of my life. Thought it would nice if I could spend my last days here."

I raised one brow. "I hope you aren't planning your demise any time soon because I have quite a few jobs for you to do."

He shook his head but there was no hint of humor in his person. "Not soon, no."

"Great." I stood up and slipped out from behind the desk. He rose as well. "Why don't I show you around and you can get started."

His low chuckle, halfway between a cough and a wheeze, made me turn at the door and look back. "Did I miss something?" I asked.

"Just think it's funny you feel the need to show me around."

"I meant -- show you what I want you to do. Unless you're clairvoyant. In that case, I won't bother."

He inclined his head. "Lead on."

I strode out through the open door, nearly having a head-on collision with Sally as she met me with a fresh cup of coffee in hand, her way of finding out what was going on without appearing nosey. "Sorry. I thought you might need this," she said, slightly off-balance.

I shook my head regretfully. "Thanks, but I have to go out for a bit."

Sean Parker followed me out of the winery and across the yard to the house. I stopped at the open door of the garage; glad to see Mother had taken the car into town for her salon appointment. "I need you to cut the grass around the house and winery, prune the shrubs, and tend the flower beds. Don't bother with the roses; my mother is an expert in that area. You wouldn't happen to know where the lawn equipment is stored, would you?" I asked, my recent ownership glaringly obvious.

He nodded and pointed toward one of the sheds. "All that stuff should be in there."

"Okay. Well, then you know where to look." My lame answer elicited a small snort from Mr. Parker that I chose to ignore. I showed him the garage door opener that I'd purchased, still in the box. "I'd like to have that installed as soon as possible. Do you think you can manage on your own or do I need to get a professional?"

He bent over the open box, peering at the instructions. "Looks pretty simple to me. I'm sure I can manage," he said.

"Good. But first I have a little job I'd like you to do. Could you bring that ladder?" I pointed toward the back of the garage. A ladder leaned precariously against a rolled up garden hose hanging in a coil on the far wall. He got it and followed me to the house.

"In the living room," I said, as I held the door wide and pointed.

The painting I'd purchased was not great art, but simply a pretty landscape that complimented my new furniture. The fancy frame from Uncle Jack's large abstract fit the new canvas perfectly. After messing with it the night before for over an hour, switching frames, I left it propped against the wall behind the recliner.

Sean Parker stood in the middle of the room, the ladder resting on one booted foot, staring up at the empty space above the fireplace mantel. I stepped around him and over to the picture. "I'd like you to hang this up there," I said, tipping it up straight. "I just bought it the other day. What do you think?" My question hung in the air between us like a cloud of nonsense. The man did not look anything like an interior decorator, but rather more like a demolitionist by the surly expression on his lips.

"What happened to Jack's painting?" he asked, ignoring my question and dropping the ladder against my new leather couch.

"Hey, don't put that there. That's glove leather; easily damaged."

I may have imagined the look of loathing when his eyes met mine, but as his gaze dropped to the picture beside me, relief was the emotion my overtired mind registered in his face. "My frame," he said, the hint of a smile on his lips.

"Your frame?" I raised my brows and tightened my grip. "What are you talking about?"

Sean Parker set the ladder up in front of the fireplace before answering, his back to me. "I made it for Jack's thirtieth birthday. It was a gift."

"Then that makes it my frame."

He turned around and glared, and this time I knew I wasn't imagining the animosity he felt toward me. "If you say so."

I slid the picture forward and he lifted it in both hands, carefully examining the frame as though reunited with an old friend after many years. Without another word he stepped up the ladder, braced his knees against the top rung, and lifted the picture in place. I couldn't help remembering the day his son helped me lift it down. Sometimes I'd catch a glimpse of Handel in this man, but more often than not they seemed worlds apart.

He pushed the bottom left corner up a quarter

inch and tilted his head to look down at me. "Is that straight?" he asked in his raspy voice.

I nodded. "It's fine." I hated the attitude he was displaying. I was his employer, after all. The man was a bum and out of the kindness of my heart I gave him a job. He could at least appear grateful. "Is there some reason you dislike me, Mr. Parker?" I asked as he stepped down from the ladder.

He took his time folding the ladder, a surly slant to his lips. "Ms. Fredrickson, my family owned this winery once and by all rights still should. Instead, my son and I work for you, a woman who has no idea what's she's doing. Damn straight, I have reason to dislike you." He looked up at the painting once more, satisfaction showing in the set of his shoulders. "Does everyone have to like you, or can I just get paid for a job well done?"

His sarcasm left me tongue-tied, which wasn't the impression I liked my employees to have of me. Taking my silence for acquiescence he picked up the ladder and started walking away. I stared up at the pretty landscape, and wondered why I'd ever thought Jack's abstract too severe. Right now I could definitely use a dose of anger art to validate my rising feelings.

"I'll hook up that garage opener now if you don't have anything more pressing," he mumbled snidely over his shoulder as he headed out.

Shocked immobile, I stood and stared after him. The bang of the front door made me jump an inch or two. I drew a deep cleansing breath and slowly released it. "Love stinks," I said, to the empty room. Handel really owed me on this one.

*****

After retreating to the kitchen, I sat down at the table for a moment and rested my head on my arms.

The next thing I knew Mother was shaking me awake.

"Honey, are you all right? What are you doing home from the winery already? Don't you feel well?"

I rubbed my hands over my face and blinked sleep away as I straightened up, frustrated that the only time I slept was by accident and never for long. "What time is it?" I asked, ignoring her barrage of questions.

She set a grocery sack down and looked at her watch. "Almost three. Did you come over for lunch?" She pulled a carton of milk and a small bag of apples from the sack and stowed them in the refrigerator, then faced me with a frown of disapproval, her hands on her hips. "I see you have that man mowing the lawn. I wish you wouldn't have let Handel talk you into hiring him. I don't trust him. And neither should you."

I removed the remaining items from the sack, pleasantly surprised by the purchase of a large bar of dark chocolate. The distant hum of the mower indicated that Sean Parker had finished with the installation of the garage door opener and started in on the grounds. Good. At least I wasn't paying him just to like me. "I never said I trusted him. Handel and Margaret wanted me to give him a chance, and I am."

"A Christian hand can only go so far with men like that," she said as she folded the sack and slipped it in the cupboard under the sink.

"I can't believe you said that. What ever happened to forgiveness?" Mother always insisted the world would be a much better place if folks would just learn to forgive.

She shook her head. "I'm sure that man has had more than his share of forgiveness from family and friends over the years. Look at his kids offering it to him once again. Like lambs to the shearer. He'll leave them bloodied and bruised and their coats stolen."

"That sounds awfully cynical coming from you, Mother. Didn't Jesus say we should forgive up to seventy times seven? You insisted on it. I'm pretty sure I was forced to forgive Adam more times than that. He was always doing something rotten." I stood up and stifled a yawn.

Mother reached out and brushed my hair behind my ear. "I didn't force you to forgive your brother, honey. And Adam wasn't that bad. Mr. Parker, on the other hand..." She stopped as though losing her train of thought, then shook her head. "Don't listen to me. You're right. Forgiveness is the high road."

I narrowed my eyes. Mother was a forgiving person under normal circumstances. But when it came to people who hurt children, she wasn't nearly so willing to forgive and forget. Her own father had been somewhat of a bully and a perfect candidate for anger management classes. Being the youngest, she didn't connect with that anger as much as her older siblings but saw firsthand how destructive it could be.

"Did you eat lunch, Billie? You look as if you're losing weight and you don't have any to spare."

I laughed. "Was that a backhanded compliment? A couple months ago you were telling me I needed to watch what I eat."

She shook her head and took the bar of chocolate from my hand. "Yes, watch the junk food. You need to eat healthier. Being busy doesn't negate the need for a well-balanced diet."

"Then why'd you buy that? You know I can't resist temptation. It calls to me in the night." I tried to snatch it out of her hand but she was faster than I.

"Oh no you don't! This is a bribe."

"You're bribing me with chocolate? What am I, a child?" I went to the window over the sink and looked out as Sean Parker made a pass on the riding mower. The engine noise rattled the pane of glass and grass clippings fluttered in the air, but the man remained stoic, staring straight ahead.

"You may not like what I've done, but I did it for you."

I 'd heard those words before. Always in the name of unselfish sacrifice, Mother declared causing me pain was for my own good. Examples: braces, summer camp, iodine on open wounds. I turned to face her and crossed my arms, a feeble barricade against what was sure to come.

"What have you done, Mother?"

"Joan and I were talking -"

"Joan?"

Mother nodded and slipped into a chair at the table, her glance darting safely away from mine. "The woman who did my nails this morning," she said, tapping them softly against the tabletop. They were now a lovely shade of mauve that matched her top. "Her niece suffered from recurring nightmares and thoughts of suicide after a horrible car accident where her younger brother was killed and she walked away unscathed."

I cleared my throat, and tried to remain calm. "That's terrible, but what does it have to do with me?"

Mother reached in the pocket of her gray slacks and pulled out a pale blue business card. "She gave me the number to a local therapist. Joan swears she's the best; has credentials galore. She said the woman literally saved her niece's life." Mother met my furious stare and licked her lips nervously. "I made an appointment for you tomorrow."

Taught at an early age not to raise my voice to my mother, I had to literally clench my teeth to keep from screaming. I also shut my eyes like a child having a temper tantrum, wishing myself far from the kitchen. To Mother's credit, she didn't say a word but waited silently as I vented internally. Finally, after relaxing my jaw, I released a pent-up breath. My frustration mostly dissipated through the simple action, a trick I'd learned in my teenage years, I could now speak almost calmly.

My words were clear and succinct, as if measuring them twice before using. "I told you -- I don't need professional help. I can get through this on my own. And I certainly don't need you discussing my mental state with perfect strangers around town."

Mother's eyes glistened and her lower lip trembled. She shook her head slowly. "You're wrong, Billie. You do need help." She held the card toward me and when I didn't respond, set it on the table. "Please -- go see her tomorrow."

When my mother turned and walked out of the room without another word I knew I was beaten. I picked up the card. The therapist's name was Elizabeth Berger.

*****

"I have a two o'clock appointment," I told the woman at the reception desk.

"Have a seat. Dr. Lizzy will be right with you," she said, indicating the waiting area behind me.

Dr. Lizzy. Another therapist's lame attempt to give patients the illusion that they're talking to a friend rather than an over-paid quack, who probably doesn't know the difference between depression and the feeling you get when you realize you're out of toilet paper.

Comfortable looking chairs and an over-stuffed couch took up much of the room, along with two end tables spilling over with dozens of popular magazines. The walls were adorned with images of smiling people.

Whether they were satisfied patients of the therapist or random photos of happy people, the result was the same. A lot of exposed teeth. Which could actually be fearful to many of Ms. Berger's potential patients. I sat down and picked up a magazine, graced with the anorexic image of a movie star, and wondered once again why I'd let my mother talk me into this charade.

How many times had I sworn never to set foot in such a place again? I did my time, went through the stages of healing, blah, blah, blah. Apparently, they couldn't fix me then, why did Mother think it would be any different now?

The room was air-conditioned yet I felt sweat trickle beneath my arms and down my sides. Time passes so slowly in a waiting room, as if all the wasted minutes of your life have been recycled and you are forced to endure them over again. I flipped through the magazine, words and photos blurring together in my mind, simply waiting for the call of my name, the moment I dreaded.

"Wilhelmina? Dr. Lizzy can see you now." The smiling receptionist stood at the open door of Elizabeth Berger's office waiting to see me safely inside. The use of my full name made me feel a bit smug as I entered the therapist's domain.

A petite, blonde-haired woman stepped out from behind a modern glass and chrome desk to greet me. Her smile added curves to cheeks already plump and round. The grip of her hand was surprisingly strong but brief before she waved me toward a set of overstuffed, cushioned chairs. She sat in one and I in the other and we looked at one another.

"Tell me why you're here," she began, her voice chirpy and light like the early morning chatter of Robins in the yard outside my window. "Not why your mother called and set an appointment, but why you came."

I couldn't help but feel as if I was meeting with a sorority sister, although I'd never joined a sorority and had no idea what we'd talk about. She crossed her legs and leaned slightly forward in her seat, her attention rapt upon my face, as though eager to hear what I'd been up to since graduation.

I cleared my throat. "I came because my mother and the woman who does her nails think I need help. I guess you could say it was a salon intervention that got me here."

Dr. Berger's pleasant expression erupted into hearty laughter, her round cheeks so like the Cheshire cat that I also smiled. "That Joan! I can always count on her for referrals. I'll probably never have to solicit new clients as long as she's in business."

I frowned. "You know Joan?" I asked.

"Well, certainly. Her niece was a client of mine." She smoothed a wrinkle from the lap of her skirt. "She's a very nice lady, but probably not the real reason you're here."

"Why do you call your patients, clients?" I asked, curiosity overriding my earlier intentions not to be sucked into another therapist's alternate world of reality.

She brushed at an imaginary piece of lint on the arm of her silk suit jacket as she spoke. "They pay for services as any client does and most aren't very patient about getting their money's worth. So it seems rather silly to call them patients. I try to help them as quickly as I can, and if I feel they would be better off with someone else - " She waved a hand toward the door. "I say, good luck and God bless. I'm not in this business for the money. I know that sounds corny and insincere, but it's true. There are a lot of hurting people in this world, and I just want to help as many as I can."

She was right. A therapist saying she wasn't in it for the money was either lying or crazy. Either way, she probably wouldn't be much help to me. I nodded as though I'd heard it all before. "Of course. You want to help me. Well, why didn't you just say so? Give me a prescription for insomnia, and I'll be on my way."

"Insomnia? Is that really what you came here for?" She tilted her head to the side, watching me in a thoughtful squint. "Or do you want to deal with the reasons behind why you can't sleep? Drugs may mask the problem for a time, but even they can't keep the demons at bay forever."

I expelled an exasperated breath and stood up. "I'm sure my mother already went through this with you," I said. "I was just trying to shorten the preliminaries and get to the end result."

She didn't appear flustered by my attitude but merely sat back in her chair and nodded. "Your mother did say you were having nightmares that were keeping you both awake. Perhaps I should give her a prescription, also."

I blew a soft laugh through my nose and looked away. The woman was quick, I had to give her that. I bit at my bottom lip a moment and then sat back down. "All right. Let's talk."

She folded her hands in her lap and smiled, the creases in her round cheeks curving mischievously. "You go first."

Thirty minutes later I realized I'd rehashed Paul's attack on me, my father's dismissive attitude, my mother's over-protectiveness, and my recurring nightmares. Lizzy asked what triggered the dream's return and I shook my head.

"I don't know." I'd kicked my shoes off earlier, at

Lizzy's insistence, and now had my feet on the edge of the chair with my knees drawn up to my chin. The overstuffed chair seemed to poof around me like a giant marshmallow. "Maybe the stress of coming here, learning a new business, meeting people from my past. It is strange to return to a place you once knew so well yet have only vague memories of."

Her eyes lit with excitement at my innocent admission; I let myself hope that she would now speak the magic words, and I would be healed. Or at least sleep peacefully without dreaming. But she didn't have any magic, just more questions. I answered them to the best of my ability and then sat back and waited for her to pronounce sentence.

"What sort of relationship did you have with your father prior to the date rape?" she asked instead. Her pantyhose made a swishing sound as she uncrossed her legs and leaned forward with her elbows on her knees. "Were you close or was he always a distant parent?"

I released a weary breath and glanced at my watch. The session had run longer than an hour. Didn't she have other individuals waiting for their turn in the inquisition?

"You don't need to worry about time. Unless you have a pressing appointment. I have all afternoon open," she assured me.

Time seemed to be all I thought about anymore. Forgotten time, wasted time, and now interminable time. I'd already counted the slats in the window blinds and the pinstripes in the fabric of the chairs. "No, he wasn't always distant," I said. Images of time spent with my father suddenly flooded my mind: playing catch, shooting baskets, tossing horseshoes. He taught me to swim, and how to put a wriggly worm on a fishhook. He took our family to church each Sunday and let me snuggle against his side as the sermon lengthened and my eyes drooped. He read bible stories to Adam and me at bedtime, and then both Mom and he would kiss our foreheads and tuck our blankets to our chins, before turning out the light. How could all of that be negated by the last few weeks of his life?

"Your father died less than two months after the incident?"

Lizzy's soft voice brought me out of the fog of memories I was sinking into. I must have spoken aloud and didn't realize. "What -- ?" I cleared my throat and shifted in the chair. "Yes, my father died of a massive heart attack after playing a round of golf on a Saturday afternoon."

"When did the nightmares start?" she asked. A question already asked and answered an hour or more ago. I wondered if she played this game with all her patients, trying to slip them up and force them to admit they really weren't crazy at all, just lonely people that wanted someone to talk to.

I stood up and stretched; then walked to the window and looked out at the street below. "You already asked me that." My voice was weary as were my emotions. I didn't want to speak of the past anymore, see my father lying there in the coffin, hear those words of tribute spoken at the service, while I sat staring unblinkingly at the cross at the front of the church, anger and bitterness tearing at my insides while forgiveness hunkered down in the corner of my heart and cried.

She watched me a moment, not saying anything. "Did you have a nightmare the very next night after Paul's attack on you?"

I turned from the window and shook my head. "I don't think so. I can't remember the exact day and hour,

Doctor. Maybe you should ask my mother. She probably penciled it in her calendar. Billie had breakdown between ten and ten fifteen last night."

"I think your answer will suffice," she said. She stood up and crossed the room to her desk. So far she hadn't written anything down, but now she picked up a tablet and pencil as she faced me, leaning her hip against the desktop. "Do you think the first nightmare occurred before or after your father's death?"

The question startled me, but I wasn't sure why. I pressed two fingers to my throbbing temple. "All of this happened when I was fifteen years old. I can hardly remember the day I graduated from law school, let alone what day I started having nightmares." That wasn't entirely true. I did remember the day I graduated. What I remembered was how much I missed having my father there to see it.

"If you had to guess," she said, leaving the question hanging in mid-air.

I threw my hands up in surrender. "Okay! Backed into a memory corner, I would say after, but I won't swear to it."

"You're a lawyer all right." Lizzy continued to write, scratching away at the tablet as though I had given a full confession and she didn't want to miss a word.

"What are you writing?" I asked, curiosity overpowering me once again. I sidled close and peered over her shoulder.

She wasn't taking notes at all, but sketching a picture of me. She looked up from her drawing and smiled. "My therapy," she said in explanation. "It helps me think. You know -- like all great mystery solvers. Sherlock had his violin, and I have a sketchpad and pencil."

I laughed lightly. "Make sure you airbrush the cellulite from my hips." I flopped back into my chair and sighed. "So what's the verdict, Doctor? Am I curable or not?"

She lowered the tablet to her lap and pursed her lips in thought. "If your nightmares didn't start until after your father's death, I think perhaps there is something else going on here other than memories of a thirteen-year-old date-rape attempt." She set the pad and pencil on her desk and returned to her chair. "Your father was your protector in life, at least for the most part." She sat down, her gaze direct. "All daughters think their fathers are indestructible, part super-hero, part super-dad. Once he was gone, you no longer were protected from your greatest fear."

"What are you talking about? My fear of what?" Dark images of the thing I struggled with in the night filled my thoughts, pressing in upon me with the overwhelming tendency to suck the breath from me. I breathed in deeply through my nose.

She shrugged. "You have a block of time missing. Granted, many children forget much of their childhood, but this was a special trip taken when you were eight. By all accounts it should be ingrained in your mind as one of your favorite adventures. But instead of good memories when once again you return to your uncle's winery, you have nightmares."

My eyes widened as I stared at the woman before me, seeing the circumstances with sudden clarity. "I can't believe I didn't think of this before. Something happened when I was eight, and I blocked it from my mind." Frightening images flooded my imagination; my father bending over Uncle Jack's bloody body; my father carrying me to the house and telling me to pack, because we were going home where I'd be safe. Or was it imagination? I couldn't be sure. I met the doctor's gaze unblinkingly, a sudden overwhelming urgency filling me. "I need to know. Can you hypnotize me or something? I have to know what I've been blocking all these years."

Lizzy slowly shook her head and steepled her fingers beneath her chin. "Digging for memories is often a dangerous thing. They have been lying dormant for a reason. You couldn't deal with them at the time and shut them out. Pushing to the fore what God allowed you to forget is asking for trouble."

I gasped. What kind of therapist prefers not to dig up the root of the matter? "What are you talking about? Isn't that what I'm here for?"

"I'm just saying you need to take it slowly. Forcing things often leads to more confusion and destructive behavior, in your case, probably also escalating nightmares. It sounds like you've already been having minor breakthroughs, glimpses of the past that you're safe in remembering. Eventually..."

"At this rate, eventually could be ten years from now. I won't be a prisoner of nature taking its course any longer. I need the truth now."

Lizzy pressed her lips together and calmly nodded. "What do you think will be accomplished by knowing?"

I ran a hand through my hair, pushing it back from my forehead. "For starters I can get some sleep." Sleep was actually the farthest thing from my mind. I wanted to know what my father had been protecting me from for all those years. And why he suddenly quit.

She sat back in her chair and folded her hands in her lap. "You do realize that after this long any recall is a process of reconstruction. Returning memories will be distorted to some degree. How you perceived things at the age of eight may not look the same to you now."

"So, what are you saying?"

"Just be careful. The past can be a big, mean dog. The bite is always worse than the bark. Your nightmares are only the bark."

Chapter Seventeen

My mother's eagerness to know the outcome of my session with Dr. Berger was annoyingly obvious as she very carefully skated around the topic at dinner. She prepared my favorite meal of steak, baked potatoes, and garden salad, with fresh peach cobbler for dessert, plying me with food as though buying my confidence.

"You don't have to try so hard, Mother." I put down my fork and swallowed a bite of warm peach covered in whipped cream. "But I'm glad you did. This is delicious."

She dabbed at her mouth with a napkin. "I don't know what you mean. I just wanted to make you something nice for dinner. You haven't been eating properly. But I thank you for the compliment."

I knew what she wanted to ask and so I told her. "Dr. Berger was helpful. I'm actually glad you set up the appointment with her. I don't agree with everything she said but now I have a new perspective."

Mother stood and carried her dishes to the sink, trying not to appear too eager. "About your dreams?"

I nodded and handed her my plate and glass. "Yes,

and I think she's right. But I need to ask you something."
I waited until she faced me again; tiny lines of worry
forming across her forehead. "When did I start having
the nightmares? Before or after Dad died?"

She looked startled by my question, much as I'd
felt when Lizzy asked the same of me. Then she released
a breath and closed her eyes, recollecting memories like
a fairy sweeping up scattered dust. "I remember the
night after the funeral," she said slowly, her eyes still
tightly shut. "You woke screaming about two a.m. I'd
taken something to help me sleep, so had a hard time
pulling out of my groggy state." She paused as if the
years had taken her away. Her voice cracked when she
continued. "You were huddled against the wall in the
corner of your room, between your bed and the
window, whimpering like a beaten dog."

I held my breath, bated feelings in check, not
allowing past pain to swallow me alive. I was no longer
beaten, lost in fear of the unknown. Power to act had
come to me and I intended to use it fully. With or
without help from Dr. Berger. "And that's the first
episode you remember?"

She opened her eyes and nodded. "I think so. Did
Dr. Berger imply there was a connection?"

"Actually yes." I explained the scenario and
watched as a stunned expression filled my mother's
face. She turned away and began washing the dishes at
the sink. Her image of my father was now blurred with
questions. If something happened to me and he was
aware of it, why didn't he tell her? I put my arm around
her shoulders and squeezed as she stood with her
hands in soapy water. "Don't worry, Mom. I'm going to
find the truth."

*****

After lying in bed for two restless hours, I decided

there was no use in trying to sleep. Dr. Berger's words kept crashing through my head like a gorilla let loose in a hall of mirrors. I climbed from bed and pulled on jeans and a sweatshirt. The house was nearly silent as I paused outside Mother's open door and listened. Her quiet, even breathing could barely be heard above the soft whir of the ceiling fan. I padded down the hall to the kitchen where I slipped on tennis shoes and retrieved the flashlight.

The dark hulking shape of the winery filled my vision as I rounded the corner of the house and hurried along in the cool night air. Gravel crunched beneath my shoes and I glanced nervously around, half expecting something to slink out of the trees and follow. Once inside the building, I reset the alarm and used the flashlight to find my way, not wanting to alert Mother to my absence if she should happen to wake and look out the window.

Searching the cellar again would help me pass the night hours and perhaps lead to something more. Since my return to the winery, my dream had mutated. Beginning with the groping assault on my bed, where clinging vines held me down, it progressed to another scene that frequently played, that of the faceless man waiting for me at the cellar door. In this new addition I was still a little girl, and I believed it was closer to reality than the other. I intended to haunt this place like the ghost of Marley until my memories came out of hiding.

I unlocked the door at the top of the stairs and paused with my hand on the knob. "And the truth will set me free," I quoted in a whisper. The words didn't inspire courage as I hoped they would, but rather cynicism. Belatedly, I thought to whisper a prayer for help. Was God listening? I hadn't spoken with him for so long, I wasn't sure if he remembered my name. But Dr. Berger implied that God allowed me to forget what I couldn't deal with, and I hoped he would now allow me to remember.

The doctor refused to use hypnosis, wanting the memories to surface in their own time. But time was no longer an option to me. I wouldn't know peace until the shroud surrounding my past was lifted away. The good memories of my father were also in limbo, and I wondered if holding fast to anger and resentment had destroyed any chance of reconciling them. Thrust back into the past by my uncle's last will and testament, I now had the chance to clarify, conquer, and banish what had been hidden for so long.

I closed my eyes and willed images to appear, needing to rediscover that time lost to me through self-induced amnesia. I pictured myself standing there, as in my dream, waiting expectantly. The way I'd waited each morning by the door of the cellar for Uncle Jack to come and teach me more. An excitement felt only by the very young, joy of discovery, happiness in the moment, filled my chest and limbs as I remembered being eight-years-old again, ready to start a new day.

I recalled the feel of sweet, ripe grapes popping and squishing beneath my bare feet, warm juice sliding between my toes as Uncle Jack allowed me to hop around in a tub of the succulent orbs one morning while he explained the crushing process people used in days gone by. Jack watched me, his eyes lit with laughter at my contagious joy. I remembered slipping and nearly falling, but he reached out and caught me just in time. We laughed and laughed. My feet were purple for days after.

I opened my eyes, supplanting memories with the here and now as the knob turned easily in my hand. The bulb had been replaced in the stairwell; seventy-five watts worth of courage to get me down the stairs. I glanced back, but no one followed. The temperature dropped as I descended, and I shivered regardless of the heavy sweatshirt I wore. Rusted hinges creaked as I swung the door open at the bottom of the stairs and peered into the dark room, my eyes adjusting to the gloom.

I managed to find the light cord without turning the flashlight back on. The naked bulb shed a yellowish glow over stone walls and cardboard boxes, sickly fingers of light poking into corners. I gazed around the crowded chamber with an eagerness that belied my inner trepidation. The boxes were first. I sorted through the contents and then restacked them in an orderly way, giving my hands something to do while my brain whirred trying to rewind.

Since my return to California, the lucid memories I'd dredged up had been pleasant enough: Uncle Jack teaching me, Handel and I in the vineyard, swinging on the tire; while dreams became more frightening as though my self-preservation techniques weren't strong enough in repose to keep them at bay. Perhaps a stint alone in the cellar would be the catalyst I needed to reveal the source of my nightly terrors. Would I be able to box them away when I was done, like the things Uncle Jack left behind, or would they follow me to the end of my life and go down to the grave to be worked out in eternity?

Hours later I sat back on my haunches and took a deep breath, hot and tired after moving everything around. The boxes now resided in one corner, stacked neatly in rows nearly to the ceiling. That opened up quite a lot of the cellar floor space and gave me access to a huge monstrosity of metal, some kind of separating machine left over from years gone by, that had blocked access to Uncle Jack's desk on the far side of the room. With all the other things stacked in front of it and on it, the desk had been hidden well. I stood up and wiped sweat from my forehead with the sleeve of my shirt, then glanced at my watch. Still three hours before anyone should arrive at the winery. I had time to finish cleaning up and go through the desk.

Pushing against the rusty machine with all of my strength, it finally moved a mere two inches. I grunted and shoved again, but made no headway, the solid steal monster standing its ground. I couldn't very well pull out the desk without moving the machine and I couldn't move the machine without help. I was at an impasse.

For the last ten years I jogged three or four miles each and every morning to stay in shape. Obviously, I needed to work on my upper body strength as well. But leg strength would do for now. I wedged myself against the wall and slid down to a sitting position, braced my feet against the machine and pushed with all my might. It began to move, the metal grinding across the floor in a loud screech.

I stood up, wiping dusty hands on the legs of my jeans and smiled at the small accomplishment. The cheap office desk had a laminate top and metal frame, a pullout file cabinet on one side and three sliding drawers on the other. Once I scooted it away from the wall, the drawers opened easily.

The top drawer was filled with five-year-old sailboat magazines. The middle drawer was empty except for a few stray rubber bands and paperclips, but the bottom drawer stored snacks. Or at least it once did. Two empty boxes of crackers lay on their sides, small holes chewed through the cardboard containers, mouse droppings leaving a trail of evidence as to the culprits.

I glanced beneath the desk as I shut the drawer and spied a small square box hiding in the shadows. Squatting down, I pulled it toward me. Bottles clinked together as it slid out. The open flaps revealed another case of empty wine bottles, but lying on top was a small piece of black cloth. I lifted it up and as quickly dropped it. A plump, brown spider scuttled away, disappearing under the corner of the separating machine. Again I lifted the cloth, holding it tentatively in two fingers to make sure there were no more creepy crawly things hiding within its folds.

The shiny material had two small tears and I wondered if rodents had gnawed through it as well, but then I saw the large opening at the bottom and realized it was a kind of mask you pull over your entire head, like a stocking. A small sound escaped my lips, a child trapped in a corner, a squeak of terror. I dropped the cloth mask as though it were Satan himself and pedaled away with my hands and feet till my back was pressed against the smooth stones of the wall. I felt the chill of the cellar's foundation inching up my spine.

I squinched my eyes tightly shut, hiding from the truth. But blocking out the familiar sight of the room sent my mind careening into the past. *I saw a man bending over me, his head covered in the tight, black mask, his eyes gleaming through slits, clearly revealing his intent. He held me down and I flailed hopelessly and then whimpered like a beaten dog as he pressed himself upon me.*

"No! No!" I yelled out, unwilling to endure the horror again. I opened my eyes and looked wildly about the room, sucking in great gulps of air as I fought hysteria.

"Is somebody down there?" I heard a voice call from the top of the stairs and then the soft thud of footfalls as they started down.

I quickly wiped my tear-streaked face and stood up, clutching at the desk for support, my knees feeling as though they might buckle beneath my weight. The mask lay crumpled at my feet, a ghoulish reminder that dredging up the past can have a painful bite. Doctor Berger was right.

Charlie's stocky form filled the doorway as he looked around the now orderly room, his eyes wide with curiosity. "Ms. Fredrickson, are you all right?" he asked finally, squinting across the dimly lit cellar.

I made my way around the desk and separation machine, taking the moments to compose my face and emotions. "I'm fine, Charlie," I assured him, not meeting his eye. "Just cleaning up the mess my uncle left. What are you doing here so early?"

He adjusted the baseball cap on his head and took another step into the room, his attention fixed on the desk. "Been thinking about what you said. Thought I'd go through some of the books and get a better feel for the business end."

I nodded absently, and wished he'd just turn around and go away.

"Appears you've been at this for some time. The place looks almost livable." His brows drew together. "Were you looking for something?"

His astute assumption brought my gaze to his and I trembled still at what I'd found. I cleared my throat and tried to smile. "Just the past," I said, bravado pushing to the fore.

"Well, I guess I'll get back to the office then. If you don't need me." He sneezed and pulled a handkerchief from his back pocket as he turned toward the door. "I think you stirred up a dust storm down here. Woke up my sinuses."

I watched him go, waiting for the closing of the door at the top of the stairs before I let myself relax. I drew a shaky breath and sat down on an upturned crate. Charlie couldn't know how true his words were. But he certainly had it right when he said I'd stirred up a dust storm. When the particles of my past settled, I hoped I wouldn't be covered in a film of regret.

Releasing a heavy sigh, I rose to my feet and looked toward the desk. Uncle Jack's desk. The man taught me joy in creating, let me stomp on grapes with wild abandon, and left me a legacy of family interest, business, and friendship. But was he also the man who left that mask atop a box of empty bottles? Was he the sort of man who could play loving uncle one minute and black-hearted molester the next? The thought made me feel physically sick.

Piecing the past together from dreams, fragmented moments in time, and other people's perceptions was a lot like working a jigsaw puzzle backwards. Normally you start with what you know, the smooth-edged frame, and work your way in. But when you don't even have that, the picture is a mess of stray parts, looking for a connection in color or shape to clarify the whole. I had a lot of parts, but none were connected. Not yet.

I moved around the desk and picked up the mask, crumpling the material in my fist as though I might destroy the wearer. Rage spread throughout my limbs, mixing with life's blood in veins and arteries and pumping through my heart. The truth was getting closer, and yet I felt no sense of freedom.

*****

Handel took me to the symphony that night. The usual calming effect of stringed instruments on my nerves was lost amid questions that wouldn't still, drowning out Mozart and Bach with tunneling persistence. Handel took my hand midway through and smiled at me, concern evident in his eyes, but I just gave a slight shake of my head as though to say, later.

I let my wrap hang slightly off my shoulders as we walked to the car. A gentle breeze blew, refreshing and cool against my heated skin. After being in an auditorium full of warm bodies, dressed to the nines, I needed relief. It had been quite some time since I'd been out on the town. Even in Minneapolis I preferred to stay home, spending nearly all my evenings in the quiet of my apartment. I loved music and concerts but the jostling crowds, waiting in lines, and lack of manners and civility that went with being in such situations usually gave me pause.

Handel opened the door of the Porsche and I slid into the leather seat. He climbed in behind the wheel and started the engine before turning toward me. "What's going on?" he asked, reaching out to trace the curve of my cheek with the pad of his thumb. "You didn't appear to be enjoying yourself like I thought you would. You seem distracted."

I reached up and took his hand, pressing his palm against my cheek, needing the nearness, the calm assurance of his skin against mine. "I'm sorry. I usually love the symphony, I really do." I released his hand and he put the car in gear and backed out.

"Why don't we take a drive and you can tell me about it." He didn't wait for an answer but headed out of town, the lights of the city fading behind us as the car sped into the night.

After a few minutes I leaned my head back and spoke with eyes closed. "I've been having nightmares since I came back here, Handy," I said, his pet name rolling off my tongue easily as though we were children again sharing confidences in the vineyard. "I haven't been sleeping. And I'm starting to remember things..."

"You mean your memory is coming back? That's a good thing, isn't it?"

I made a small sound of derision. "What don't you understand about the word nightmare?" I asked, then instantly regretted my hasty words. "Sorry," I said, opening my eyes and turning my head toward him. "I don't mean to take it out on you."

He glanced my way, his eyes searching. "These nightmares and memories are related?"

"Yes." I turned to look out the window on my side of the car, watching the dark scenery rush by, a blur of incoherence. I didn't know how to tell him that I suspected my uncle, his friend, of committing a crime so heinous that I'd blocked it from my mind for twenty years. Would he believe me, or think I was deranged?

The silence between us was palpable, a third entity hovering thick and black as the night outside. Finally, he cleared his throat. "What sort of nightmares?"

The headlights cut a swath of brilliance before us on the two-lane highway as the car ate up mile after mile of road, never exhausting its appetite. Handel listened gravely, his hands tightening on the wheel when I told him what I'd found in the cellar and the memories that surfaced because of it. I glanced at his profile in the dark, afraid of what he must think of me, his opinion suddenly looming more important than anything.

My voice shook, as I put into words the awful feeling I had that Uncle Jack was not what he seemed to be, but a monster, completely evil with no redeeming virtue. "The cellar was his private domain. No one else had a key. The mask was there. It happened there. I remember." I stopped and drew a deep breath, clasping my hands tightly together in my lap. My heart beat a ragged tattoo within my breast, anticipating Handel's reaction.

He kept his eyes on the road but reached out with one hand and covered my own, the warm pressure of his fingers reassuring and calming. I told him of my visit to Dr. Berger, wanting him to see that my perception of reality had a clinical seal of approval.

Finally, he slowed the car and pulled off onto a gravel turnabout area. The road was empty, no sign of approaching traffic in either direction. He opened his door and climbed out. I didn't wait for an invitation but followed his lead, stepping out on the loose gravel in stiletto heels. I tripped and nearly fell but he was suddenly there to right me. He walked me to the front of the car and lifted me up to sit on the hood. "I don't let just anybody sit on my Porsche," he said, his voice serious as taxes. "But you're a special case."

"I appreciate that." I tried to smile but failed.

He gazed up at the sky a moment as though collecting his thoughts. "You said Dr. Berger told you there may be discrepancies between what you remember and the actual circumstances."

I shook my head, putting up my hands to defend myself. "No. She said I might perceive things differently. That doesn't mean I'm not remembering the truth."

He caught my hands and held them still between us. "Okay, but you said the man who attacked you was wearing a mask. You couldn't see his face. So, you can't be sure if it was Jack or someone else."

"Yes." My answer was soft, a breath of insecurity. "I admit that, but the mask was in Jack's cellar," I said, my voice gaining back some firmness. "Why would it still be there?"

He shrugged and released a weary sigh. "I don't know. Maybe the man dropped it and Jack threw it in a box, not knowing the significance." His explanation didn't ring true but I knew he wanted to believe it.

I nodded. "Okay, I'll give you that scenario, but then what do we do with the fight between my father and Jack?"

"What do you mean?"

"It happened the same day. I know that now. My father found me and took me to the house. He told me to pack, that we were leaving. Do you really think it possible that the attack on me and their fight are unrelated?"

He ran a hand through his hair, and then stared off into the distance shaking his head. "I honestly don't know."

"I'm sorry. I know Jack was your friend and you trusted him. Obviously, at one time I trusted him too."

Handel leaned in and lifted me down from the car. We stood for long moments that way, his arms wrapped around me. When he spoke his voice was low, hesitant. "Sometimes in cases like this, after many years, a victim's memories can be muddled. They sincerely believe they've recovered a memory of abuse by a particular person, accuse them, and then find out they're wrong. The law is a funny thing, Billie. A person is innocent until proven guilty. I know you think it's an open and shut case, but could you hold off publicly accusing Jack until we have definite proof?"

I stiffened in his arms, feeling he'd somehow turned against me with the question. Apparently, he didn't believe me. I felt as though I was the accused and I didn't like it. I pulled away from his embrace. "How dare you?! I was raped as a child, the whole thing was obviously covered up, and now you act as though I'm somehow wrong in pursuing the truth." I turned and started away, not knowing where I was going or how I would get there. In fact, my heels had no intention of letting me have a graceful and proud exit but immediately tripped me up and I twisted my ankle. "Damn!"

Handel was beside me in an instant, helping me back into the car and closing the door as though I might try to escape again, hurt myself, and then sue him. He hurried around to the other side and slid in behind the wheel, a worried expression on his face as he glanced my way.

"I'm sorry. I just don't want to see you get hurt all over again. Jack's dead. Questions about the past might tarnish his reputation, but they can't hurt him. On the other hand, you'll be living with those repercussions in real time, probably on the front page of the local newspapers." I felt a moment of regret for doubting him, but stared out the window, stubbornly refusing to acknowledge the chance that he could be right. I didn't know how to do that without feeling as if I were giving part of myself away.

The ride home couldn't have been quieter if I'd been the passenger in a hearse. But my thoughts were anything but quiet, tumbling about like rocks in a polisher, my feelings for this man becoming clearer and more vibrant. I felt I could trust Handel and yet I still held him at arms-length, lingering cynicism from past relationships clouding my confidence meter.

He pulled up to the house and parked the car. "Billie." He shook his head slowly. "I hate that this happened to you and I wasn't there to stop it."

I swallowed the lump in my throat and bit my lip to keep it from trembling.

Handel leaned over and cupped my chin in his

hand, turning my face toward his. He could probably see tears in my eyes, but I no longer cared. "Give me the chance to protect you now. Don't close me out. Please."

Knowing he cared was almost enough for me to give up, crawl into his arms, and hope the future turned out better. But I didn't. I blinked back the tears and very gently pushed his hand away. "I don't need a protector, Handel. I need someone to believe in me, to stand by me no matter what. Someone who doesn't doubt my mental state."

"I never said that."

"I know. But you were thinking it." He didn't argue my point. I glanced toward the house and saw my mother at the window looking out. "I've got to go. Thanks for the symphony." I pushed open the door and stepped out on the sidewalk. He started to get out to walk me to the door but I shook my head. "Goodnight, Handel."

At the front steps I looked back. He still sat watching me. I went in and shut the door.

Chapter Eighteen

The following week was uneventful as far as new memories cropping up or new evidence surfacing. I finished cleaning out the cellar, going through all the nooks and crannies, looking for proof that my dreams and fragmented memories were sure, and not just a figment of an overactive imagination. Even with the mask I'd found as tangible proof, I still had my doubts.

The phone rang while I was at the house for lunch Wednesday. Mother picked it up so I wouldn't be disturbed from my break. I thought at first it was her banker friend from Minneapolis, the way she blushed and appeared flustered by the call. Her voice chirped like a spring Robin looking for a mate.

I picked up my tuna sandwich and took a bite, trying to hear what she was saying as she stepped around the corner of the kitchen into the hallway. When she hung up and joined me at the table, my curiosity was almost more than I could bear, but I managed to swallow the food in my mouth and fork a dill pickle from the jar on the table as though lunch was the only thing on my mind.

"Do we have anymore of those pretzels I bought the other day?" I asked, knowing perfectly well I'd finished them the night before on one of my nightly walkabouts.

"Hmm?" Mother lifted her water glass, a smile still hovering over her lips as though she were mulling a secret.

"So, who was that?" I asked, patience waning.

She patted absently at her hair with one hand. "Oh, that was just Antonio. He asked if I'd like to go out Friday night," she said, not meeting my eye.

"Antonio? You mean that man at the restaurant? The one Handel said is only forty-two years old?" My tone implied he'd just been weaned from comic books and video games.

"There is nothing wrong with dating a younger man. They do it all the time here in California."

"They who, Mother? Hollywood celebrities? I didn't think you took much stock in their anomalous lifestyles." The thought of my mother dating was bad enough, but to think of her with a man young enough *not* to be my father was excruciating. I set my sandwich down half eaten, my appetite gone. "What did he say when you turned him down?" I asked, my words pointedly obvious.

Mother's brows flew up as her eyes opened wide and innocent. "Why on earth would I turn him down? I haven't been out of this house except to get my nails done for days. I don't even have a garden to keep me busy. A night out will rejuvenate my soul."

I shook my head at her melodrama. "If you date younger men, it's not your soul that needs rejuvenating. And I thought you wanted to be here. I said you should go home. Tend your rose garden. Bond with the banker. Watch over Adam. But no! You insisted that I needed you. Now you want to go out partying with some wild Italian Stallion."

"Billie, why would you begrudge me a night of fun?" she asked, an inquisitive frown replacing her earlier smile. She reached out and patted my hand and I felt a moment of confusion as though the tables had been turned and I was now the mother. "Perhaps if you went out with a younger man you might not come home so depressed."

She'd been hurt when I wouldn't go into detail about my date with Handel and what caused me to come home in a darker mood than when I left. But I still couldn't bring myself to tell Mother what she already surmised, that my father had shielded her and lied to her that day twenty years ago to protect me. His thoughts must have been muddled; basic emotions blown to horrific proportions at the sight of me crouched in the cellar, crying. Perhaps he couldn't bring himself to say out loud what he suspected with near certainty, even to my mother. Instead, packing us up, and taking us away from the source of the pain was his quick fix. No need to ever talk about it again. What my mother didn't know wouldn't hurt her, and what I couldn't remember wouldn't haunt me for the rest of my life. But quick fixes seldom hold.

I sighed. "I don't want to begrudge you anything. I just don't know if it's such a good idea to go out with a man you haven't even met. He could be a serial killer for all you know," I said, tossing one of her favorite fears back at her.

Mother laughed as she stood up and went to the sink to refill her glass. "Well, do you think if we'd had a proper introduction first he would have said, 'hello, I'm Antonio, a serial killer and restaurateur'?"

I threw my hands up and leaned back in my chair.

"Fine. Just don't say I didn't warn you."

A glance at the clock reminded me there was work to be done. I helped Mother clean off the table and gave her a quick kiss on the cheek. "Thanks for lunch. I'll probably be in the office till five. Don't start dinner. It's my turn tonight."

Before I was out the door, she called me back. "Billie, wait." She hurried off down the hallway but returned momentarily, a familiar manila envelope in her hand. "I found this jammed up under the footrest on the recliner when I vacuumed the rugs this morning. I don't know how it got there but it has your name on it."

I shook my head as I took the envelope. "Can't believe I forgot about this. Must have dropped it the other night."

"Well, you've had lots on your mind, honey."

Mother's words were a definite understatement. I nodded. "Thanks."

I took the envelope and headed out the back door. On my walk to the winery I spotted Sean Parker standing on a ladder, painting one of the sheds. He didn't acknowledge me, although I lifted a hand in greeting. The man was infuriating, and I wondered how Handel could stand to live with him in the same house.

Sally beckoned me over as I tried to slip past her desk to my office. She had the phone pressed to one ear and was writing something on a pad of paper. I leaned with one hip on the edge of her desk, idly swinging my foot back and forth while she finished up the conversation.

She finally put the phone down and smiled across at me. "Guess what?"

I made a face and shrugged. "Why don't you tell me. My sixth sense doesn't seem to be working today."

"You're not going to believe this. The Post wants

to do an article about us. They're interested in small, family-owned wineries. Not super-rich multi-million dollar places, but little struggling businesses that have something no one else has. A special wine, only made in small quantities, perhaps never even sold in the outside market."

I narrowed my eyes as I listened. "How would they know we had a small quantity of wine never sold in the outside market?" I asked.

She opened her mouth and shut it again, her gaze fixed on something over my left shoulder. I turned and saw Charlie standing there. He cleared his throat, a sheepish look on his face. "That would be my fault, Ms. Fredrickson. I took a bottle of Jack's wine the other day. I was curious to know if it was everything he always bragged about, and if it was why he didn't put it into production? I had a friend over for dinner. She thought it was fantastic."

I straightened up and faced him, hands on my hips. "Let me guess. This friend of yours works for The Post."

He nodded. "Yep."

"So, what you're saying is that you owe me for an old bottle of wine?"

"I guess I do." His look of chagrin was almost more than I could bear. The man was a miniature horse and Teddy bear all rolled into one.

"Then I'd say we're even. Free publicity beats cash any day of the week." I picked up the envelope and left them both staring after me as I retired to my office.

Five message slips greeted me from the surface of my desk, two from Handel, three others from Jody. Jody's cryptic words were full of doom and gloom. In my absence, the law practice was coming apart at the seams. I never anticipated staying away this long.

Clients were getting antsy. They expected face-to-face time, and assurance that I was in their corner. The time had come for me to think about handing them off to another attorney. I hated to let go, but I no longer knew when, if ever, I would return to practicing law.

I called Jody and set things in motion. The tone in her voice assured me that she was not pleased. Her hope lay in my return and everything resuming, as it should.

"I'm sorry, but things are still unresolved here, and I'm seriously thinking of making a permanent move." I pushed the hair back from my forehead and set my elbows on the desktop. "I'll call Hank Ingebretsen and see if he'll take on some of the clients."

Jody's silence lasted a good twenty seconds. When she spoke her words were clipped and angry. "You never said this was forever, Billie. What happens now? Am I out of a job?"

I knew her true concern was taking care of her family. Three teens to feed and board, put through college, and send out into the world was a heck of a lot of responsibility for a single mom. People lost their jobs every day but I didn't like being the catalyst.

"I won't lie to you, Jody. I'm still not sure if the winery business is for me, but at this point I'm equally unsure of law. I have some serious thinking to do and I'm sorry you are left hanging, waiting for my decision. I won't hold it against you if you put your resume out there. In fact, I'd be glad to write a glowing reference." I paused but she didn't say anything. "Look, I know this isn't the news you want to hear, but it's the best I can do at this point. You're not just a secretary; you're my friend. Believe me, if there was a kinder way of doing this, I would."

Jody sniffed and then blew her nose loudly.

"Sorry," she said. "It's been a hard week."
I silently conceded.
The rest of our conversation went better. Fifteen minutes later I hung up, confident that things would work themselves out. Without further ado I picked up the manila envelope and slit the top with a letter opener, then tipped it upside down and watched the contents slide out. A small stack of Polaroid pictures, held together by a rubber band, hit the desktop along with a folded piece of notebook paper. The pictures were facedown, black squares framed in white. The rubber band was old and brittle and fell apart when I lifted the bundle and pulled on it. The pictures slipped from my fingers, scattering across the top of the desk, some landing face up, others down.

Before my brain registered what I was seeing, I picked up the nearest photo and stared stunned into the eyes of a young girl. Completely naked, she sat on the edge of a bed, her eyes wide and pleading, staring back at me with the look of an injured animal, not quite sure if help would be forthcoming but still innocent enough to beg. Along the white edge of the Polaroid was a name printed in block letters. ANGIE

I gasped, and stared fearfully down at the remaining photographs. Half a dozen young girls somewhere between the ages of eight and twelve, blue eyes, brown eyes, green eyes, all staring back with the same beaten despair. Names like: CINDY, TINA, LORI, and...

Tentatively, my hand shaking, I reached out and flipped one, SARAH, and then the remaining picture right side up.

"Oh God," I breathed out, the words escaping of their own volition, a desperate prayer for strength.

An eight-year-old, dark-haired cherub, curled

naked on the floor of the cellar, eyes scrunched tight to block out the sight of the photographer holding her down, his arm caught in frame. My finger rubbed across the image as though somehow to erase her pain. A tear fell at her feet and I wiped it away, the dampness smearing the name printed along the edge. BILLIE

I don't know how long I sat there, memories rising in revolt, segments of time born anew, the resurgence of a virus, aching and angry. But a glance at the clock on the corner of my desk confirmed that the afternoon was waning.

I made a conscious effort of separating myself from the moment as I scooped the pictures into a pile and slipped them back inside the envelope, no longer able to bear the look of anguish in those six pair of eyes. The folded notepaper still lay unread. With hands trembling, I picked it up and smoothed it open. The Polaroid images were by all accounts at least twenty years old, but the note was much more recent. Jack dated it just two weeks before his death.

Dear Billie,

I made a visit to the doctor on my last trip to Germany. He said my heart was worn out and needed replacing. I guess your father and I suffer from the same ailment. Since there is little chance of a timely replacement, I am tying up the loose ends of my life.

The past haunts me still, as I'm sure it does you. I certainly don't blame James for beating me that day. Not knowing the facts, I probably would have done the same.

I've kept these pictures hidden away, but now it's up to you. Do with them what you will. I'm so sorry for any suffering I may have caused you, and beg your forgiveness. Setting things right was probably the honorable thing to do, but I couldn't bear the thought of more children being hurt because of it. I hope you can

forgive me.
> *Your loving uncle,*
> *Jack Fredrickson*

My loving uncle? How dare he use those words! I crumpled the letter in my hand and threw it across the room. The lightness of paper being what it is, it inflicted no damage on the wall where it hit, giving me zero satisfaction. But rage being what it was, I could no longer hold it in. I swept the contents of my desk to the floor with both arms. Papers, pens, tissue box, paperweight, and adding machine went crashing down as my arms flailed wildly. My brain infused with vengeance, I turned in my chair and stared into the painted eyes of my Uncle Jack. His self-portrait held no inkling of the evil that lurked within the man. Like Dorian Gray's portrait after his death, it showed a pleasing likeness. In fact, he appeared almost benevolent and perhaps thought of himself that way in his twisted mind.

I pulled my chair close and stepped up on the seat, balancing precariously as I reached up and yanked the portrait from the wall. The weight of it nearly tipped me over backward, but I managed to drop it to the floor and climb down without falling. My heart beat faster as I lifted the framed canvas and smashed it ruthlessly against the corner of my desk. The frame splintered apart, and the canvas split across Jack's nose, leaving a bloodless gash.

Sally suddenly appeared, the door thrown wide in her haste to see what was going on, her eyes round with shock and her mouth hanging open as though she'd never been witness to impotent rage before. Her glance took in the floor, strewn with papers and objects, then came back to rest on me as I grasped hold of the ripped canvas and tore my uncle's image asunder.

"Holy moly, boss! I could hear you all the way down the hall. What in the world are you doing?"

Her question struck me funny and I started laughing. I dropped the painting into a crumpled pile on the floor and collapsed back into my chair, laughing so hard my stomach hurt. Concern for my mental wellbeing showed in the way her mouth pressed tight and her nostrils quivered. She blinked rapidly as though the picture might change like channels on a remote. Tentatively she approached, one hand outstretched. "Billie? Are you all right?" she asked.

My laughter died rapidly when I saw the envelope at my feet, one of the pictures lying exposed beside it. Tina's green eyes regarded me oddly from her ground level view. I bent and scooped her back inside and pressed the envelope to my chest, a safe, secure place for our sisterhood of sadness.

"Billie?"

I looked up. Charlie stood in the doorway now, staring around the room. I thought I detected a satisfied glint in his eye when he saw the bashed and ripped painting on the floor. I smiled first at Charlie and then up at Sally who stood by my side now.

"I'm cleaning house," I calmly explained. "Out with the old and in with the new. God save the queen?" I shrugged and stood up, the envelope still clutched in my hands. They stared blankly at me as I kicked the painting out of the way and walked toward the door. "Well," I said with a sigh, "I think I'll call it a day. See you tomorrow."

*****

Ignoring Mother's questions at my early return, I went to my room and climbed in bed, expecting sleep to avoid me as usual. But weariness took hold as soon as I closed my eyes.

Dad's smile, bright with pride, filled my dreams. We ran through the field by our house, pulling against the tug of a kite. The wide expanse of blue, bright with sunshine, made a perfect backdrop for the green and yellow lizard that swooped and dove with the wind's erratic current. I pointed across the field where another kid flew a red and white kite shaped like Mickey Mouse, and we laughed together, father and daughter.

An ominous, black cloud began to grow and spread across our sky of blue; rumbles of danger menaced the lizard-shaped kite and we began to bring it in, giving it less line to bounce and fly, the string taut as we wound it closer and closer to the ground. Then suddenly, snap! The kite was gone. Taken higher and higher by a fierce wind of change, into the storm, perhaps to be torn asunder with rage.

Dad smiled and turned away, heading for home. I stared after him. How could he let go so easily, not even look for our kite where it might land? I yelled for him to stop, wait for me, but he didn't turn around.

I heard my name called. Billie! Billie! The boy across the field ran toward me, his blonde hair bouncing over his forehead. He held the red and white kite in his hand. When he reached my side, he placed it at my feet and walked away. I bent and picked it up, unsure what to do. Should I run and give it back or accept the gift with joy. I looked up at the angry sky, dark and heavy with the brewing tempest, and felt the first drops of rain splash over my face. Drops began to fall in earnest now, pinging upon the slick surface of the kite and rolling away. I lifted it over my head and ran for home.

Dad had left the screen door unlatched, and it banged open and shut in the wind. I hurried toward it, holding my kite high. Thump. Thump. Thump.

I sat up in bed and stared around the room, trying

to place the sound. Thump. There it was again. It came from the door.

"Honey," Mother opened the door and stuck her head through the opening. "Aren't you feeling well? I made some chicken soup and grilled cheese sandwiches if you're hungry."

I exhaled a long, relieved breath, and nodded. "I'll be there in a minute."

"Okay but don't take too long. The food will get cold." She smiled and pulled the door closed on her way out.

I slid to the edge of the bed and dangled my legs over the side. Perhaps it was time to confide in Mother. Keeping her in the dark about Jack and Dad and all the rest of it, would only make things worse when she eventually found out. And she would find out, because she was my mother. Even when I tried to hide things from her, she knew.

The nap had done me good. I felt refreshed. I went into the bathroom and splashed cold water over my face and wiped it dry. The mirror reflected a woman I barely recognized wearing rumpled clothes, one bright-red cheek indented with sleep lines. We had the same chocolate-brown hair, the same wide cheekbones, and the same bump in the middle of our nose from getting cracked with a softball in eighth grade. But gone was the self-assured attorney, cynical and proud, gone was the chip on her shoulder, the one she'd been carrying for far too long. The woman staring back at me now had no idea who she was. All these years I'd worked to be strong, forged like metal, able to cut men in half with biting rhetoric. But inside I was still an eight-year-old girl, shutting my eyes to block out the truth. And the truth was...I was afraid. Afraid of life. Afraid of love. Afraid that even God no longer cared.

I closed my eyes and shut out the woman in the mirror.

"Billie, aren't you coming to eat?" Mother called again from the bedroom door.

I stepped out of the bathroom and flipped off the light. "Yes, I'm coming. I finally get to sleep and now you want me to wake up," I muttered under my breath.

Mother stood outside my door, her arms crossed. She pursed her lips as though she had something to say and then shook her head.

"What?" I threw up my hands in a shrug. "I know it was my turn to make dinner. I'm sorry I fell asleep, but I really needed a nap. I promise to do it tomorrow night. And since you're going out Friday, I'll make dinner Saturday too."

"Tomorrow is Friday, honey." She stared at me as though I'd grown two heads. "You slept through the night and well into the afternoon today. Sally called this morning to see if you were all right. She said you seemed unwell yesterday." Mother put her hand over my forehead and held it there, the human thermometer. "You don't feel feverish," she said, a slightly suspicious tone to her words as though I were still thirteen and trying to skip school with a fake case of Malaria.

"No, I'm not sick." I gently removed her hand and tugged her toward the kitchen. "But at the news that I slept through nearly an entire day without eating, I suddenly feel famished. Where is that soup you were talking about?"

Mother dished up two bowls of steaming chicken noodle soup and sat across from me. We ate in silence, except for the slurping of noodles, which I exaggerated just to get a rise out of her, but she ignored me. Finally, after I'd eaten one bowl and started on another, she asked, "Are you going to tell me what happened, or do I have to pull it out of Sally? Which shouldn't be too hard. She sounded rather eager to talk about it, but I had just stepped out of the shower when she called and was dripping wet."

I swallowed the last bite of my sandwich and looked up. Concern etched my Mother's face, little lines of worry stretching from nose to mouth and puckering the space between her dark, arching brows. She looked every day of her fifty years, and I blamed myself.

Up to now, time had been kind to Mother, washing over her with soft breezes and gentle ripples of change. She was carried with the waves rather than being buffeted. I'd heard her say more than once that God blessed her with resilience and great skin. I agreed with both. I hoped she was resilient enough now to hear what I was going to tell her.

"I'm afraid Sally and Charlie think I've lost my mind," I began.

Mother raised her brows at that but didn't comment.

"Perhaps I should start with what I found in the cellar."

*****

"Jack sent you pictures?" Mother asked, her voice shaking with rage and disbelief. "Why would he do that? How could he do that? I don't understand any of this." She slipped out of her chair and looked wildly around the room as though searching for something, a reason perhaps; but there wasn't one forthcoming.

"Maybe he was looking for absolution," I said, watching her.

She started to put things away, pouring the remaining soup in a container and storing it in the refrigerator, her movements jerky and robotic. As she lifted the heavy soup pan to place it in the sink, she lost

Entangled

her grip, dropping it to the floor. Two ceramic tiles cracked on impact and the pan clattered noisily to a slow spinning stop. Mother covered her ears as tears swam in her eyes.

"Mom, are you okay?" I jumped up and went to her, reaching for her hand to check for burns, but she held them tight against her ears. "Mom!"

She finally looked at me and began to shake with sobs. "I'm so sorry, Billie. I'm so sorry. I should have been there to protect you. I should have stopped him. I'm your mother, for God's sake."

"I know. I know." I pulled her into my arms and we slid slowly down to sit on the floor, our backs against the refrigerator. "It's not your fault. You didn't know. Dad didn't tell you; instead he covered it up," I couldn't help adding.

She leaned her head on my shoulder, her tears dampening the fabric of my t-shirt. "Why did he do that?" she asked softly, as though I held the answers to my own pain.

With eyes closed I leaned my head back and released a soft sigh. The dream of my father and I flying a kite together had left me wishing for a reconciliation that could never be. Most of my memories of him were joyful, filled with love. I adored my father. As a child, I was wise enough to know God hung the moon and stars, but suspected Dad had the inside track to turn them on. Why he would intentionally keep such a horrific thing from Mom and basically ignore my trauma, not get me the help I needed, but tamp down any lingering memory with a firm hand, was beyond me. "I'm afraid motives are nebulous. I'm sure he did what he did out of love – for me, for you."

She sniffed loudly and wiped at her face with the back of her hand, oddly inappropriate actions for someone so attuned to etiquette. "Trust is part of love and what he did wasn't trustworthy."

I sensed the hurt she felt slowly turning to anger. Having lived with resentment against my father since before his death, the good memories packed away in the cedar chest of my mind, I certainly didn't want mother to fall into the same trap. Time had a way of clearing things up or fogging things over. Perhaps we needed a little of both.

"Humans often do things in the name of love that aren't trustworthy." I took Mother's hand and laced it with my own. "Daddy wanted to protect me from the pain of remembering. He wanted to protect you from ever having to know. Maybe he was also protecting himself by pretending it never happened. Whatever the reasons, I have every confidence that he did it out of love." I lifted her hand to my cheek and held it there, reestablishing the age-old connection of mother and child. "Remember...I was there. He picked me up and carried me to the house. He said we were going home, and I'd be safe."

Mother's lips trembled and she pressed them firmly together, as though holding something back.

"What?" I said, releasing her hand.

"I'm just so angry! How could he do this to us? His silence has caused more repercussions than the actual truth would have twenty years ago." She pressed her palms against her cheeks and shook her head. "It eroded our marriage, and it damaged the relationship a mother should have with her daughter. You never trusted and confided in me when you were a teen." She held my gaze, her eyes red and pooling with tears.

I reached out and brushed a stray lock of hair behind her ear. "Mom. The damage is not beyond repair. And I didn't confide in you because I was a *teenager*. But

I'm still young and we have years and years to work on what needs to be fixed. Please don't hold bitterness in your heart against Daddy."

She broke down crying again, sobs racking her body, but this time as her arms came around me and we wept together on the floor, I knew her tears no longer stemmed from anger. She wept for my lost innocence, for her inability to change the past, and for the man who failed to keep me safe. Suddenly a picture in high resolution flashed on in my brain. My father made a promise he was unable to keep; and being a man of his word, perhaps that's what killed him. His brother Jack being what he was, lived another twenty years. As Billy Joel wrote in his hit song, *"only the good die young."*

Chapter Nineteen

Mother took a pocketful of tissues and left for a walk. She said she needed to be alone for a while to talk with God, something she'd done since Adam and I were kids. Whenever she was upset she would get God on the line and have it out with him, ask the unanswerable questions of *the man upstairs* and hopefully come to terms with the past and the present, in her heart if not in her head. What she thought she knew, had always known, was not the reality she faced. I knew what she was dealing with, from a different perspective. The cost of discovering the truth was becoming more than I wanted to pay. If I'd heeded Dr Berger's warning and let things unfold slowly, things might be different today, but what about tomorrow? Wouldn't tomorrow come eventually, bringing to light the same dark moments of time, exposing the same evil residing in the heart of a man?

I felt responsible for the other girls in the Polaroids, to seek out their identities and set things right. Of the five, only one name was familiar. SARAH. I was almost certain I knew the girl. I'd never met her, played with her, or seen her picture before, but the fact that Charlie Simpson had a daughter named Sarah and she committed suicide as a teen, made me confident she was one and the same.

I dialed Handel's office number and waited as his secretary connected me. A soothing sonata played softly in the background as I sat on hold. I stared at the cracked tiles beneath my feet, and wondered how something so broken could ever be repaired.

"Handel Parker." Handel's businesslike voice startled me for a second and I lost my nerve. "Hello?" he said.

"It's me." I hesitated. Was I doing the right thing, getting Handel involved? Would he help me or would Sarah's inclusion in the list of victims be too much for him to deal with? "I need to talk to you. Are you available this afternoon? I could come there."

He was quiet a moment. "Does this mean you're not mad at me anymore?" he asked.

"I wasn't mad at you," I said, a tad too quickly. He made a sound of disbelief on the other end of the line. I couldn't help smiling. "Okay, I was a bit mad, but I'm over it now. How's that?"

He laughed. "Very convincing. I'd like to talk to you too, but I have to be in court in a few minutes. I was just on my way out. And tonight Margaret planned a family dinner, so that's not an option. Is tomorrow afternoon too late?"

Disappointment vied with relief at the reprieve. Waiting one more day couldn't hurt. These girls had waited over twenty years to see justice. "No, tomorrow would be fine. Actually, Mother is going out with your friend Antonio tomorrow evening. Would you like to come over for dinner? We could talk then."

"Are you okay with that?" he asked.

"What - my mother going out with a younger man? Why wouldn't I be? I've been informed that lots of people in California do it."

He laughed again. "Is that right? I'm glad you're so accepting of the situation," he said, the irony in his voice coming through loud and clear.

I pushed my hair back with one hand and turned to look out the window over the sink. "I didn't say I was accepting. But she is over twenty-one and there's nothing I can do about it."

"You're starting to freak me out. For a second there I thought I was talking to your mother."

"Hey! I don't know if I want you to come for dinner now," I said, turning and leaning against the counter.

"Sorry. I've got to go Billie, but I promise to call Antonio and warn him to keep his hands to himself, or else." His voice was teasing but I suspected he would do just that.

"Good luck in court."

"Babe, what I do is not luck. It's all skill."

I set down the phone, a smile still playing over my lips. The man was incorrigible and I was definitely conflicted, one minute pushing him away and the next wishing he'd move faster.

*****

"I don't think I should go out tonight," Mother said for the second time Friday morning. She'd moved about the house since dawn, straightening, dusting, and making herself a nuisance.

Lowering the newspaper to the table, I watched as she polished the stovetop and wiped the counters down -- again. "Would you quit obsessing over cleaning and sit down? You're making me crazy," I said.

Mother turned around, rag in hand and waved it at

me. "Things don't get done if I sit down. In fact, instead of going out tonight, I should clean all the windows. They have a film of dust on them after the way the wind picked up yesterday."

I expelled a frustrated breath. "Mother, you are not the maid. If the windows need to be done, I'll do them when I get around to it, or hire them done. Please sit down and have a cup of coffee with me. I need to be at the office soon," I said, looking down at my watch.

She glanced around the spotless kitchen as though searching for something else to polish, then reluctantly turned and rinsed the rag out in the sink. I stood up and poured a fresh cup of coffee for both of us, setting them at the table.

Mother sat down and I studied her across from me. "What's going on? You were all excited about dating the young stud and now you're trying to back out."

She cradled her cup with both hands, staring into the hot liquid, avoiding my eyes. "I just have more important things to do, that's all," she said, lifting the cup to her lips.

I frowned. "You do not. The house is perfect, cleaner than it's probably ever been. You've been shut up here for days. You said yourself, you needed some fun. Well, this is your big chance before you return to Minneapolis."

That got her attention. She set her cup down, slopping coffee onto the saucer. "What are you saying? That you want me to leave?" She leaned forward, her gaze intent on my face.

With just a look she could make me feel guilty for a month. I shook my head. "I didn't say that. But in Minneapolis you have a life, friends, things you love to do. You're just passing time here, waiting to see if I'll fall apart and then you can pick me up. But guess what? I'm not planning a breakdown anytime soon."

Mother pursed her lips in the look she gave when I wasn't cooperating with her agenda and then appeared to deflate, sat back in her chair, and released a sigh. "Perhaps you're not the one ready to break down," she said.

That got my attention. I leaned forward with my arms on the table. "I know you're dealing with a lot right now. But you're strong. Stronger than I'll ever be. And you know what they say about those things that don't kill you..."

"Makes you stronger?" She shook her head. "Don't believe it. I thought when I broke-up with Jack and miscarried the baby, if I just got through that, I'd be strong enough for anything. Guess what? I'm not." Her voice shook and she cleared her throat and looked away. "I let you down because I'm a terrible judge of character. The two men I trusted with your life both wore masks of deceit."

"Mother, don't say that. Dad loved us. I've been blaming him for screw-ups in my life for years now. Hiding from the past took its toll on him as well. He lived with guilt and regret while we lived in ignorance. I think the last weeks of his life he was struggling with his conscience. His heart couldn't take anymore and it gave out. I assumed he didn't care about me because of the way he acted those last weeks, but now I look back and believe he cared too much. Too much to show. So he hid behind indifference."

She sniffed and wiped at the corners of her eyes with a napkin. "But what about Jack? I thought I was in love with him once. And although it didn't work out, I still believed he was a good man. How could I have been so wrong?" Her words were wracked with pain, and fresh tears spilled down her cheeks.

"I don't know. But you have to quit blaming yourself." My voice hardened with determination. "I blame the perverted man who molested six children. No one else. Not you, not Daddy, and not me. It's time to set the record straight."

"What are you going to do?" Mother asked, worry filling her eyes. She lifted her cup with a shaky hand.

"I want to find the other girls. See if they need anything." I spread my hands. "I don't know, but I have to do something. When I look at those photos, I just want to cry. I know they're adults now but maybe they need a friend, someone who understands."

Mother got up and carried her cup to the sink and poured the coffee down the drain. With her back to me she spoke. "You have a soft heart, Billie. Thank God you still have a soft heart."

I went and put my arms around her. "Handel's coming over tonight to talk. And you're going on your date. And I don't want to hear anymore arguments about it."

My mother laughed and turned to kiss my forehead. "You sound so much like me, it's scary."

I rolled my eyes. "That's the second comment I've heard like that. Maybe it is time for you to go home."

*****

"Billie!" Sally's surprised greeting made me smile. "How are you?" she asked from behind her desk. She let her hands slide off the computer keyboard and drop into her lap.

"I'm just fine, thanks. Mother said you called yesterday to see if I was well. That was very thoughtful of you," I said, setting my hip on the edge of her desk and crossing my arms. "Did I miss anything important?"

She shook her head, her gaze openly curious. "I guess not. Did you really sleep the whole time?" she asked.

"Yes, I did. And I feel great." I stood up and started backing away, hoping to get my office picked up before anyone else saw it. "No messages for me?"

"I left them on your...desk," she said, her face flushing pink to clash with her hair.

I grinned. "Then I ought to be able to find them. I don't believe I left anything else on my desk," I said, then turned and hurried down the hall.

I usually left the door open when I went home for the night, so that the cleaning crew could vacuum and dust, but someone had pulled it closed and posted a stick-it note at eye level that read, Do not disturb. I silently thanked God for Sally and turned the knob.

The room was just as I'd left it, the floor strewn with papers and odds and ends from my desktop. Uncle Jack's painting lay smashed and torn in a crumpled heap where I'd kicked it against the far wall. I stepped into the room and quickly closed the door.

Three pink slips greeted me from the corner of my desk as I pushed my chair in place and sat down. I picked them up and glanced over them, then let them drop to the floor with the rest of my things. I drew a deep breath and slowly released it, gathering my courage for the day.

Ten minutes later a soft tap at the door interrupted me as I tried to stuff the broken pieces of the frame into my garbage can. "Yes?"

Charlie opened the door but hung back as though unsure of his invitation. He pulled off his hat and scratched his scalp. "Mornin', Ms. Fredrickson. Good to see you back."

"Thank you, Charlie. Is there something I can help you with?" I asked, as he hesitated.

He shrugged and replaced his cap. "Actually, I was

wondering if there was something I could help you with."

"What do you mean?" I straightened and crossed my arms.

"Well, I've been sensing that you're not very happy working here. And although we'll all sure miss you if you go back to your law business, I just wanted to encourage you to follow your heart. You're a lawyer. I can tell you were a good one too. You've got that bulldog mentality. I don't believe it's right for someone else to plan your life for you just by leaving a will."

His grudge against Jack was obvious but what about the rest? "Why do you think I'm not happy here, Charlie?"

He inclined his head toward the painting, half in and half out of the can, answering my question with one of his own. "You want me to get rid of that for you?"

I smiled. He was a man of few words and he'd used them up. "That would be nice. I'd prefer never to see it again."

Charlie advanced into the room and lifted the full can as well as the remaining pieces of the portrait. "I'll take care of it."

I was a little surprised he didn't ask why I'd destroyed it but perhaps he didn't care. "Charlie?"

He stopped and turned, his pale eyes narrowed with interest.

"Why do you blame Jack for the loss of both your daughters? If you don't mind my asking." I leaned against the front of my desk and held his gaze.

He licked his lips and set the can down, straightened up and ran a hand thoughtfully over his clean-shaven chin. "Most folks don't remember my daughter Sarah. She drowned when she was seventeen." He didn't mention suicide and I wondered if the omission was deliberate or subconscious, his mind unwilling to wrap around such a horrible truth. "She started having nightmares when she was ten. Told my wife a man in a black mask hurt her. We were never sure if it were true or her imagination. In the light of day, she always denied it. But she became withdrawn and moody, not like the girl she was before."

"Did she ever spend time at the winery?" I waited expectantly, my hands gripping the edge of the desk behind me as I fought the urge to purge my soul and tell him what I knew. Sarah had endured the same nightmare as I; only she didn't live to overcome it. But a father shouldn't have to hear such a thing, especially since there was nothing he could do.

Charlie glanced up sharply. "Yeah, she did. I brought her with me a couple times when she didn't have school. She wanted to see where I worked." He breathed heavily through his nose, as though emotion weighted his chest. "The next time I asked if she wanted to come, she started crying and begged me not to make her." He cleared his throat and sniffed. "My wife started acting as if I'd done something wrong. She accused me of horrible things and eventually filed for divorce. Alexandria sided with her mother and refused to speak with me after Sarah's death."

"That's terrible." I shook my head, my heart going out to the man. He'd lost everything. "And Jack? Where does he fit in?" I asked, trying to hide my impatience.

Charlie stared down at the ripped canvas, his mouth set into a grim line. "I don't have any proof about the man in the mask, but Jack treated Sarah real special that day she came to the winery, taking her on a personal tour while I worked." He drew a shaky breath and blew it out through his mouth as though expelling years of bitterness. "After Sarah died, he came around befriending my family and asking if he could help out. Said he wanted to set up a college fund for Alex in her sister's name. I suspected something wasn't right about his request, like he was paying off a debt. But my wife and Alex let him into their lives with open arms, and pushed me out. Shortly after that, he moved me to the position of manager," he said, a wry twist to his lips. He bent and lifted the garbage, then headed out the door. "I'll burn this in the barrel out back," he said, sounding quite pleased at the prospect.

"Thank you, Charlie," I called after him.

I shut the door and turned toward the empty wall behind my desk. Jack's face was gone, but in my mind's eye I could still see the faces of every one of those girls staring back at me, looking for justice, release from the past, and hope for the future. Sarah's hope was gone but perhaps the others were still out there searching.

*****

When I slipped in the back door of the house, I immediately knew something was wrong. The teakettle was whistling fiercely on the stovetop, steam pouring from the spout. I heard something clatter to the floor in the other room, followed by Mother's loud groan of disapproval. I smiled and turned off the burner; glad it wasn't me going on a blind date.

When I peeked around the corner, she was brushing at the back of her hair with short, jerky movements, holding up a small mirror to reflect the larger mirror behind her. Angry mutterings burst from her lips every few seconds until finally she tossed the brush into the sink and let out another miserable groan. "Why can't my hair turn out decent the one time I have a date?" she ranted into the mirror.

"You look great to me, Mom," I said, trying to ease her stress.

She jumped about six inches and pressed her hand to her chest. "Billie! Do you have to sneak up like that?" I laughed. "I didn't know I was. Sorry."

She shook her head, then leaned forward over the sink to touch up her lipstick, her face about three inches from the mirror. I refrained from reminding her that she needed glasses. "That man will be here in just a few minutes and my hair is a mess. I don't know what to wear and I'm scared out of my mind," she confessed, meeting my reflected gaze.

"You look beautiful, Mother. And what you have on is perfect." I reached out and turned her to face me, nodding with approval at her black slacks and silk top. "You have no reason to be scared. Besides, that man has already seen you and he obviously liked what he saw or he wouldn't have called."

She drew in a cleansing breath and slowly released it. "You're right. I've got to relax. It's just a date."

"You keep telling yourself that, Mother," I said, patting her on the shoulder.

The doorbell rang and Mother's eyes widened in panic. "I'm not ready yet," she said, thrusting me out the door and slamming it behind me.

I laughed and went to let our guest in.

When I opened the front door, I was surprised to see Sean Parker standing at the bottom of the steps, chatting with Mother's date as though they were old friends. It was after six and I wondered why he would still be hanging around. He should have already gone home for the night. At sight of me, he turned abruptly and stalked away. Antonio stared after him, a shocked expression on his face. But when he turned to meet my gaze, his lips curved up into a brilliant smile.

"Hello. I'm Antonio Franzia. You must be Billie.

Handel has told me so much about you," he said smoothly, replacing Sean's rudeness with pure grace. In a black suit with a bold pink, black, and white striped tie, he looked every inch the successful businessman. I stepped back to let him in.

"What sort of things did Handel tell you?" I asked. I sat on the couch and he took the recliner across from me.

He smiled and gave a small shrug. "Oh, you know. The usual."

I raised my brows. "And that would be?"

He shifted uncomfortably in the chair, and straightened his tie unnecessarily. "Just that you're old friends and he's glad you're back."

The sound of heels clicking on the wood floor brought us to attention, and we both stared in amazement as Mother made her grand entrance. "Quit torturing my date, Billie," she said with a dazzling smile. She had changed into a knee length wrap-around black dress, with a scooped neck and cap sleeves. With pearls dangling from her ears, she was stunning.

"Sabrina. You look beautiful." Antonio was on his feet and moving toward Mother in an instant. He took her hand and kissed the tips of her fingers. "It's wonderful to finally meet you in person," he said, his deep voice as smooth as a grand piano.

My mother soaked up the attention like a hothouse flower feeling the rays of the sun for the first time. She let him take her arm and they hurried off. At the door, I watched, feeling as if I'd just sent my daughter out on her first date.

Handel tore up the driveway in his Porsche just as Antonio drove Mother away in his Mercedes. I saw them both wave as they passed. I stood on the steps waiting as he strode up the walk toward me, a bouquet of bright yellow sunflowers in his hand.

"For you," he said, presenting me with the flowers, "the lady that lights up my life." He bent and kissed me lightly on the lips before I could find my voice.

"Wow. And I thought Antonio was smooth."

He laughed. "Antonio? He's just a novice," he said, and followed me into the house.

In the kitchen, I cut the stems down and arranged the flowers in a large canning jar, unable to find a vase. I then set the arrangement in the middle of the table. The bright yellow heads, heavy and tilting, lit up the room.

"How's that? It's the best I can do. We aren't prepared for formal occasions around here. I think Jack must have given away everything worth keeping." I fell silent, an odd feeling coming over me as though somehow betraying those other five girls by speaking my uncle's name aloud.

"What's wrong?" Handel sensed my discomfort and reached out to pull me close. He smiled down at me and kissed my forehead. Oddly, it reminded me of my father and I buried my face in his chest, soaking up the strength of him. He stroked my hair for a minute and then pulled back to look into my eyes.

I brushed my hand down his blue polo shirt, smoothing away the wrinkles I'd caused. "I have more information that points to my uncle," I said without preamble.

He pulled out a chair at the table for me and took the seat opposite, his mouth grim. "You recovered another memory?" he asked, leaning with both arms on the table.

Knowing that he thought recovered memories were as reliable as a stoolie testifying in court, I shook my head. "No. Solid evidence."

He rubbed one finger back and forth over the

stubble on his upper lip making a scratchy sound with the motion. I could almost see the wheels turning in his brain, trying to come up with something to discredit whatever I had. Resentment filled me as I imagined he thought more of upholding my uncle's reputation than helping me discover the truth. I pushed back from the table and went to the stove. The water in the teakettle was still hot. Needing to keep my hands busy, I poured two cups and hung a teabag over the side of each.

"Are you going to tell me what it is?" he asked finally. His attorney patience was obviously wearing thin.

I turned around. He'd crossed his arms and leaned back on the legs of the chair, waiting. I nodded. "A letter and some pictures. Alex brought me an envelope when she came to the office the other day. She said Jack left it with her a couple days before he died. I'll get it."

I hurried out of the kitchen and to my bedroom, relieved to get away from Handel's piercing gaze. Why did his scrutiny make me feel as if I were intentionally hurting him?

The envelope was right where I'd left it that morning, under my pillow. I tipped it over and poured the contents on the bed. The one picture I couldn't put into evidence was my own. I slipped it out of the pile and safely back under the pillow. Then took the rest and returned to the kitchen.

Handel stood at the stove stirring sugar into his tea. He carried the cups to the table and we sat down. He smiled as though to give me confidence. I reached out and pushed the envelope across the space between us.

He tipped it over and let the contents fall out. I could see shock wash over his face, and a flush of anger mount his cheeks at the sight, just as once had mine. His hands shuffled the Polaroid images, arranging them in a straight row, and then his mouth opened but nothing came out, as he stared at ten-year-old Sarah Simpson.

"I'm sorry, Handy," I whispered. "I didn't know how to tell you."

He closed his eyes and swallowed hard. I reached out and gathered the pictures into a pile and quickly turned them over. When he opened his eyes, his lashes were damp and I looked away, afraid of reading too much there.

He cleared his throat. Then smoothed open the letter and read through it. His gaze narrowed. "Why would he say that if he was guilty?" he asked, pointing at a line of print.

"What?" I tried to read it upside down but my uncle's handwriting was hard enough to read right side up.

"He said he didn't blame your father for beating him, he would have done the same, not knowing the facts. That sounds like he's saying your father falsely accused him." He looked up, a childlike eagerness in his face. "Maybe someone else was to blame and Jack was just in the wrong place at the wrong time. Your father assumed the worst and wailed into him."

I shook my head. "No. My father was not easily provoked. He would never..." I stopped, and tried to control my growing anger. Handel was looking for a way to vindicate Jack. There was no use arguing with him; he was a criminal lawyer.

"What about this? He says he didn't set things right because other children would have been hurt." He tapped the pictures. "Obviously, these are the other children."

"What does that mean? He's innocent because there were other children? That makes no sense. Most child molesters are not one-time offenders. They repeat their crime over and over again, until someone stops them."

He was silent, staring blankly somewhere over my shoulder. "You're right," He finally admitted. "So, why aren't there more pictures?"

"More pictures? How many more do there have to be for you to believe he did this?" I flipped over the picture of Sarah and pointed at it. "Charlie told me that Sarah came with him to the winery when she was ten. Jack took her on a special tour, alone. What other proof do you need?"

He stared at the image of the little girl for long moments and then he straightened and looked up, his eyes alight with more wishful thinking. "She isn't in the cellar," he announced, his voice sure. "You said you were attacked in Jack's cellar. She's sitting on a cot of some kind." He flipped the picture around for me to see. "Does any of the background look familiar, like a room in the winery or the house? It doesn't to me."

"Handel, it was twenty years ago. Things may have changed."

"I've lived here all my life. Been in and out of this house and the winery more times than I can count. This room is not here."

I threw up my hands. "Fine! The room doesn't exist, therefore my uncle is innocent." I stood up and jerked the chair back. It toppled and fell over, landing with a loud crash against the floor. My eyes filled with tears and I turned away, not wanting Handel to comfort me. Right now he felt like the enemy and I knew what court would be like with me on the witness stand.

He sighed. "I'm sorry. I'm trying to help. I really am. I know it doesn't seem that way, but –"

I spun on my heel and faced him. "No, it doesn't. It

actually seems like you have already made up your mind that Jack is innocent and I'm crazy and now you just have to talk me into it."

"I don't think you're crazy. You say you were attacked in the cellar and I believe you. But where is the picture? If Jack collected these, then he would have taken one of you."

His reasonable assumption hit me like a cold wind at two a.m., chilling me to the bone. Of course he would realize that my picture was missing from the pile. I shriveled into a ball of nerves at the thought of Handel seeing me that way, vulnerable and wounded, a child of abuse. I swallowed down my pride.

"He did."

The look on his face didn't make me feel vindicated, but only sad. I took his hand and led him to my room. He stood awkwardly in the doorway as I went to the bed and slipped the Polaroid out from under my pillow. Like a shameful secret I'd held it back, but now I was ready to share the truth and be set free.

I handed it to him. His eyes narrowed as he examined the photo and I had to look away. "Do you have a brighter light?" he asked after a moment.

I pointed toward the bathroom. "In there."

He stepped in the bathroom and flipped the switch on. "Oh my God," I heard him say and then he stood in the doorway, his eyes wide with horror. "It's my grandfather's watch," he said, his voice husky with emotion.

"What?" I took the picture and minutely examined it in the bathroom's brightly lit interior. The arm of the man holding me down was in frame. He wore a gold watch with a dark band. But to me that watch looked like any other. I shook my head, completely confused. "What are you saying?"

"I'm saying that is my grandfather's antique watch," he said, pointing to the picture. "He gave it to me before he died, but my father stole it from me."

I reached out and pressed my hand to the left side of Handel's chest, certain that I would feel his heart breaking. But instead, I felt it beat strong and sure beneath my fingers. He slipped past me and strode toward the kitchen. I hurried after him; afraid he'd do something crazy. "Where are you going, Handel? You can't just run off and confront him. What happened to innocent until proven guilty? You were willing to give Jack that, why not your father?" But I knew the answer. Jack had treated him like a son; his father treated him like dirt.

He scooped up the rest of the pictures and the letter and stuffed them inside the envelope. "I'm not confronting him. I'll let the police do that." He was out the front door and nearly to his car before I'd grabbed my cell phone, punched in the security code, locked the door, and ran after him. It might be his father, but it was my fight.

Chapter Twenty

The drive to town was silent except for the soft purr of the car's performance engine and the whine of rubber on asphalt. The sun had set and darkness fell quickly as we drove along. Headlights pierced the interior, shining briefly over our faces as cars passed. The grim set to Handel's mouth remained unchanged as he guided the car toward our destination.

"Where exactly are we going?" I asked finally.

He glanced in the rearview mirror as a motorcycle advanced upon us and quickly passed, the thumping of pipes drowning all else out for a moment. "The police station. I have a few friends there. They can pull his record. I should have done this before I allowed him to move back into our house and into our lives." Bitter self-recrimination came through loud and clear in his voice and words.

I reached out and ran my fingers through the hair above his collar. "It's going to be okay," I said to him, to myself. "We'll find the truth one way or the other."

We hurried up the steps of the station and down a brightly lit hallway. A uniformed officer sat behind a desk facing a waiting room, reading a newspaper. He didn't glance up at our approach, but grinned and snorted at the article before him.

"Hey, Mike. Is Sam around?" Handel asked, without waiting for the officer's attention.

Mike took a gulp of coffee, and grimaced. He tipped his head toward the double doors to the right. "I think he's in his office," he said.

"Thanks." Handel took my hand and we entered a large room filled with desks in double rows, with just enough space to walk between. Plainclothes officers sat at a couple of the desks but most were empty. Handel pulled me along toward the rear of the room and knocked on a closed office door. We heard a muffled grunt that could have been, *come in,* and Handel pushed the door open.

"Parker! Hey, good to see you, buddy," the man behind the desk said, his voice weak but welcoming. He stood and held out a hand.

Handel stepped forward and clasped it firmly. "Hi, Sam." He turned to me, "This is my friend, Billie Fredrickson. Billie, this is Lieutenant Sam Harper."

"It's nice to meet you," I said, trying not to look surprised by the frail image of the man before me.

The Lieutenant inclined his head and grinned, revealing a set of overlapping teeth reminiscent of spokes in a bicycle wheel. Even standing he was shorter than me, and skinny as an anorexic teenage girl, obviously unwell.

"So, what brings you here tonight, kids? Looking for a good time at the old police precinct?" He resumed his seat and waved us to the stiff-backed chairs across from him.

"I need a favor," Handel began.

Sam coughed, covering his mouth with a

handkerchief. The sound was brutal and seemed to sap his energy. He finally caught his breath and smiled. "Well, now would be a good time, buddy. I may not be around next week. And I do owe you one."

I glanced at Handel. His eyes said what words could not. He shook his head slowly. "How's Janie doing?" he asked instead.

"She's baking me stuff I can't eat, trying to fatten me up for my grave clothes I guess." Sam leaned forward and folded his skeletal arms on the desk. "She's not doing too good. She's going to need her friends around when I'm gone," he said, raising his eyes to Handel.

Handel nodded. The room was quiet as a tomb.

"What's the favor?" Sam asked, curiosity flaring in his sunken eyes.

"I need you to bring up any record you can find on my father."

Sam raised his brows but didn't ask any questions. He turned toward his computer and started typing. "How's that sister and nephew of yours?" he asked after a moment of silence.

"Fine," Handel said shortly, "and I want them to stay that way."

Sam gave a low whistle. "We've got quite a record here." His eyes met mine for just a second and then flashed back to Handel. "Did you know he spent some time in the Arizona state pen?"

"No - but I'm not surprised." Handel didn't pull away when I reached out and took his hand, squeezing his fingers reassuringly. He swallowed. "What was the conviction?" he asked, his voice tight.

Sam looked up from the screen. "Sexual assault of a minor."

Handel's grip made me wince. He released my

hand and leaned forward. "Anything else?"

"He was released on probation last month. Looks like he's already screwed that up," Sam said, his voice grim. "He didn't check in with the probation officer. There's a warrant out for his arrest." He turned the computer screen so that Handel could read it.

My cell phone rang and I quickly apologized and stepped out of the office to take the call. The voice on the other end of the line asked, "Is this Wilhelmina Fredrickson?"

"Yes," I said, holding a hand over my other ear to block the office noise.

"This is Breckinridge Security. We have an alarm going off at 14409 County Road 7."

I gasped. "Someone's breaking into my house?"

"We've already dispatched police to the scene. Do you know if anyone is at home and could have set off the alarm accidentally? We rang the residence but there was no answer."

"No, I don't think so. My mother went out and I don't expect her back this early." She knew the code and had used it before without mishap. I glanced in Sam's office but Handel's attention was still on the computer screen.

The dispatcher directed me to return home and speak with the officers at the scene.

When I entered the room, the men were in the middle of a heated discussion, their voices low but intense. I saw the envelope of pictures between them on the desk. They looked up at my return, cutting off their conversation mid-sentence.

"What's going on?" Handel asked immediately, my face no doubt bearing signs of shock. He stood and reached out for my hand.

"That was the security company. Someone is

breaking into my house right now," I said, still unable to believe it was happening.

Sam stood up. "You better drive her home, Handel. The officers will be there. They'll need her to help fill out a report." He smiled. "It was very nice to meet you, Billie."

"It was nice to meet you too, Sam," I said, knowing in my heart that it would be the last time I'd see him.

Handel took Sam's hand and held it for a long moment. "Thank you, Sam. For everything." He followed me to the door then looked back one last time. "Give Janie my love."

The drive home was tense and uncomfortable. Handel didn't speak, but drove at reckless speeds, as though exorcising his demons through hairpin curves. I closed my eyes and tried to relax, although I gripped the sides of the seat with both hands. My thoughts were a jumble with the past as well as the present. Images and faces swirled round and round in my head, Uncle Jack, Sean Parker, my father.

I remembered being in the cellar waiting for Uncle Jack to come that morning. He was late and I started snooping through his desk. I found the pictures of my mother and him kissing and holding one another. It made me want to cry. I didn't know why, but it felt wrong. I took and hid them in the hole behind the file cabinet. When I turned around a man stood behind me; I hadn't heard him come in. His head was covered with a black stocking, two slits cut for his eyes. I was scared, afraid to move. He reached out and touched my hair, then my face. I pulled back and he laughed, a horrible muffled sound that chilled me to the core. I wanted to scream, but he pulled me against him and clamped a hand over my mouth. "You'll do whatever I say or I'll kill your little friend, Handy," he whispered in my ear. And he did things to me

*while I clenched my eyes shut and listened to the tick of
the clock on the wall.*

*I counted 729 ticks of the clock before there was a
scrape of a boot on the stair and the door creaked open. I
refused to open my eyes even when I heard Uncle Jack's
voice raised in anger, "I'll kill you, Sean! How could you
do this to her? You're a sick animal!" The man moved
away and I pressed myself against the wall while sounds
of fists hitting flesh and grunts of men in a struggle over
life and death went on above me. Then someone pounded
up the stairs and the room fell silent except for heavy
breathing. "You'll be okay, Billie. You'll be okay," Uncle
Jack said breathlessly as though reassuring himself.
"Here," he said, placing my scattered clothes beside me.
"Put these on while I go get help." I heard him run back
up the stairs and I slowly opened my eyes and started to
dress. When I heard a light step on the stair a moment
later, I cringed back against the wall and scrunched my
eyes closed, praying the bad man had not returned. But it
was my father. He helped me finish dressing and cradled
me to his chest, then carried me to the house like a
precious package, covered and secure.*

"We're back," said Handel, and I opened my eyes.
"The police are still here. I hope they caught whoever
did this."

The police cruiser sat parked before the house,
lights flashing. We hurried up the steps and through the
open front door. An officer put up a hand. "Are you Ms.
Fredrickson?" he asked.

"Yes," I said, looking wildly around my living
room. "What happened?"

"Looks like you've had vandals, Ma'am. Look
around and see if anything is missing, but as far as we
could tell, the perp spent most of his time in here."

I gasped as I saw the damage. My brand new glove

leather sofa had been shredded. Someone had taken a knife to it, cutting huge slits and pulling out chunks of stuffing. The picture I'd spent so much time reframing had been pulled down and smashed against the fireplace. It lay in a twisted, pile at the foot of the hearth.

I bent down and lifted one side of the shattered frame, reminded of the portrait I'd destroyed myself. This one was much lighter. The bottom section was hollow. I wondered why I hadn't noticed earlier. Taking a closer look, I saw something that made my eyes widen.

"Handel, come here," I said, gesturing for him to come quickly.

"What is it?" He stood over me.

I lifted the section of frame. "This was made with a secret compartment. I think whoever broke it was trying to cover up that fact."

"Who but Jack would know something like that?" he asked, and then went still. "My father used to work with wood."

I nodded and stood up. "He told me he made this frame for Jack's birthday."

"What could possibly have been so important that he would break in here to get it?" Handel dropped the pieces, his face suddenly pale with shock. "His wood working shop. The big shed behind the winery. I wasn't allowed in there. Sometimes he would spend the night, too drunk to go home. He had a cot in the corner." He paused. "He was probably looking for the pictures."

The officer stood nearby listening. "You know the person responsible for this?" he asked.

Handel glanced up. "There is a warrant out for the arrest of Sean Parker. He's the man who broke in here."

The officer narrowed his eyes. "How do you know that?"

"He's my father. And he's a dangerous criminal."

After the officer left, Handel called his sister on the phone in the kitchen and I looked around the house to see if anything was missing. Sean Parker had obviously come for one thing. Whatever was in that frame. Although he wasn't in too big of a hurry to destroy my couch while he was there.

"Margaret's a mess. She can't believe this is happening." Handel ran his fingers through his hair and expelled a weary sigh. "She said her car was missing. She didn't know he'd taken it. He never came home for supper."

I nodded. "He was out front when Antonio came. He must have been watching the house and realized tonight was his chance, with everyone out for the evening."

He looked down at the ruined couch. "I'm sorry about that."

I shook my head and put my arms around him. "It's not your fault. Besides, things can be replaced, people can't," I said, thinking of his friend Sam. "I'm just glad Mother wasn't here."

The phone rang and I ran to answer it, Handel following close on my heels. "Hello?"

Margaret's voice was shrill and agitated. "Davy is missing! I just checked his room. He's not there." She sobbed hysterically into the phone and I handed it quickly to her brother.

"It's Davy. He's gone," I said, covering the receiver.

His eyes widened, but he spoke calmly to his sister, trying to get all the information. Finally, he said, "You know how he likes to sneak out and hide. He's probably here somewhere. We'll find him."

"Should we call the police?" I asked when he hung up.

He licked his lips and looked around the kitchen. "Do you have a flashlight?"

"Yes." I dug in the drawer and handed it to him. "Here."

"You stay here and I'll take a look out in the vineyard where he likes to hide. If I don't find him in half an hour, we'll call the police then," he said. He flipped the flashlight on and off to check the battery and opened the back door. "Don't worry. He does this all the time."

I stood at the window, unable to see into the dark night and wished for the hundredth time that Handel would burst through the door with Davy in tow, and this day would end on a happy note. But the door didn't open. I glanced at my watch and realized only ten minutes had passed since he left.

I paced to the living room and looked around at the destruction Sean Parker had wreaked once again upon my life. Like a black cloud he continued to rain down grief. I prayed the police would catch him before he ruined any more lives.

The drapes were open on the front window and I went to pull them closed. I started to tug on the cord but a flicker of light caught my attention across the yard. Was Handel over by the winery now, searching for Davy around the sheds and buildings?

I reached out and switched off the lamp, darkening the room and making it easier to see outside. I stared unblinkingly into the night. Suddenly a light went on inside the winery. I could see it through the glass of the front door. Someone was in there. I bit my bottom lip and waited. The light disappeared. Could I have been mistaken?

Only three people had the code for the security system: Charlie, Sally, and me. Would either of them be

wandering through the winery on a Friday night? I
didn't think so, but then Charlie had admitted to taking
a bottle of Jack's wine without permission. Perhaps he
came back for another.

My cell phone rang and I flipped it open, my
attention still on the winery.

"This is Billie."

"Ms. Fredrickson." It was Charlie. "I think there's
something over here at the offices that you should see."

"Charlie, why are you at the winery after hours?" I
asked. I pressed my fingers against the front window
and squinted into the night. There was no sign of his old
pickup parked in the drive. Did he park in back of the
shed?

"I found some discrepancies in the books the other
day and wanted to double check." His voice sounded
funny, sort of halting and unsure. Was he insinuating
that someone in the office was cooking the books? Or
perhaps his daughter Alex. As the accountant for the
winery, she certainly had access.

I bit my lip. Handel wanted me to stay here and
wait in case Davy showed up, but I'd just be across the
yard and I had my cell phone. "I'll be right over." I
flipped the phone closed and pushed it into my back
pocket.

I went out the front door and marched across the
drive, gravel crunching briskly beneath my shoes. At the
winery, I punched in the code and let myself in.

The hallway was dark and I wondered if Charlie
was in the back. I waited for my eyes to adjust to the
dim light before heading toward my office. The door
was closed. I distinctly remembered leaving it open for
the cleaning crew, but perhaps they closed it on their
way out.

I turned the knob and stepped inside, flipping the

light switch on as I did. The brightness made me blink, but then I stared in horror at the room around me. Bottles of Jack's special wine had been carried to my office and smashed against the walls, desk, and bookcase with apparent rage. The carpet, soaked and splattered with red wine, looked as if a massacre had taken place upon its tan surface. A rich, heady fragrance filled the air, almost overpowering, as though the room itself was on a binge.

I took a step forward and felt the crunch of glass beneath my shoes. Moving carefully across the room, I approached the desk. The drawers were all yanked out, the contents dumped unceremoniously to the floor, wine and shattered glass sprinkled liberally on top like decorations on a cake.

I reached down, my hand shaking, and lifted a broken piece of bottle, the label with the clock I'd designed still intact. Why would someone do this? It made no sense. Charlie and Sally were excited that the local paper was doing an article about the winery and this wine, a special vintage never before made public, and could give us the publicity we needed to attract new customers. Certainly they wanted the winery to become a success as much as I did.

Glass and wine covered the desk's surface as well as the seats of the chairs. My legs felt weak but there was nowhere to safely sit. I clung to the back of a chair and took a deep breath. My heart beat heavily as though I'd been running. I felt violated once again. Vandalized twice in one night.

Of course. Sean Parker. He hated me and I knew he bore a grudge. He resented the fact that Jack left the winery to me; had said as much to my face. How he got in here, I had no idea, but he wouldn't get away with it.

I flipped my phone open and dialed 911. The

sound of crunching glass made me look up. Charlie stood in the doorway, his expression horrified as he glanced around the room and back at me. "What did you do, Ms. Fredrickson?" he asked, his voice overloud in the quiet room. He wore a black t-shirt tucked neatly into a pair of dark jeans, and a black stocking cap rolled up on the sides to cover the top of his head, making him appear a stocky cat burglar.

I shook my head. "I'm calling the police. Sean Parker did this. He also broke into my house earlier tonight," I tried to explain, listening for the call to connect.

"911. What is the nature of your emergency?" The dispatcher said.

"Yes, I'm at...

"Ms. Fredrickson, you don't have to do this. I can help you," he said, his voice cutting me off, speaking loud enough for the dispatcher to hear on her end of the line. He reached one hand behind his back as he stepped closer and I felt a tingle of apprehension run up my spine, self-preservation screaming my name.

Instinctively I grasped the neck of the broken bottle lying there on the desk. When he brought his hand forward there was a gun in his grip. As he hesitated, I lunged forward and swung my weapon, slicing deep into his wrist. He yelped and dropped the gun to the floor, as blood spurted from the wound, running down his fingers and mixing with Jack's chardonnay.

I pushed past him and ran down the hall. I'd dropped my cell phone and knew I had to call for help. Charlie could bleed out and I'd be responsible. I had no idea why he would try to kill me, but I didn't want his death on my conscience. Gasping for breath, I stopped at Sally's desk and lifted the receiver.

There was no dial tone. I yanked up the cord and saw it was disconnected.

"Put that down, Ms. Fredrickson," a calm voice ordered.

Alex Becker stood in the doorway, her dark figure silhouetted by the light filtering down the hall. She stepped closer and I saw that she now held the gun her father dropped in my office. "What are you doing? I need to call an ambulance. Charlie's been hurt, " I said, my voice pleading.

She didn't seem overly worried about the circumstances, but waved the gun at me. "Let's go back to your office now, Ms. Fredrickson," she said.

I moved away from the desk and toward the door, keeping my eye on the gun she held. She stepped back and let me walk ahead of her, as I retraced my steps down the hall. "Why are you doing this? I don't understand."

She reached out and pushed the small of my back with the barrel of the gun, prodding me to move faster. "Just walk."

At the office door I stopped and stared. Charlie sat on the glass-strewn carpet with his back against my desk. He held his bleeding arm to his chest, his belt tied tightly above the wound as a tourniquet. He looked about ready to pass out.

"Get in there!" Alex ordered, her voice rose at the sight of her father lying still. "It's time to finish this."

Charlie turned his head slightly and looked up. "Alex. I'm sorry. I just couldn't do it."

The repugnance she felt for her father was a tangible thing. With lips twisted she made a sound of disgust. "Of course, you couldn't. Mother was right. You're worthless! You can't do a simple thing right. I planned this to the last detail and you can't even follow directions. Just shoot the bitch, put the gun in her hand, and leave!"

His breath was short and raspy. "Its too late now, Alex. Get out while you still can. I'll take the blame," he said, still desperate for his daughter's love even in the face of her undisguised loathing.

I moved to his side and knelt down, examining his wound. It was still bleeding, the belt not tight enough to stop the flow. His face was pale and his skin felt cold and clammy. He needed to get to the hospital immediately or he would die.

She laughed bitterly. "It's too late for you. Not me. With both of you dead, there won't be anyone to contradict my story. Jack wanted me to have this winery. He told me so. He wrote a preliminary will. If she's out of the way, I'm next in line."

I turned my gaze on her, fury beating out fear. "You'd let your own father die for this?" I opened my arms wide and shook my head. "I would give it all to you free and clear for one moment back with mine."

"It's a deal," she said, her lips curved into a tight smile. She stepped close and raised the gun to my head. "I'll send you to your father and you can leave me the winery."

I heard the click of the trigger as Charlie shoved me to the floor. The loud blast so close to my head was deafening and made my ears ring. I felt a spray of dampness hit my cheek and turned to see Charlie lying slumped behind me, not moving.

Alex stood over us, rage turning her features ugly. She cursed at her father, who could no longer respond. Then turned her attention to me. Her lips pulled back like a dog baring his fangs and she raised the gun again.

"Drop your gun!" a voice yelled from the doorway.

Moments later, Alex Becker was cuffed and on her

way out of the winery while her father was being placed on a stretcher to be taken to the morgue. Handel pushed past the room full of officers and scooped me up in his arms, holding me so tight I thought I might pass out.

"Where's Davy?" I managed to gasp out.

"Margaret called," he mumbled against my ear. "He was camping out in his closet. She found him asleep, curled up on a pile of clothes." He pulled back, his mouth grim.

I couldn't help smiling despite the current circumstances. Little boys play hide and seek and life goes on. Handel leaned down and kissed me hard on the lips and I held him there.

*****

The following week was a blur. Discovering the depth of Alex Becker's plan to make me appear depressed and suicidal was frightening. Getting Charlie to go along with her scheme was not so surprising. He desperately wanted his daughter back in his life. But when he got involved I don't think murder was part of the plan. Planting the mask in the cellar where I would find it, thus jumpstarting my dormant memories and sending me packing back home to Minnesota, was probably as far as he wanted to go.

Alex admitted having an affair with Jack the year before he died. He confided in her about his guilt in hiding Sean Parker's crimes. Jack made his friend sign a confession and used it and the pictures he found to blackmail him into leaving town, the two things Sean had obviously been looking for in the secret compartment of the frame.

The one thing Jack didn't tell her was that he was dying. Jack promised Alex that if I refused to run the winery, he would have it revert to her in six months; although, he died before he got around to actually changing the will that way. Or perhaps he never really intended any such thing. Only Jack knew and he wasn't talking. But Alex figured with my history at the winery, I would never want to stay, and with her ability to forge Jack's handwriting, she would make things work out in the end.

Sean Parker's surprise return was a windfall of good luck for Alex. With him around, she was sure that I would fall apart and make her job easier. But as gamblers know all too well, good luck is never a sure thing.

Chapter Twenty-One

The setting sun melted into the horizon like molten iron, glowing reddish orange, tinged pink at the edges. Mother and I sat on the front steps of the house watching the day slowly wane, enjoying the evening breeze and the quiet time after everyone had gone home from the winery.

It reminded me of the day our family visited California twenty years before. Uncle Jack had waved to us from the steps as we pulled up in our rental car. After introductions he bent down to my level and pointed at the setting sun. "You like orange sherbet?" he asked with a grin. I nodded eagerly. He reached out his hand and pretended to take a big scoop out of the sky with an imaginary spoon. "Better eat up. It's already melting," he said. I liked him from that moment.

"What are you thinking about?" Mother asked, reaching out to push a strand of straggling hair behind my ear. She hadn't let me out of her sight the entire week and I was beginning to feel that old familiar suffocation setting in.

"Family. I miss Dad and Uncle Jack."

She took my hand and squeezed. "I do too, honey. But we'll see them again."

I nodded and turned back toward the setting sun, now just faint streaks of pink fading away. "I know we will."

She stood up and opened the screen door. "You coming?"

"I'll be there in a minute. I need to do something first."

She hesitated before going in. "You want me to come with you?" she asked.

I shook my head. "You don't have to worry, Mother. The police apprehended Sean Parker two days ago and he's on his way back to the Arizona state prison. As far as I know, I don't have anymore enemies, but ..."

"Very funny." She let the door bang shut behind her.

But I could feel her eyes watching me as I walked across the drive, and entered the winery. This time I flipped all the lights on. I avoided my office, not ready to see it quite yet. I knew professional cleaners had come and torn out the carpet, cleaned the walls and furniture and left things somewhat restored, but there would still be the memory of Charlie lying there in death, soaked in wine and blood.

I made my way to Jack's cellar. The cold, stone stairwell no longer felt frightening to me, but rather inviting, our passageway to adventure as Jack called it. The creaking door sent a shiver along my spine, the kind you get when chugging slowly up the steepest hill of a rollercoaster, knowing you'll soon be shooting straight down the other side.

Charlie and Alex had destroyed much of Jack's special stock, but I discovered a dozen dusty bottles at the far corner of the wine rack, back underneath where cobwebs obscured them from view. I took one and wiped it clean on the tail of my denim shirt. The label of the clock was simply drawn, a child's rendition of keeping time in a bottle. Uncle Jack told me to draw our time together and I drew the clock I saw on the wall of the cellar, the hands set at six for that early morning hour we met to laugh, and live, and learn together.

I held the bottle to the light and watched the chardonnay sparkle, remembering all the precious moments spent with those I loved that summer when I was eight.

"You were right, Uncle Jack," I said, my voice a mere whisper. "You *can* save time in a bottle."

*****

Mother finally flew back to Minneapolis, after I bribed Adam to call and say he wanted to live at home for the summer. She couldn't resist washing and cooking for a helpless male. Apparently, it was even more fun than taking care of me.

I pulled into the garage and shut off the engine. The drive back from the airport had been stressful. Traffic was hectic and I was no longer accustomed to dealing with rush hour on a regular basis. I stepped out of the car thinking of the night ahead and a certain sense of freedom I felt without Mother looking over my shoulder.

Handel had promised a memorable evening in celebration of my decision to stay and run Fredrickson Winery. Perhaps we would also celebrate the subtle change in our relationship, moving us closer to what my mother and father once had. Handel was a man I could trust, a man I could love if I let myself. Some of the old walls had already come down and I looked forward to the day he smashed through the last of my reserves.

The garage door shut behind me as I pushed the button and walked toward the house. I heard the crunching of gravel from behind and turned to find Davy following close on my tail. "Hey, kid. Haven't seen you around here lately. Your mother chain you to the house?" I teased.

He shook his head and wiped his nose with the back of a hand. "Nope. But Uncle Handel said if I scare her like that again I'll have to go to Juvie." His blonde brows drew together in a frown. "What's Juvie anyway?"

"Not a good place." I held open the front door. "You want to come in and have ice cream?"

"Sure. But I better call Mom and tell her where I am."

I smiled. "Good idea."

Davy dug into his bowl of chocolate ice cream as though he'd been stranded in the desert for a week. I watched him from across the table. "How old did you say you were?" I asked, sitting back and crossing my arms.

He stuck his tongue out and licked all the way around his face as far as he could reach. "Eight and a half." He sniffed and wiped his nose with the back of his hand again.

I regarded him thoughtfully. "Ever think of learning a trade?" I asked. "I bet you'd make a great wine maker. I could teach you."

Davy took another bite before answering. "Do I get paid?"

ABOUT THE AUTHOR

Barbara Ellen Brink lives in the great state of Minnesota where the mosquitoes are so large they fear nothing but tornadoes. She enjoys motorcycle trips with her husband, hiking with their dogs, Rugby and Willow, and of course writing novels.

Made in the USA
Charleston, SC
13 October 2016